POWDERSMOKE RANGE

POWDERSMOKE RANGE

William Colt MacDonald

Chivers Press • G.K. Hall & Co.
Bath, England Thorndike, Maine USA

This Large Print edition is published by Chivers Press, England, and by G.K. Hall & Co., USA.

Published in 1997 in the U.K. by arrangement with the author.

Published in 1997 in the U.S. by arrangement with Golden West Literary Agency.

U.K. Hardcover ISBN 0–7451–8946–6 (Chivers Large Print)
U.K. Softcover   ISBN 0–7451–8957–1 (Camden Large Print)
U.S. Softcover   ISBN 0–7838–2048–8 (Nightingale Collection Edition)

The text of this Large Print edition is unabridged.
Other aspects of the book may vary from the original edition.

Set in 16 pt. New Times Roman.

Printed in Great Britain on acid-free paper.

British Library Cataloguing in Publication Data available

Library of Congress Cataloging-in-Publication Data

MacDonald, William Colt, 1891–1968.
  Powdersmoke range / William Colt MacDonald.
  ISBN 0–7838–2048–8 (lg. print : sc)
  1. Large type books.   I. Title.
[PS3525.A2122P69   1997]
813′.54—dc21   96–48190

To Wallace James Howells

CONTENTS

CHAPTER ONE

'I'M TAKIN' A HAND'

Crossing the lofty, saw-toothed spine of the Escabrosa Range while the morning sun was still high in the turquoise sky, the Guadalupe Kid drew rein to a more leisurely, safer, pace to negotiate the tumbled, lower slopes of the mountain descent. At spots the procedure was a distinctly dangerous affair requiring a firm hand on the dun cowpony that its hoofs might not slip from some narrow ledge thus precipitating itself and rider into the tangled brush bottoms that lay hundreds of feet below. Now and then, a quiet word from the Kid was all that was necessary to carry the little horse over some particularly perilous bit of footing. More often than not the Guadalupe Kid left matters to his mount's own sense of good judgment.

By mid-morning the way became much easier despite the beating down of the torrid rays of a Southwest sun, now higher in the sky than when Guadalupe had crossed the crest of the range. Scrub oak and piñon were left behind. The timber, though still sparse, grew to greater dimensions. Tumbled heaps of granite barred the trail from time to time but the footing in all directions was now secure.

Prickly pear and yucca became more profuse, small clumps of blue-stem commenced to appear among the rock, the rock itself, in time, giving way to easy-rolling, grass-covered foothills. Good grazing lands here; the Kid spotted several white-faced bunches of Hereford cows bearing on the left ribs the long-remembered Tresbarro brand: a figure 3.

By noontime, the Kid had pushed his sweating pony among the cottonwood trees lining either side of the south fork of Santone Creek which rose high up in the Escabrosas and branched northwest and southeast back of Old Baldy Mountain before descending to the triangular valley that lay between the V-shaped juncture of the Escabrosa and Little Escabrosa Ranges. The Kid drew up his high-heeled booted feet as the dun pony pushed belly-deep into the cool, gravel-bottomed stream and stopped to bury its nose in the limpid waters.

Splashing out on the opposite bank a few minutes later, the Kid pulled to a halt, dropped reins over his pony's head, and swung his slim-hipped, broad-shouldered form to the ground. The pony was quick to take advantage of the long grass, when the Kid had loosened its cinch and took from the roll back of the saddle a couple of cold biscuits and a fried slice of beefsteak. Pushing back the sombrero from his unruly mass of tawny hair, the Kid seated himself cross-legged on the earth and

2

commenced to eat. He murmured, once, between bites,

'Two-bits to a plugged peso, Don Manuel don't remember me. Bet he'll be plumb surprised.'

He paused to shift to more comfortable positions the twin Colt forty-fives at his overalled thighs and resumed certain meditations, 'Only for Tucson, I wouldn't be comin' here like this.' His face grew momentarily grim as he added, 'Nope, not like this.' A slow flush crept through his olive coloring, bespeaking the quarter-Spanish ancestry, and a grin curved his lips: 'Ten to one if I come through a-tall, I'd been comin' fast with a sheriff's posse huggin' my trail like a burr in a broom-tail's hair.'

The Kid's dark eyes roved about the landscape. They were good eyes, the kind that could meet, with no shifting, the gaze of any man regardless of how penetrating the gaze might be. It hadn't always been so. The Kid finished his meal, raised the neckerchief at his throat to wipe his lips, rolled and lighted a cigarette. Then he rose, crossed the intervening yards between himself and the pony, tightened the saddle-cinch and swung lithely up to the horse's back.

Three-quarters of an hour of easy riding through lush grass brought him to the crest of a low rise of land from which he glanced down a long slope toward a thick clump of huge cottonwoods from among which rose the whirling sails of a tall windmill. Below, seen through leafy branches, were several buildings. The Kid touched spurs to his pony and moved into a faster gait, murmuring, 'I didn't realize the place was this near.'

So thickly were the trees bunched about the buildings that the Kid didn't notice he was approaching the ranch house from the rear. The clanking of the windmill came clearly to his ears now, together with certain squeaks and grindings. 'Needs oilin' bad,' he muttered automatically.

Breaking through the trees he noticed three good-sized corrals, one of which contained several saddlers. The gates of the other two hung open. The buildings were of adobe and timber. There wasn't anyone in sight about the place. No smoke curled from the chimney of the combination mess-house and cook shanty. Nor was anybody to be seen near the other buildings—blacksmith shop, stables, hay barn, wagon shed. The Kid had a better view of the ranch house proper now. It was a huge, one story rambling affair. The back door was shut. Above the slanting shakes of the roof spread leafy branches of the huge gnarled cottonwoods commanding the front approach to the house.

The Kid shook his head a bit dismally as he noted the peeling paint and general air of neglect about the buildings. Refuse was

4

scattered about the yard at the rear of the house. 'Certain looks like the Tresbarro iron had gone haywire,' he muttered disappointedly.

Passing the rear door, he walked his pony around the corner of the building before he heard voices coming from the front. Certain angry tones reached the Kid's ears. Quietly he pulled rein. He didn't want to put himself into the position of eavesdropper. Still, on the other hand, if any sort of help was required...

The Kid's thoughts were interrupted a second time by that cold voice, determined, forceful, decisive. The voice of an old man, but that of a *man*, nevertheless.

'I do not wish to speak further of the matter, Señor Ogden,' the voice was saying. 'I've given my answer, once and for all. You will now be so kind as to remove yourself from my premises.' The words were spoken in perfect English.

'Now, look here, Tresbarro,' a heavier, bullying voice put in, 'you can't talk thataway to us. Big Steve has made you a neat and proper offer. Anybody will tell you that Steve Ogden is the most generous hombre what ever—'

'I have told you I do not wish to sell,' the old voice interrupted coldly.

'What you want and what you'll get—' the bullying tones commenced.

A third, quieter voice cut in, 'Leave be, Brose. Mr Tresbarro doesn't understand the

5

situation. I'll handle this.' The tones weren't raised above normal, but there was something evil in the soft, silky way in which they were uttered. The voice continued, 'See here, Don Manuel, it must be clear that you can't continue to operate your brand. You're losing money hand over fist. Your taxes aren't paid. Your hands have left you—'

'I'd like to know just how much you know about that too.' This time the speaker was a girl. She sounded angry, her voice full of hot scorn.

There came vigorous denials from two of the speakers. For a few moments a rush of angry words became unintelligible to the Guadalupe Kid. He touched spur lightly to his pony and moved toward the front of the house bringing the four speakers into view.

None of them noticed the arrival of the Kid. He sat his pony quietly, taking in the scene on the long gallery that fronted the width of the old ranch house. A spare old man with a thick mane of white hair, a hawk-beak nose and bushy eyebrows sat in a chair a few feet away from the open front door. The Kid recognized him as Don Manuel Tresbarro.

Standing at his side, one slim hand resting on the chair stood a tall slim girl with reddish-brown hair, in worn corduroy riding skirt, mannish flannel shirt and riding boots. Offhand the Kid would have judged the girl as decidedly pretty, though it was a bit difficult to

6

tell right now. Her features were flushed crimson, her determined chin set firmly, her eyes flashing as she faced two men who had gained their feet in the heat of the moment.

Of these two, the taller instantly caught the Kid's attention. His eyes were a pale blue and held hard, vicious lights. Above the straight, thin-lipped mouth was a wisp of dark mustache. In one hand he held a wide-brimmed fawn-colored sombrero, thus disclosing a head of brown curling hair with streaks of gray at the temples. His complexion was a dead white, showing no traces of tan. As he talked a diamond glittered on one of the fingers of his long thin hands. Listening to the conversation a moment, the Kid gathered this individual to be Big Steve Ogden. The man's build bore out his name. He was at least six feet tall with powerful shoulders contrasting strangely with his thin white hands. His linen was immaculate, a black string necktie being tucked under the fancy vest. A long square-tailed coat reached to his knees. His striped trousers were tight-fitting, the bottoms coming to the ankles of his black riding boots.

The man's gestures were full of grace as he talked, 'Now, look here, Miss Sibley,' the cool tones were caressing, 'you're sure mistaken, thinking we had anything to do with your hands leaving. Trouble is, I'm afraid you've misjudged me. Don Manuel has had a run of bad luck—no two ways about that. But surely you can't maintain I'm responsible. The very fact that the Tresbarro outfit has lost cattle should prove that Don Manuel is getting too old to operate an outfit—'

The old Spaniard was on his feet now, eyes blazing. His voice trembled with anger. 'That,' he said, 'is entirely my concern, Señor Ogden. I haven't asked your advice. It goes against the grain of hospitality to again request you to leave my premises, but you give me no other alternative—'

Again the girl burst out, 'Oh, if we only had some semblance of law here, we might have a chance—'

'Hey, Miss Sibley, that's me yo're hittin' at,' the man at Ogden's side said gruffly. 'I represent the law—'

'You!' scornfully from the girl. 'Deputy-Sheriff 'Brose Glascow!' A bitter laugh curved her lips. 'The only law you represent is that made by Big Steve Ogden. Ask any decent man what that law stands for, what Steve Ogden stands for, and he'll—'

'Seems to me,' Ogden smiled thinly, 'I'm standing quite a bit—and Deputy Glascow as well.'

Brose Glascow growled an affirmative. He was a chunkily built man with a heavy mustache, eyes placed too closely together above a nose that had once been broken, and a narrow strip of forehead beneath rumpled thinning hair of an indiscriminate shade. He

8

wore a skimpy open vest on which was pinned a tarnished deputy-sheriff's badge, a woolen shirt, open at the throat, and none-too-clean belted overalls. A six-shooter hung low on his right leg.

'We're standin' too damn much, if you ask me.' Glascow growled. 'Tresbarro, you better do business with Steve. He's treatin' you fair and aboveboard. It's yore last chance. Things on this outfit won't get no better. They're a heap li'ble to get worse. Is that clear?'

The Guadalupe Kid cut in promptly, 'I'm danged if it sounds clear to me, Mister Deputy. 'Bout all's I can make out is that you and this Ogden hombre has been asked to leave and you don't nowise understand a hint—'

The four on the porch turned swiftly. The girl faced the man on the pony, something of distrust in her features. Don Manuel's face was a frowning mask as he tried to place the stranger. Ogden glanced quickly at the girl and the old man, saw that the Kid was a stranger to them. He started to speak, checked himself, and remained silent. A stranger here, at this time, might mean anything—or nothing. It would be best not to commit himself for the time being.

Ambrose Glascow's beetle-brows constricted to a heavy frown. 'You.' he growled, 'who invited you into this game?'

'Me,' the Kid said easily, 'I'm takin' a hand.'

'On whose invitation?' Glascow persisted.

9

'Deputy,' the Kid laughed, 'you're sure lackin' in civic pride. Usual, a stranger enterin' a growin' community gets some sort of welcome. Ain't you got no sense of the social amenities?'

Without waiting for an answer, the Kid swung down from his pony, dropped reins over the horse's head and vaulted over the railing that bordered the long gallery. He was laughing easily as he approached the group, at the same time not missing a movement on the part of Ogden and Glascow. A movement of Ogden's long coat had disclosed the holstered six-shooter suspended from a cartridge belt.

'I'm askin' who you are,' Glascow grunted warily, somewhat taken back by Guadalupe's assurance. 'We'll discuss the social 'menities after I've got yore moniker. As deputy-sheriff of Tresbarro County I'm demandin' that you talk fast.'

'Yeah?' The Kid laughed shortly. 'All right, deputy, you can have it all in the space of a breath. I'm known as the Guadalupe Kid or Guadalupe Ferguson on any old reward bills you happen to have in your office. My friends know me as Jeff Ferguson.'

Don Manuel half gasped, 'Ferguson—Jeff Ferguson.' The name stirred old memories in his ancient brain.

'Remember me, now, Don Manuel?' the Kid asked, nodding.

Something clicked in Glascow's mind. 'By

10

Gawd!' he exclaimed. 'You got a nerve. There's rewards posted for you—dead or alive!'

The Kid nodded coolly. 'Somethin' of that sort was put up,' he admitted. His cool-eyed glance narrowed. 'You cravin' to collect any rewards, Glascow?'

Glascow eyed uncertainly the lithe figure poised waiting, thumbs hooked into cartridge belts, before him. 'You—you got a nerve,' the deputy sputtered.

'Because if you have got any illusions about gainin' sudden wealth easy,' the Kid continued insolently, 'I'm warnin' you that you're proddin' into a hornet's nest.'

'I—I ain't so shore of that,' Glascow growled.

'That bein' the case,' and the Kid's laugh was challenging, 'the next move is up to you, Mister Deputy-Sheriff. How you playin' 'em?'

Glascow swore under his breath, made a sudden movement toward his holstered gun— then stopped abruptly. He hadn't seen the Kid's arm move, but, somehow, as though by magic, he found himself staring into the round black muzzle of Guadalupe's Colt gun.

The Kid's voice had turned cold. He said again, 'How you playin' 'em, deputy? Have you got the nerve to try and collect on those old posters?' His eyes flashed sidewise to Ogden who hadn't made a move, then swiftly back to the deputy whose arms were now dangling at his sides. The Kid's words were scornful,

11

'Shucks, deputy, you'd just be wastin' your time, anyway. Better give up the thought. You're not the first peace officer who thought he'd grabbed a sure thing. It's plumb probable you won't be the last.'

Glascow swallowed heavily but couldn't locate his voice. Ogden asked coldly, 'How so?'

'Those posters are deader'n last year's brand scabs,' the Kid snapped back. 'My accounts are square—and so is this deputy's head, I reckon, or he'd know that much.'

Ogden couldn't detect any bluff in the statement. He nodded shortly. 'Leave be, Brose,' he ordered. The deputy relaxed with some relief. Guadalupe's six-shooter slipped back into holster.

Old Tresbarro's hand was reaching for Guadalupe's now. 'Ygnacio Pizarro's grandson,' he was saying wonderingly.

'Right, Don Manuel,' the Kid nodded.

The old Spaniard's keen eyes gazed uncomprehendingly at the Kid. 'But—but you are the complete *Americano*.'

'Three-quarters *Americano*, Don Manuel,' Guadalupe corrected. 'I wondered if you'd remember me. It's almost twenty years since my grandfather brought me to visit—'

The girl broke in with certain words. The old man continued, 'Your pardon, Señor Jeff Ferguson—' he indicated the girl, 'my ward, Miss Caroline Sibley. I might almost say, my daughter.'

The girl's hand came out to meet Guadalupe's. He found himself liking the cool firm strength of her fingers, discovered that her eyes were a deep violet. Mentally, Caroline Sibley was telling herself that this Guadalupe Kid person had a 'darn good set of features.'

Brose Glascow cleared his throat loudly. Ogden interrupted to say something relative to unfinished business. Caroline turned to Don Manuel, 'I think, grandad, you do not care to talk business any longer today. Mr Ogden and Deputy Glascow will understand we have a guest to—'

'Exactly, exactly,' Don Manuel said quickly, turning to Ogden. 'Nor do I care to go any further with the business which brought you here, *señores*. The matter is settled.'

'Just a minute,' Ogden persisted, striving to keep the anger from his voice. He turned to Guadalupe, 'You won't mind, I hope, if we take up just a few more minutes of Don Manuel's precious time.'

'Seems like,' Guadalupe drawled, 'I heard Don Manuel mention somethin' to the contrary. Howsomever it's up to him.'

'Thanks,' Ogden's tones were sarcastic. 'I'm making an offer for this property. It will be to Don Manuel's advantage to accept it.'

The Kid laughed easily. 'That bein' the case, I reckon I'll take a hand in the biddin' myself. I didn't know the Tresbarro holdin's was for sale, but—' Without finishing, the Kid turned to the old Spaniard, 'Don Manuel, I'm willin' to double Ogden's bid!'

Tresbarro looked startled, his eyes widened. Caroline frowned, her gaze searching Guadalupe's face to learn if he were speaking in earnest. Glascow's jaw dropped in an exploded 'Huh?'

'Cripes!' Ogden snapped scornfully. 'Fool's talk. Or just a bluff. See here, Don Manuel—'

'Bluff?' the Kid clipped out. 'All right, Ogden, call me.'

'Bluff or fool's talk, either one,' Ogden said angrily. 'No one in his senses would make an offer of that sort without first learnin' my bid.'

The Kid was grinning widely now. 'Ogden,' he drawled softly, 'did you ever hear a rattler buzz his tail at you?'

'Naturally,' Ogden said impatiently. 'What's that to do with the question? Why do you come here and interrupt?'

'So have I,' the Kid continued a bit wearily, ignoring the latter part of Ogden's question, 'heard one buzz right recent. A feller can usual tell by hearin' a snake rattle just how far he's goin' to strike. I reckon I ain't misjudged your strikin' distance any. I heard some of your *habla*. I know your kind. You wouldn't pay near what a property like this is worth.'

'You makin' war talk to me?' Ogden demanded coldly.

'We were talkin' business,' the Kid reminded, meeting steadily Ogden's

14

challenging glare. 'Take it any way you like. My offer stands. You ready to raise the ante?'

'Bosh!' Ogden jerked out. 'This outfit as it stands ain't worth more than ten thousand. Because Don Manuel is an old friend I'll raise my bid to fifteen thousand. We can ride into town right now. At the bank I stand ready to pay Don Manuel five hundred dollars to bind the bargain, until final papers are signed.' Ogden paused, a confident sneer on his dead-white features. 'Well, Guadalupe Kid, you ready to double my bid?'

The Kid's grin widened now. He scarcely heard the words while his reassuring glance answered the pleading look in Caroline Sibley's eyes. Reaching to the right hip-pocket of his overalls he produced a leather bill fold, a much worn bill fold, from which he extracted and unfolded a narrow green slip of paper which he handed to the astounded Don Manuel.

The Kid's voice sounded slightly bored as though this were an everyday occasion. He explained languidly, 'Cashier's check on the First National Bank of El Paso. One thousand dollars. I'll endorse that, Don Manuel, just as soon as you've accepted my offer of thirty thousand dollars for the Tresbarro iron!'

CHAPTER TWO

SHOTS IN THE NIGHT

Ogden's dead-white face went suddenly scarlet. Glascow broke into a torrent of inarticulate protests. Sudden, relieved joy swept across the girl's features. The old Spaniard looked steadily at the Kid a moment, then nodded decisively.

'I'll be very proud to accept your offer,' he said.

'Now look here, Tresbarro,' Ogden advised, 'you better go slow. One thousand dollars isn't thirty thousand. You know me, know my standing in Los Potros. My word is good throughout this country. What do you know about this Ferguson hombre? Ten to one he ain't got the other twenty-nine thousand—'

'I'm takin' a thirty day option,' Guadalupe said calmly. 'Don't worry, Ogden. If the money don't get here—well, Don Manuel will be a thousand bucks ahead and still have time to consider any offer you might make—'

Glascow broke in to say, 'If that check is good I'll eat my Stet hat.'

'That a promise?' Guadalupe grinned. 'If it is, you better get ready for a diet of boiled felt. Or mebbe you like your hats fried? Offhand I'd guess you went in for stews. Stews sure do give a man a big head now and then.'

Glascow's face went apoplectic with rage. 'I—I betcha that check's a forgery. Don't you tech it, Don Manuel. Listen to Big Steve. We're yore friends. Don't take the word of a feller that's admitted rewards is offered for him—'

'*Was*, not *is*,' Guadalupe corrected.

'That's what you say,' Glascow raged. 'I ain't so sure. You can't prove that check is good—'

'That check can be proved good on any bank in the country,' the Kid said calmly.

'That's what you say—' Glascow continued.

'Leave be, Brose,' Ogden cut in. Spots of angry color still showed in his cheekbones, but he held his temper in check. He turned to Don Manuel. 'It's like this, Tresbarro, I don't want to see you accept an offer that may not work out to your advantage. I'll raise my offer to twenty thousand—'

'You're too late, Señor Ogden.'

'Thirty thousand—cash—money in hand tonight. No monkey-business with thirty day options or—'

'You're too late, Señor Ogden,' the old Spaniard repeated. 'I've passed my word to Jeff—'

'Don't let me stop a sale,' Guadalupe interrupted.

Tresbarro shook his head. 'My word stands good,' he said firmly.

Ogden glared at the Kid, turned again to

Tresbarro. 'Thirty-five thousand—cash in hand,' he offered. 'That's my last word on the subject.'

Guadalupe laughed. 'Listen, Ogden, didn't I hear you orate a spell back that the Tresbarro iron wa'n't worth more than ten thousand?'

Ogden, waiting for Tresbarro's reply, ignored the words. For the last time, Tresbarro shook his head, said for a third time, 'You're too late, Señor Ogden. The word has been passed. Between gentlemen.' A momentary gleam of triumph appeared in the old eyes. 'I scarcely expect *you* to understand that, of course. However, the subject is closed. I think I will spare you the embarrassment of having further offers rejected when I tell you I prefer that the Tresbarro iron stays out of your possession. That, also, is final. *Adios, señores.*'

Ogden raised one clenched fist as though to strike the old Spaniard. But Tresbarro had turned his back, as though bringing the subject to a close. Caroline Sibley took one step forward, but the Kid placed himself quickly between the girl and Ogden.

The Kid said quietly, 'That's all, Ogden. You can say "good-bye" any time you feel like it.'

Glascow cursed in low tones, stopped abruptly when he saw the Kid's right hand slide toward six-shooter butt. The Kid said, 'Don't say that again, Glascow.' The words were even-voiced, level.

'Leave be, Brose,' Ogden snapped. 'C'mon, we're leavin'.'

He stepped from the gallery to the ground, followed by the deputy and headed toward the two horses waiting in the shade of a tall cottonwood. The two men climbed into saddles, spoke to their ponies, then drew rein abruptly as Ogden called to the Guadalupe Kid:

'Ferguson, I'd like to speak privately with you a moment.'

Guadalupe's eyes narrowed, then he nodded. Carelessly, he sauntered out to the two horsemen. Behind him he caught words of warning from Caroline Sibley. He didn't turn around, nor reply to the low tones of the girl.

He stopped a few feet from the two horses. 'Well?' coldly.

Ogden said, 'You goin' through with this deal, Ferguson?'

'Them's my intentions.'

'You got backing?'

The Kid said easily, 'Enough to take care of any obstructions *you* can think of.'

Ogden flushed. Glascow maneuvered his pony to get behind Ogden. The Kid quickly shifted position, so as to keep the deputy in sight. Glascow dropped his eyes before the Kid's challenging stare.

Ogden went on, after a minute, 'You want to make some money out of your deal, quick money?'

Guadalupe said flatly, 'I'm not open to any offers, Ogden. You heard Don Manuel say, didn't you, that he didn't want his brand in your name?'

'You're talking, and acting, like a fool,' Ogden said harshly. 'Folks in this country don't buck Steve Ogden—not and make it stick!'

'You mean,' the Kid asked mildly, 'they haven't in the past?'

'I'm talkin' about now!'

The Kid yawned and replied, 'I'm open to conviction, Ogden.'

'Said conviction—' and Ogden swore, '—may arrive before you look for it.'

'That,' the Kid said quietly, 'sounds like war-talk.'

'It's only a warning,' Ogden stated in deadly tones. 'If you're wise you'll take it. I've never yet failed to get what I've gone after. I want the Tresbarro Ranch. I'm going to have it. New blood ain't welcome in this country. You get a crew of hands in here and you'll start a range war, sure as hell. We've run out more than one band of rustlers. We don't want no new crews comin' in.'

'Anybody I bring in here,' the Kid said steadily, 'will throw a straight rope. You won't have no argument on that score.'

'You're a stranger here. I can't take chances. If you insist on goin' through with this deal, there'll be a heap of powder burned.'

The Kid laughed scornfully. 'So far as I'm concerned this range can be hazy with powdersmoke. I'm goin' through with—'

'You'll never leave here alive with that option,' Ogden rasped.

'That,' the Kid said, 'is mighty strong *habla*. It wouldn't sound good in court.'

Ogden laughed confidently. 'Try and prove anything against me. It'd be only your word against mine and Glascow's. I'm givin' you your chance. You can be sensible and avoid trouble. Travel—and forget you ever stopped this side of town. I'm bein' patient, but I'm trying to make you see how strong I stand in this neck of the range—'

'Furthermore,' Deputy Glascow could contain his words no longer, 'unless you do listen to reason I'm aimin' to do somethin' about those reward bills, Gaudalupe Kid.'

'Yeah, I'd advise you to,' the Kid said sarcastically. 'I told you my accounts were all squared.'

'Who squared 'em?' Ogden snapped.

The Kid grinned and said, 'Ever hear of a man named Tucson Smith? He's back of any move I make.'

Ogden's eyes narrowed in thought. He glanced sidewise at the Kid, then shook his head.

Guadalupe grinned. 'Don't lie, Ogden. Your face give you away. And don't forget that Tucson Smith has got plenty influence—'

21

'He a friend of yours?' Deputy Glascow was looking rather put out.

'Friend of mine!' The Kid laughed joyously as though eager to admit the fact. With the Kid it was almost akin to confessing a belief in a Supreme Deity. That was how he felt about Tucson Smith. 'Oh, shucks, travel, hombres. You're brayin' a little louder every time you open your traps.'

Ogden asked warily, 'Where's this Smith hombre now?'

The Kid said frankly, 'Last letter I had from him was posted down in Mexico.' The Kid didn't say what the letter had contained.

Ogden smiled thinly, confidently. 'We're getting off the trail,' he changed the subject. 'I've made my talk. Better take heed, Kid. C'mon, Brose.'

The two wheeled their horses and broke into a swift lope, but before they passed over the next rise of land, Guadalupe saw them slow pace and draw close together.

'Yeah,' the Kid chuckled, 'I've give 'em somethin' to think—and talk—about now. They're sure due for a surprise if they figure Tucson is still in Mexico. He ought to be gettin' pretty close to this country, 'bout now.'

Guadalupe retraced his steps to the long porch and dropped into a chair beside Don Manuel. The old Spaniard looked worried. 'I greatly fear, my son, that you are about to embrace trouble with wide open arms. What did they have to say?'

'Nothing that matters,' Guadalupe replied absent-mindedly. He was looking for Caroline who had stepped into the house a few moments before the Kid returned to the gallery. 'Where's Miss Sibley?'

'She left to find our cook, thinking you might wish something to eat, some hot coffee—'

The Kid looked surprised. 'I had an idea you and Miss Sibley were alone.'

'We still have a cook—Sourdough George Jenkins. I don't know why he stays. I can no longer afford to pay wages. My other hands left long since—those who were able to leave.'

The Kid looked up rather quickly. 'Meanin'?'

'Three of my *vaqueros* were found out on the range,' the old man explained grimly. 'They had been shot from ambush. My cattle have been run off. There are a few horses in the corral. How many are left on the range I can't state with any certainty. Being unable to afford help has made the yearly round-ups impossible. In short,' and the old man forced a wistful smile, 'the glories of the Tresbarro brand are all in the past.'

'Who's responsible?' the Kid asked and immediately sensed the reply.

'Steve Ogden—but I can prove nothing. The man is insane with the greed for money and power. Gradually he is gaining more and more

23

of the range—'

'You should have accepted his offer when he upped my bid.'

'In the first place,' Tresbarro said grimly, 'he would have found some way of avoiding payment. I don't trust him. He practically dictates politics in Los Potros—that's our nearest town. I'm getting too old to fight him, though had I had the money—' He broke off, then added, 'I fear, my son, that you are making a bad bargain. If there are left on my range, fifteen hundred cows bearing the Tresbarro brand I'm much surprised—'

'I'm not worrying about that. I know a bargain when I see one. Don't forget that I know something about this layout. The minute I heard Ogden offering money I knew it was worth-while. Furthermore, if you care to stay on, here, I don't reckon it's going to be necessary for you to move. We'll try and make you comfortable—'

Guadalupe broke off, embarrassed at the gratitude in the old man's tones, and said something about Caroline Sibley.

Tresbarro explained. 'She's an orphan, like yourself. The daughter of a man who once worked for me. When her mother died, I took the responsibility of bringing her up. Now that I'm alone in the world, it's been good having her here. She takes care of me like a daughter of my own would have done. I grow old, Jeff. I haven't many more years. Someday, any

24

money I have left must go to her.'

The conversation turned to other subjects, Guadalupe asking questions about the ranch, Ogden and his cohorts, the town of Los Potros, and so on, and advancing certain information of his own life during the past years, until Caroline appeared in the doorway to announce that food was on the table and the coffee piping hot.

With her was a lanky, bald-headed individual with sweeping mustaches and a long red nose whom Caroline introduced as Sourdough George Jenkins. Jenkins must have been close to sixty years old and wore, in lieu of an apron, an old flour sack.

'See ye, when ye come past my shack,' Jenkins said, shaking hands, and looking dourly down his long nose at the Kid. 'Figgered ye could find yore way. Corns been a-frettin' me all mawnin', so I didn't bother gittin' up. Muh corns always warn me ahead of trouble comin'. Oh, well, one more spud in the pot an' another plate on the table. Thet's 'bout all there is to life, these days—allus pervidin' ye got that extra spud.' He added a moment later, 'I'll put up yore hawss an' give him a bait while ye're eatin'.' And Guadalupe, with that, knew he had passed the cook's favorable inspection.

'Thanks, Sourdough,' Guadalupe grinned, 'and you won't make that crowbait mad if you mix a mite of grain with his fodder.'

'I'll do that,' Sourdough nodded, 'pervidin' I

can scratch up said grain someplace.'

He took the horse away and Guadalupe followed the girl and Don Manuel into the big main room of the ranch house which was comfortably furnished with solid oak furniture, Navajo rugs and wild animal skins. In one wall was a huge rock fireplace. A door opened into a dining room, through which Guadalupe could see a long table and plates of steaming food.

The two men talked long at the table. By the time night fell and Caroline had lighted the kerosene lamps, she had a pretty good idea of the Kid's history and that of his friends. The talk was continued when they had left the dining table for the easy chairs in the main room where a blazing fire now crackled in the fireplace.

Finally, Don Manuel mentioned the drawing up of the paper covering the option on the ranch. This was dictated by Guadalupe and signed by the old Spaniard, being witnessed by Caroline and Sourdough George. The Kid endorsed the check and passed it over.

'And that is that,' Don Manuel said, with considerable relief in his voice when the cook had left the room. 'You'll find things pretty generally in need of repair, Jeff. Caroline manages to keep the house clean, but—well, you see how it is. It's too much for one girl. George keeps up his end. I'm not good for much, anymore.'

'You're good for a great deal, grandad,' Caroline said earnestly. 'Now, with this worry off your mind, you can really commence to live—'

Her words ended in a shrill scream. There came a sound of shattering glass. Outside a rifle barked sharply. A second shot whined through the broken window!

Don Manuel started to rise, then stiffened and sank back in his chair, clutching his breast. Guadalupe leaped toward Caroline, one hand sweeping the lamp from the table as he moved. The room was plunged into darkness as he forced the girl toward the floor.

'Stay down—down!' he ordered sharply. 'Don't move!'

In the flickering lights cast by the fireplace he saw the dark crimson blot welling on Don Manuel's breast. The old Spaniard's eyes were open, but were already growing glassy.

Another shot burst through the window, followed by two more, to thud harmlessly into the adobe walls. By this time, Guadalupe had reached the dining room where he'd left his gun belts hanging on a peg. Seizing a gun in each hand, he dashed back into the darkened main room, crossed the floor with quick strides and flung open the front door.

A veritable hail of lead greeted the opening of the door, but Guadalupe had been prepared for that: he shifted rapidly to one side, three orange flashes of fire burst from his right hand.

In the yard fronting the house came a shrill cry of pain. Horses moved rapidly through the darkness. There came a creaking of saddle leather. Another burst of explosions shattered the night. The horses were getting swiftly under way now.

From the rear of the house came the hoarse voice of Sourdough George. A shadowy figure flashed past the doorway. The gun kicked in Guadalupe's hand—once, twice! A horse screamed, the sound drowning out a human cry of anguish. Then, from another angle, came three crimson lances of flame. Another horse pawed the earth, got under way with a rush.

Guadalupe staggered back from the door, guns dropping from his hands, then crashed full-length on the floor!

Sourdough George rounded the corner of the house at a gallop, bearing a double-barrel shot-gun, loaded with buckshot. The gun roared twice in the direction of the retreating riders, but, apparently failed to score a hit.

George swore fervently, started toward the front door of the house. Halfway there he stumbled against something and fell to the ground. His voice came through the darkness after a minute, 'Finished complete. There's one hombre won't never need to buy no more cornsalve ... Hawss, too. What the hell's happened?'

The drumming of horses' hoofs was dying

rapidly away. Sourdough stepped to the gallery, peered through the darkness beyond the open front door, dimly made out movement in the feeble flickering of the dying embers in the fireplace.

'Everythin' all right in there?' The cook's voice sounded shaky, as he struck a match.

Caroline's steps sounded, as she groped for the upset lamp. Her voice held a sob, 'I—I think they're both—dead. Sourdough—' Numbly she examined the lamp which still held some oil.

'Cripes Genimity!' The cook pushed into the room, helped the girl relight the lamp. He looked at Don Manuel, then avoided the girl's eyes. 'You jest take it a mite easy now, Car'line. Better go to yore room. I'll take care of this.'

Caroline swallowed heavily, her eyes brimming. 'Maybe—maybe Jeff isn't—'

'I'll see to thet too.' The cook crossed back to the doorway, knelt at Guadalupe's side, turned him on his back. 'Dang nasty scratch 'long side his head. If thet's all, he's lucky. Who done this?' continuing the examination of the Kid's unconscious body.

'I don't know,' the girl said bitterly, 'but I might make a close guess. You could too.' She explained what had happened in quick terse sentences. Sourdough nodded grimly, said, 'Yeah, I could make a guess too … Say, can you get me some water? I'll wash this wound on Guadalupe's head. Mebbe we can make to pull him through. I don't find no other holes.'

Glad to escape from the room even for only a few moments, Caroline hurried for a pan of water. The Kid was still unconscious when she returned. Sourdough washed the wound and asked for some bandaging cloth. Caroline procured that too. Sourdough splashed water on the Kid's face, then rose and crossed to Don Manuel's cold form. In a moment he returned to the Kid, shaking his head. A groan issued from the Kid's lips, but his eyes remained closed.

'Reckon he'll be comin' to in a jiffy,' Sourdough said. He spied the Kid's guns on the floor, picked them up and placed the weapons on a chair. Caroline didn't say anything.

Hoof beats sounded through the night. Sourdough shut the door quickly, seized Guadalupe's guns. The girl's eyes were wide with fright, but she didn't give voice to her fear. Men dismounted outside. A moment later their footsteps thudded on the gallery floor, then came a knock on the door.

Caroline said, fighting to hold the words steady, 'Who's there?'

Steve Ogden's voice replied. 'Deputy Glascow is with me. What's happened here? We heard shots. There's a dead man outside.'

Caroline and Sourdough exchanged quick glances. Caroline said, 'Let them in.' Sourdough opened the door.

'Good God!' Ogden cried. 'What's this?'

'Somebody's shot old Tresbarro,' Glascow chimed in.

Caroline said steadily to Ogden, 'You don't know anything about this?'

Ogden looked surprised. 'Certainly not, Miss Sibley. We heard shots—'

'What brings you here now?' the girl cut in.

'I came to make one last effort to persuade Don Manuel to sell me this place. I was prepared to raise my price. I may of course be too late—'

'Do you expect us to believe that story?' Caroline asked scornfully. 'You don't know a thing about any of this, I suppose—'

'Great Scott!' from Ogden. 'Why should I?' He added, 'We heard shooting, of course—'

'But you didn't meet the men who did the shooting?' the girl persisted.

'Certainly not. We just came from Los Potros—'

'The killers,' Caroline said sternly, 'left by the trail that leads to Los Potros.'

'You're mistaken, Miss Sibley.' Ogden smiled thinly, shaking his head.

'Come to think of it,' Glascow broke in, 'seems like I heard horses headin' west. Yep, you're plumb-mistaken, Miss Sibley. Howsomever, things is comin' a mite clearer to me now.' The deputy glanced at Guadalupe who was commencing to stir.

'What you hinting at, Brose?' Ogden said.

31

'It's all mighty clear,' Glascow nodded. 'This Guadalupe Kid had a gang with him. The gang bumped off Don Manuel so they wouldn't have to make good on any option. It's a plan to steal the outfit. One of the shots went astray and hit Guadalupe—'

Contempt showed in Caroline's eyes. 'Anybody with a half a brain could see Jeff was shot defending the house—'

'You don't know his record like I do, Miss,' Glascow growled. 'I'll be takin' him in. He'll hang for this, shore as blazes—'

'Brose,' Sourdough said angrily, 'yo're a bigger fool than I thought if ye think ye can make that story stick. Thet's a wounded man ye're plannin' to take prisoner. He don't move if I can prevent it. He needs medical 'tention fer thet head—'

'You, Sourdough,' Glascow rasped, 'put away them guns plumb pronto. Yo're resistin' the law. I'll shoot if I have to. This Guadalupe hombre sleeps in a cell tonight. That plain? Steve, you keep an eye on Sourdough. I'm authorizin' you to plug him if he tries to prevent me doin' my duty. The Guadalupe Kid gets a charge of murder placed against him. That settles the matter.'

Reaching to a hip pocket he produced a pair of handcuffs, slipped them on the Kid's wrists and yanked him upright. 'Yo're comin' with me, see, Kid,' he rasped triumphantly, 'and don't give me no back talk.'

32

But the Kid was still too far gone to resist. Ogden had his gun out, covering Sourdough George. Caroline had the back of one hand pressed against her open mouth as though stifling a scream. The two men, half carrying their semi-conscious burden, backed toward the doorway.

'I'll send the undertaker out here, when we get back to Los Potros,' Glascow said.

Caroline didn't reply. Sourdough mouthed feeble oaths under his breath. The door slowly closed at Ogden's heels. From outside came the sounds of horses getting under motion. Faint, triumphant laughter, illy suppressed, floated back through the closed door. Then all sounds, except the quiet sobbing of the girl in the ranch house main room, tapered off to silence...

CHAPTER THREE

THE THREE MESQUITEERS

Three riders traveled west along the old stage road that ran between Los Potros and Chancellor, the latter being the seat of Tresbarro County. The hoof-chopped and wheel-rutted trail wound snakily through the rolling, grass-covered foothills of the San Mateo Mountains. The road was easy to follow under the brilliant mid-morning sun.

Clumps of cactus and sage dotted the hills at intervals. Occasionally, outthrusts of huge granite blocks bordered by the spiny yucca were seen. Tiny lizards and horned toads darted, from beneath the hoofs of the easily moving horses, across the dusty trail. All this was viewed and accepted automatically by the three riders. The Southwest country was an old story to the trio of mesquiteers, as Tucson Smith, Lullaby Joslin and Stony Brooke were known to their friends.

Tucson Smith rode between his two pardners, his lean, muscular length moving easily to the motions of the sorrel gelding under his saddle. He was a rangy individual with brick-red hair, slate-grey eyes and a long bony face. His nose was hooked; the straight-lipped, wide mouth was determined, with tiny quirks at the corners, as if he enjoyed and got a great deal from life as he viewed it. There was something stern, implacable, about his face, and, if the small laugh wrinkles radiating from the eyes had anything to do with the matter, at the same time considerable tolerance in his make-up.

Smith's companion on the right was Lullaby Joslin who was lanky, sleepy-eyed and soft-spoken. Joslin's leather-like features were long and funereal-appearing, his hair as straight and black as an Apache's. There was something slouchy about his clothing—like his two companions he wore a typical range

34

costume: riding boots, bibless overalls, woolen shirt, vest, neckerchief and sombrero—something ill-fitting, as though the sleeves which exposed bony wrists were too short, the neckband of his shirt a size too large. Even his seat in the saddle of the black pony between his long legs was loose, careless, as his drowsy hazel eyes surveyed the twisting trail ahead.

Stony Brooke, the third man of the trio, was shorter than the other two, but what he lacked in height was more than compensated by exceedingly wide shoulders and a barrel-like torso. He was dark complexioned with innocent blue eyes and a snub nose. A wide, mischievous, gargoylish grin covered his good-natured features at nearly all times. Stony's one ambition in life seemed to be to stir up some *real* excitement, and this ambition had been amply realized on a good many occasions in which he shot his way through perilous situations with a blazing gun and a cheerful grin. It was said of Stony Brooke that he would, undoubtedly, crack jokes at his own funeral.

Brooke and Joslin were about thirty years of age; Tucson Smith a trifle older. One thing all three possessed in common: from the criss-crossed cartridge belts encircling their slim hips was suspended a brace of holstered Colt's forty-five six-shooters, in the use of which all three were remarkably proficient.

These three were known by many names:

35

The Incomparables, The Cactus Cavaliers, the Three Inseparables. Probably, the Three Mesquiteers fitted them best: like the famed musketeers of the immortal Dumas, these three were, indeed, 'one for all and all for one.' Law busters in the Southwest country feared and hated them. Their friends—and the Three Mesquiteers had made many in their various adventures—swore by all the gods of the cow-country that Tucson and his pards were 'ace-high all through the deck.' That they would, in short, make good hands on any man's spread.

The three horses trotted on. Stony Brooke lifted the neckerchief at his throat, wiped the perspiration from his face and reached for Durham and cigarette papers. Half way through the operation of rolling a smoke, Lullaby turned his head and said, 'Pass that Durham to Tucson so I can have it, will you, Stony?'

Stony frowned. 'Thought you put in a supply of 'makin's' before we pulled out of Chancellor.'

'Did,' Lullaby admitted lazily, 'but I'd have to reach into my pocket for it.' Then, at Stony's indignant outburst, 'Oh well, let it go.'

Tucson smiled and said nothing. He was used to the wrangling of this pair which afforded him considerable amusement on their travels and made time pass swiftly.

Lullaby finally produced his own tobacco and papers. He smoked in silence for a time,

36

then, 'I'll be dang glad if we ever hit some town where there's food.'

'Food!' from Stony in awed-tones. 'You hungry again? Migawd! Where do you stow it? Your legs must be hollow.'

'That's an idea,' Lullaby said suddenly.

Stony asked suspiciously, 'What is?'

'If it's hollow legs that makes me eat so much, what is it that makes you ask so many questions? I'd like to think it has somethin' to do with some sort of brain process, but, where you're concerned, I don't dare.'

'You hintin' that my head is hollow?' Stony demanded belligerently.

Lullaby said sweetly, 'I didn't reckon it was necessary to *hint*.'

Stony ignored that. He went on, 'You had two orders of ham-an'-aigs before we left Chancellor, three cups of coffee, apple-pie—'

'It was dang good pie. I liked it.'

'I s'pose,' scornfully from Stony, 'you ate all that other fodder just from force of habit—'

'I didn't see no fried rabbit on the bill-of-fare—'

'I said "force of habit", nitwit,' Stony said disgustedly, missing the wink Lullaby directed at Tucson. 'You better wash your ears.'

'Not for me,' Lullaby yawned. 'I'm forced to listen to too much empty conversation as it is.'

'Hear what he said about your talkin', Tucson?' Stony asked.

Tucson chuckled, 'Don't drag me into your

arguments. You know what always happens to the innocent bystander.'

Stony continued, 'All that chuck in Chancellor, then at that stage station, ten miles back, you mooched a bowl of *frijoles* from the Mex gal—'

'She was a dang pretty *paisana*,' Lullaby defended his actions.

Stony agreed. 'I didn't say anythin' about the girl's looks. I've heard of hombres bein' driven to drink by beauty, but that's the first time I ever heard of a man takin' to beans. But that's neither here nor there. What I'm gettin' at, where do you put all the stuff you eat? You'd think your skinny frame would be swelled out like—'

Lullaby cut in indignantly. 'Never mind my frame. You ain't no Adonis, yourself.'

Stony looked disgusted. 'Now, it's doughnuts. Can't you keep your mind off food?'

'I said Adonis—not doughnuts. Not that I'd mind a coupla sinkers—but, say, didn't you ever hear of Adonis, Stony?'

'Nope,' promptly, 'and ten to one you don't know much about him either. Me, I think twice before spoutin' off talk about things I ain't familiar with.'

Lullaby said dryly, 'I often wondered why you hardly ever talked.'

Stony reddened. 'All right, Mister Wise Guy. You tell me. What outfit did this Adonis ever punch for.'

Lullaby snickered. 'Adonis was one of the old Greeks—'

Stony's face cleared. 'The only Greek I ever knew was Greek George. He drove them camels that Jeff Davis brought over before the Civil War—'

Lullaby stifled an exasperated yawn. 'Your lack of culture is somethin' terrible, Stony. Now, look, try to understand this: Adonis was a Greek god—'way back in ancient times. He was in love with a girl called Aphrodite, but before they got to marry each other, Adonis was killed by a boar—'

Lullaby broke off to guide his pony around a chuck-hole in the road. Stony said, 'This bore bein' the Aphrodite gal's lawful wedded husband, I suppose. Go on—'

Lullaby heaved a long sigh of patience. 'The word,' he said sarcastically, 'is spelt b-o-a-r. Meanin' a wild pig. Does that penetrate anythin'?'

'Well, you twisted-tongued rannie, why didn't you say in the first place that Doughnuts run a pig ranch? Go on. A swill time was had by all, I expect.'

Lullaby pretended to be nauseated. 'That one ain't so new, either.' He appealed to Tucson, 'Say, can't we leave this dumb rannie home, next time we drift places.'

'You might,' Tucson smiled, 'tell me where home is. Then mebbe I can answer your question.'

Lullaby looked sorrowful. 'There, you've reminded me of that, again. We ain't got any home. We're just saddletramps. Ain't we ever goin' to settle down any place? This boomin' around the country—'

'Can't find any *real* excitement any other way,' Stony put in.

'Who wants real excitement or any other kind?' Lullaby said sorrowfully. 'Me, I crave a nice little outfit—'

'There, you got him started again, Tucson,' Stony said disgustedly. 'Him and his settlin' down.' He grinned, 'Never heard of anybody settlin' *up*, did you?'

Lullaby said fervently, 'If you're referrin' to that five bucks you owe me, I certainly didn't.'

Stony fell suddenly silent, his mind struggling for the swift retort that wouldn't come. Lullaby went on, 'But why didn't we do as we planned? When the U.S. Government paid us that reward for recoverin' those gold bars, we was all for buyin' an outfit that we could call home.'

'Most of that money,' Tucson reminded, 'is still in the bank at El Paso, Lullaby. Why don't you take your share and—'

'What,' indignantly from Lullaby, 'and leave you two to go roamin' around, gettin' shot up?'

Tucson's eyes twinkled. 'Seems like to me,' he said gravely, 'that you was the first, Lullaby, to propose that last trip down into Mexico.'

'Not me,' Lullaby declared emphatically. 'I'm the last man in the world to suggest any such dangerous trip as that. Me, I'm peace lovin', I am.'

'Yeah,' Tucson stated dryly, 'I've seen you spread the gospel out of those forty-five Peacemakers of yours.'

'That's whatever,' Stony broke in, 'what I'm thinkin' about is why Guadalupe Ferguson didn't meet us at Chancellor, three days ago, as planned.'

'Aw, the Kid's all right,' Tucson said quietly, though in his own mind he wasn't so sure. The Kid being, in a way, a protégé of Tucson's had been the subject of considerable thought the past few days.

'You don't suppose,' Stony said slowly, 'the Kid's in any trouble, do you? No, I don't mean that he's gone to runnin' with the wild bunch again, but—'

'Shucks,' Tucson reaffirmed, 'he'll be all right. Mebbe we'll cross his trail today. His last letter said he'd be comin' this way, on the road that ran from Los Potros to Chancellor. This is it.'

'Los Potros the next town?' Lullaby asked.

Tucson nodded. 'The next town—yes. There's a stage station called Wagon Springs, about fifteen miles farther on. Nothin' there though, except—'

'Could we get a snack of food at Wagon

41

Springs, do you suppose?' Lullaby asked wistfully.

Stony groaned and quickly changed the subject. 'Tucson, you seem to know this country right well.'

Tucson nodded. 'I been through here before—when I was a button about seventeen years old. Ridin' with a crew that brought a herd of steers to deliver to the Tresbarro outfit, which was experimentin' on some cross-breeds stuff.'

'I've heard of the Tresbarro iron in the past,' Lullaby put in. 'Old brand, ain't it?'

'Yeah,' from Tucson, 'dates away back. Old Spanish grant stuff. Haven't heard much of the brand the past several years. Reckon it must have petered out, after the massacre.'

'What massacre was that?' Stony asked.

Tucson explained. 'Bunch of 'Paches took to the warpath and raided the Tresbarro place. With the exception of Don Manuel Tresbarro himself, the whole family was wiped out. The old man was bad wounded, but recovered. He carried on alone after that, but I reckon he lost interest in raisin' beef. Speaking of ranches, there's a spread that would suit Lullaby right down to the ground.'

'In what way?' Lullaby wanted to know.

'It's got everything—water, grass, buildin's. It's got anythin' that's required to raise cows. That is, it used to have. Pro'bly gone to pot, or parceled up into small outfits by this time.'

Ahead of the three riders the road curved widely to cut around a high outcropping of sandstone. Low mesquite trees dotted the landscape on each side of the trail. Cholla grew profusely among the grass that carpeted the hillsides.

'Another five miles, about,' Tucson was saying, 'will bring us out of these hills. Then there's a clear stretch of grass country until we strike the Escabrosa Range. If we don't see anythin' of Guadalupe by the time we reach Los Potros—'

He stopped suddenly in what he was saying. The other two had tensed, stiffening in saddles. A second crack of a rifle followed the first, the sound coming from just around the bend that lay ahead. There came the roar of a shot-gun. A couple of wild yells. Then more gun shots!

'C'mon,' Tucson snapped.

He jabbed spurs into the sorrel's sides and swept into swift motion, the other two being quick to catch and adopt the idea. The three mesquiteers, standing in stirrups now, strung out as they rounded the abrupt curve in the road, the hoofs of their ponies kicking up puffs of dust as they rode.

And then, the trail straightened out, throwing into plain view the scene of tragedy that had succeeded the firing of the shots:

At each side of the wheel-rutted way stunted trees and thick brush had provided an ideal location for the ambush. In the center of the

43

road stood a Concord coach, the driver of which was slumped sidewise on his seat, his body in a queer, awkward position. The two lead horses were down, dead in the dusty roadway. A lifeless man lay sprawled on the earth a few yards from the right front wheel of the coach. Another man knelt on the ground, the coach's strong box before him. He was holding his gun muzzle toward the lock of the strong box.

Even as the three riders swept round the bend the man pulled trigger. So engrossed was he in his work that he didn't catch the sounds of the approaching hoofs. An instant later he had thrown back the lid of the box and extracted a packet of letters, bound together with a length of cord. Breaking the cord he commenced looking over the letters.

At the same instant he heard Tucson and his pardners bearing down on him. Startled, he leaped to his feet, the letters fluttering from his hand to the earth. One hand started to swing his gun, then he turned and commenced to run.

Tucson's gun barked savagely, kicking up dust at the fleeing man's heels. 'Stop!' Tucson yelled. Guns roared in the fists of Lullaby and Stony, cutting a series of small dirt clouds about the bandit's flying heels. He stopped suddenly, turned, flinging his arms in the air and commenced to beg for mercy.

The three riders closed in, pulled their ponies to a halt. Stony leaned down and jerked the gun from the man's hand. Then the three dismounted.

'Look here, fellers,' the man started to whine, 'I didn't have anythin' to do with this, y'understand. I just happened along—'

'Shut up, coyote!' Tucson snapped. 'We saw a-plenty.' Stony and Lullaby had been looking around. Lullaby reported. 'No passengers, but the driver has been shot through the heart. Wonder where the guard is.'

Stony had examined the dead man on the earth. 'Reckon this stiff is a hold-up man. The driver's plumb ruined his face with that shotgun that's layin' on the footboard of the coach.'

Tucson turned to the man they had captured. 'What you got to say, feller?'

'Nothin' to you,' the man returned sullenly. 'I didn't have nothin' to do with this.'

'Don't lie,' Tucson said sternly. 'We saw a-plenty.'

The man said insolently, 'All right, try to prove anythin' against me. Me, I ain't talkin'. I want a lawyer—'

'You'll get a damn sight more than that,' Lullaby growled.

Stony had been examining the shattered lock of the strong box. He looked up to call to Tucson, 'The coach wasn't carryin' anythin' valuable, I reckon. Nothin' but U. S. Mail in this box—and that's scattered on the ground here.'

'Picked the wrong stage, eh, mister?' Tucson said to the bandit.

'Sure, if you want it that way,' the outlaw sneered. 'Anythin' to be agreeable, feller. You goin' to stand here talkin' all day? If you figure to take me to town, let's go. You'll find my hawss back in the brush.'

'Cocky, ain't you?' Stony said.

'I ain't saw no reason to be otherwise. If you hombres think you can prove anythin' against me—'

'Shut your trap, killer,' Lullaby snapped. 'We'll take you in, all right, and I reckon there won't be any trouble provin' this against you.'

Stony had disappeared in the brush. A moment later he came out leading the two saddled horses that had been hidden there. The bandit was boosted to one of the saddles and his wrists tied securely to the horn. Tucson found a blanket inside the coach which he threw over the body of the dead driver. The dead bandit in the road he put inside the coach, then unharnessed the stage horses and tethered them to the nearby brush.

By the time he had completed this, Stony and Lullaby had finished tying the captive in his saddle. Tucson noticed the letters scattered about the earth and commenced picking them up. Happening to glance at the third letter he retrieved, he noted with surprise that it was addressed to himself, care of General Delivery, at the town of Chancellor. This he thrust into a hip pocket, then continued to gather the remainder of the letters which were finally stowed safely inside his shirt.

Stony and Lullaby were already mounted when Tucson came up to them. He didn't mention the letter bearing his own name, but climbed into the saddle with the remark, 'We'll stop at Wagon Springs and tell 'em about this hold-up. Let's go.'

Lullaby said to the captive, 'Get movin', skunk—up ahead of us, where we won't have to smell you. If you feel like makin' a dash for it, go right ahead. That would suit me right down to the ground. I'm still regrettin' you didn't try to shoot your way out.'

In silence, the four riders moved away from the scene of the tragedy, the captive riding a few yards in advance of the three cowboys.

Once the horses were moving steadily along the road, Tucson drew out the envelope bearing his name, ripped it open and commenced to read the sheet of written words it contained. As he read, a strange expression crept into his usually sober features, a frown gathered on his forehead.

'Hey, you,' Stony asked, 'you openin' the U. S. Mails for your entertainment these days?'

'Happens to be addressed to me,' Tucson returned absent-mindedly. And added, 'It concerns the three of us.'

He glanced at the captive on the horse ahead, looked steadily at the other two. As though by mutual consent, the three allowed their ponies to drop several yards behind, out of earshot of the outlaw.

'Lullaby,' Tucson said, 'you or Stony know anybody by the names of Caroline Sibley or George Jenkins?'

Stony and Lullaby shook their heads, puzzled. 'Who are they?' Stony wanted to know.

'Never heard of them myself,' Tucson admitted, 'only—well, their names are signed as witnesses on this paper—'

'Witnesses to what?' Lullaby asked.

'To the fact,' Tucson said quietly, 'that we've bought a ranch known as the Tresbarro outfit—'

'Huh?' in startled exclamations from the other two.

Tucson nodded, smiling at the looks on the features of the pair. 'I don't know what it's all about, but this paper gives us a thirty day option on the Tresbarro brand, buildin's, water rights, land, stock—shucks, the whole layout. The price is thirty thousand. We have to pay some taxes—'

'Who signed it?' Stony wanted to know.

'Old Don Manuel Tresbarro, himself.'

Lullaby said, 'Do you suppose Guadalupe had anythin' to do with this business?'

Tucson's shoulders lifted in a shrug. 'It's all a mystery to me. Looks like a girl's handwritin'—except the signature.'

48

'Well, I'll be damned!' Stony said suddenly.

'I hope it's true,' from Lullaby. ''Bout time we was settlin' down—'

'Aw, you and your settlin' down,' Stony said bitterly. 'We don't ever get to see no *real* excitement if this deal goes through.'

Tucson said seriously, 'I got a hunch that we'll see plenty of excitement, hombres. That coach wasn't carryin' money. Either the stick-up men were after letters, or they made a mistake. Somehow, I sort of feel they were after this option paper ... Here, take a look at it, yourselves.'

A few moments later, the three cowboys spurred their horses to catch up to the captive who had plodded steadily along, apparently regardless of the fate that awaited him.

For a time no one spoke, then Lullaby, 'That hold-up coyote is too damn easy in his mind. I'm wondering' if he's got a stand-in with the law in this county.'

Tucson nodded. 'Such things have been known to happen. We ought to learn a heap by the time we reach Los Potros. I'll be damn glad to learn just what's happened to Guadalupe.'

'If anything has,' and Stony's usually good-natured faced was clouded, 'God help the coyotes that done it.'

CHAPTER FOUR

TUCSON TALKS TURKEY

The sun had already passed meridian before Wagon Springs station was reached. Wagon Springs wasn't much of a place—just a few buildings, corrals containing horses, and manned by several stockmen, employees of the stage company. The place was what was known in those days as a swing station, established solely for the purpose of enabling stages to secure relays of fresh horses and turn over to the stock-tenders the weary beasts which had thus far hauled the coaches over many miles of rough road.

The man in charge of the station was seated on a long porch fronting the main building when the three cowboys rode up and dismounted in the shadow of the building. He rose quickly upon noting the captive tied in the saddle.

Tucson explained briefly, 'Your stage was held-up about twelve miles back. Driver killed—'

'T'hell you say!' exploded the man whose name was Winters.

Tucson nodded. 'Two lead horses downed. Looked to me like your driver was the one killed one of the outlaws before he got his own

50

rubbin' out, though it might have been the guard done it. We didn't see any sign of a guard. Mebbe he drifted—'

'Wasn't any guard on that coach,' Winters said, looking upset. 'The regular guard has been sick. No money or passengers going through—nothing but the mail. Old Charlie has been driving the route the past two trips alone. This is a hell of a note—Old Charlie Panzer dead. Hell, stranger, he's druv this route for nigh on twenty years now.' The station man seemed stunned at the news. He added, shaky voiced, 'I'll send a man right out there.'

Tucson indicated the captive outlaw, 'Know this man—?' meanwhile explaining how they had seen him breaking into the strong box.

The station man looked at the outlaw. The outlaw glared back viciously. The station man opened his mouth to speak, then stopped, went on, 'We-ell,' uncertainly, 'he looks sort of familiar, but I can't say.'

'You sure?' Tucson persisted.

Winters changed the subject, 'I'll have to get one of my hands started.' He raised his voice, 'Hey, Taggert.'

Tucson took from inside his shirt the letters he had picked from the ground, handing them to Winters, 'Here's the mail I picked up.' He didn't say anything about the option addressed to himself.

Winters took the letters. A young fellow in

51

overalls rounded the corner of the building, looked inquiringly at the three cowboys and their captive, then said, 'What's happened to you, Sharkey?'

The outlaw's face clouded with hate. He didn't answer.

Tucson said, 'You know this man.'

'Look here, Taggert,' Winters cleared his throat hesitatingly, 'there's been a hold-up—'

Tucson cut in, 'You know this man, Taggert?'

Taggert said promptly. 'I ain't a friend of his, if that's what you mean, but his name's Sharkey—Fin Sharkey. I've seen him in Los Potros several times. Him and his pard, Puma Jeems, rode through here just at daylight this mornin'.'

'You better keep your trap closed, Taggert,' Sharkey snarled.

Taggert said, 'You know where you can go, don't you, Fin?'

Fin Sharkey swore venomously. Tucson said, 'I reckon it's Puma Jeems you'll find layin' in the coach with his face blown off.'

Winters cut in hurriedly to give brief details of the hold-up and added certain orders, urging Taggert to be on his way. Taggert glared angrily at Sharkey. 'I hope they hang you, Fin, but they pro'bly won't. I thought a heap of Charlie Panzer.'

'Get goin', now, Taggert, get goin',' Winters urged nervously.

Taggert nodded and disappeared around the building. Tucson said, 'We'll water our horses and take Sharkey into Los Potros. Who's sheriff there, now?'

'There's just a deputy-sheriff, Brose Glascow. Sheriff Morgan stays in Chancellor—county seat.'

Lullaby said, 'Glascow good enough for the job?'

Sharkey cut in, 'Winters, anythin' you don't say won't get you into trouble.'

Winters said, rather weakly, to Lullaby, 'Far's I know, Deputy Glascow is a good man. I don't get into Los Potros much. My duties here keep me busy...' His voice trailed off to silence. He cleared his throat again, changed the subject, 'I don't know what this country's comin' to. I suppose you heard about the murder.'

'Which one?' Stony wanted to know.

'Old man Tresbarro. He had a big place over west of Los Potros. It was gettin' kind of run down though.'

The three cowboys exchanged glances. Tucson asked, 'When was this?'

Winters told him, adding, 'He was buried yesterday afternoon.'

The three cowboys noted that the murder had taken place on the same day upon which the option had been signed. Tucson said, 'Did they catch the murderer?'

'I heard somebody say there was rumors to

53

that effect,' Winters replied, 'but I ain't heard any details yet. Deputy Glascow is a pretty good man. He don't talk much until he's sure.' As though looking for approbation Winters glanced quickly at the sullen Sharkey and received in reply only a cold sneer.

Taggert came riding around the corner of the building on a heavily built horse, leading a second animal of the same proportions. Winters said, 'Look here, Taggert, you don't need to take a team of leaders. The swings and wheelers will bring that coach back—'

'I ain't bringin' the stage back here,' Taggert cut in. 'Give me that mail. I'm goin' on through to Chancellor. Charlie Panzer lived there. I'll take him home. As for Puma Jeems, if anybody in Los Potros wants the carcass of that measly, dry-gulchin' vinegaroon, they can come to Chancellor for it—'

Winters protested feebly, 'I ain't give orders to that effect. You better—'

'T'hell with you and your orders,' Taggert snapped bitterly. 'What's that to do with breakin' the news to Old Charlie's wife. That's a job I ain't keen about, but I liked Charlie ... Give me that mail.'

Meekly, Winters surrendered the letters as Taggert leaned low from the horse to receive them. 'Taggert,' Winters commenced, 'you'd better learn a little respect for your superiors, or you're li'ble to find yourself jobless—'

'I'm already that,' Taggert snapped. 'I

decided to quit a few minutes back. I'm sick of workin' for a jelly-spined fossil what takes credit for the work I do. I'm through, see, Winters?' He spoke to the horses and started off.

Winters watched him in silence a few moments, then called, 'You come back here. No non-employee of the company has any right to drive company property—'

'Try and stop me,' Taggert snapped back over his shoulder.

Winters sighed and didn't say any more.

Tucson called, 'Say, Taggert.'

Taggert pulled up, rather belligerently, and looked around.

Tucson asked, 'You know anything about Deputy Glascow?'

Taggert said flatly, 'He's a louse—and I'm apologizin' to all the other breeds of louses.'

Tucson laughed softly. 'Frank and to the point.'

Taggert added, 'He'd steal the dandruff outten a dead man's hat. If you got any gold fillin's, keep your mouth shut when you get to Los Potros.'

'I ain't,' Tucson laughed, 'but I'll keep my eyes open. Thanks. Anythin' you can add about Fin Sharkey, here?'

'Last I heard he was workin' for Big Steve Ogden—and Puma Jeems too. You'll see Ogden in Los Potros. Mebbe he don't own the town, but he's got ideas.'

'Friend of yours?' Tucson asked ironically.

Taggert spat on the ground. A reply wasn't necessary in words.

Fin Sharkey swore a lurid stream at Taggert which Taggert disregarded with the remark that he'd 'better be on his way.'

'And you better keep goin' too,' Sharkey yelled after him. 'Steve Ogden will make it hot—'

Taggert smiled grimly. 'Do you think I'd talk so much if I intended comin' back. But there's a limit on how long a man can keep his trap shut—and still tell hisself he's a *man*.'

Sharkey cursed some more. Winters was pale as death, imploring Taggert to get on. Taggert told Winters to 'shut up,' then nodded good-bye to Tucson and his companions.

Tucson said, 'Taggert, if you do decide to come back mebbe I can talk job to you. I'll be in Los Potros for a spell.'

'Thanks, I'll look you up.' He grinned suddenly, 'That is, if I can get up enough nerve to return. Me, I've talked too much to make life comfortable. S'long.' He spoke to the horses and started again.

Twenty minutes later, after having seen to the horses' needs, the cowboys and their captive were again pushing along the trail that led to Los Potros, Sharkey being kept far enough in the lead to prevent his hearing the cowboys' conversation.

The way had flattened out considerably by

this time. As far as Tucson could see the road ran straight through easily rolling grass lands. Something in the atmosphere told Tucson that off to the south some distance was desert, or at least semi-desert country, but the range through which they were passing was all good grazing country with only occasional clumps of cactus and cat-claw growth. Now and then small bunches of cattle branded IXI were passed and a few rib-thin cows bearing a Rocking-R symbol were seen. Ahead, the serrated spine of the Escabrosa Range raised rugged peaks against the blue sky.

'And so,' Lullaby drawled, after a time, 'they settled down and were happy forever after.'

'You think so,' Stony chuckled, 'but I got a hunch—'

'It ain't from bearin' too many responsibilities,' Lullably said quickly, 'on that back of yours. If I couldn't look any farther ahead than you do! I didn't say we'd settle down to once. I realize we got troubles ahead—anyway, it's beginnin' to shape up thataway. I feel it in my bones—'

'Must give you a headache,' Stony grinned.

Lullaby said genially, 'All right, pal, I'll forgive that one. I remember pulling it on you first.'

Tucson said, 'Shut up a minute, you two, and talk sense.'

Stony said, 'Lullaby don't know how.'

'It looks to me,' Tucson said seriously, 'like

57

this Ogden—yes, and Deputy Glascow, too—had this country pretty well bullied.'

'I noticed that Winters didn't want to talk about 'em. In fact, he didn't want to know anythin'. If it hadn't been for Taggert tellin' us how the land lays—' Stony said.

Lullaby interrupted, 'Hell, that Winters is just a figurehead, afraid of his job. Taggert had the guts to talk up.'

'Don't overlook the fact,' Tucson pointed out, 'that Taggert, mebbe, is goin' to pull out of the country. Now, he looked like a pretty decent hombre—the kind that don't scare easy. And yet, he's got the notion to drag out and keep goin'.'

'Meanin'?' from Stony.

'That there must be a damn bad situation in this neck of the range. Mebbe we've bought a ranch. At the same time, mebbe we'll have a tough time holdin' it—'

'And us with no crew, either, and strangers in a strange land,' Lullaby drawled. 'It commences to sound interestin'.'

'We'll have to gather a crew,' Tucson said soberly. 'And among strangers as you say. That don't sound encouragin'.'

'That why you asked Taggert to look you up?' Lullaby asked.

Tucson nodded. 'We can't start buildin' an organization too soon. 'Course, there may be a full crew on the Tresbarro spread, but I doubt it. Unless that outfit is bad run down, it wouldn't sell for no thirty thousand. And if it's run down, it ain't likely there's any crew left by this time. From what I remember of the outfit though, it's a bargain at the price. I've got an idea that somebody killed Tresbarro to try to prevent him givin' this option we hold—'

'That someone bein' a hombre named Ogden?' Lullaby said.

Tucson replied, 'You heard Taggert's words.'

Stony suddenly started laughing. Lullaby said, 'What's the matter with you. What you laughin' at?'

Stony grinned. 'You—as usual.'

'Howcome?'

'You,' Stony explained, 'are the guy that's always cravin' to get an outfit and settle down. Well, you got it. Now, let's see you settle.'

Lullaby smiled sheepishly. 'I'll settle about five inches of Colt barrel alongside your head, if you don't shut up when your superiors are tryin' to think sober on a vital subject.'

'Vittles subject, where you're concerned,' Stony said. 'What's wrong, you sick? You ain't mentioned food for twenty minutes past.'

'I'm sufferin',' Lullaby said with a martyr-like air. 'I'd like a drink too.'

'One drink and you won't be able to think—sober.'

Lullaby said defensively, 'I can hold my liquor better'n you.'

'Ain't it the sweet truth,' Stony admitted. 'Last bar we were in I didn't see you let go the bottle once.'

The two were still wrangling when the tallest buildings of Los Potros were sighted as the mesquiteers and their captive pushed up a long slope of range. By this time the sun was touching the peaks of the Escabrosas, and filling the draws and canyons with deep purple shadows.

It was almost dark when the riders entered the single winding dusty street along each side of which had been erected the town. The buildings were of adobe in most cases, though several structures of wood, with high, false-fronts were to be seen. Here and there a mesquite tree raised branches above the riders' heads as they rode along the street. Squares and oblongs of yellow light shone from windows and doors along the way.

Tucson pushed up close to Fin Sharkey. 'I wouldn't advise you to signal any friends you might see, Sharkey. If there's trouble, the first slug out of my gun will have your address on it. That clear?'

'Think I'm a fool?' Sharkey growled.

Tucson nodded. 'Pretty much of a fool, or you wouldn't be in the tight you're in now.'

The riders were bunched closely together. It was too dark by this time for anyone to recognize Sharkey, or notice that his hands were tied to the saddlehorn. Several horses and wagons were tied at hitchracks along the way. Pedestrians moved on either side of the street. Now and then a rider passed through the dusk, but paid no attention to Tucson and his companions.

Lullaby said hopefully, 'There's a restaurant.'

'I see a saloon up ahead,' from Stony.

'Business first,' Tucson said. 'We got to find the deputy-sheriff's office. Mebbe you'll tell us where it is, Sharkey.'

Sharkey's reply consigned Tucson and his pards to a hotter climate. Lullaby said suddenly, 'There it is.'

On the left side of the street, fifty yards farther on, a light from a window illuminated a small sign bearing the words: 'DEPUTY-SHERIFF' with below it, 'JAIL.'

The men reined their horses toward the long, low adobe building which bore the sign. At the hitch-rack, Tucson dismounted. The others remained in saddles. Tucson approached the open doorway. Inside, seated at a desk, was Brose Glascow. A closed door at his rear led to the jail cells. The walls of the deputy's office held a rack of guns; several pairs of handcuffs on wooden pegs; three or four calendars, advertising packing houses; and a large map of the county. Several straight-backed wooden chairs stood about. The deputy was alone, a rank cigar burning between his teeth.

Tucson stepped through the open doorway. Glascow glanced up frowning. 'Well?'

'Deputy-Sheriff Glascow?'

'You called 'er correct, feller.'

'I'm reportin' a hold-up of the Los Potros-Chancellor stage, this morning', about twelve miles east of Wagon Springs. Driver killed.'

Glascow affected a certain interest. 'Is that so? Did you stop at Wagon Springs?' A cloud of cigar smoke obscured his features.

'Gave 'em the mail I found scattered on the ground, near the coach. Winters sent a man to handle the matter.'

Glascow said gruffly, ''Obliged. I'll get on the trail of the bandits soon's possible. Goodbye. Come in again.' He turned back to his desk.

Tucson smiled grimly. 'It won't be necessary to take any trails, Glascow. The driver of the stage killed one of the skunks. Feller named Puma Jeems, I believe.'

Glascow's head jerked up, startled. 'But Sharkey got away, eh?'

Tucson hesitated, then asked slowly, 'How did you know the other one was Sharkey?'

Glascow's pig eyes shifted suddenly as though seeking escape. The cigar dropped from his mouth as he fumbled with words. He choked. 'Why—why,' his speech stumbled awkwardly, 'I don't, of course. Only those two was always together—thicker'n thieves. I figured—you know, jumped to a conclusion— well, you see—'

'Sharkey's outside,' Tucson said quietly. 'He didn't get away.'

Tucson turned toward the street. Behind him he heard Glascow's chair crash to the floor as the deputy hurried to follow. Outside, Tucson said, 'Untie that skunk, fellows. This is Deputy Glascow.'

Fin Sharkey was released. Glascow stepped promptly up, jerking a pair of handcuffs out, and pinioned Sharkey's wrists. Then, 'Well, Sharkey, what you got to say for yourself?' he growled.

'What do you think, Brose?' the prisoner answered coolly.

'None of your lip, Fin,' in ugly tones.

'All right, it was this way. The stage was held up. I happened to be ridin' along there and these three dumb cow nurses grabs me as one of the hold-up men. It's all a mistake.'

Stony laughed sarcastically. 'A damn bad mistake.'

'You, feller,' Glascow glared at Stony, 'keep yore mouth shut 'till yo're spoke to.'

'My,' Lullaby drawled insultingly, 'ain't the deputy got a sweet nature.'

Glascow swore an oath and commenced hustling Sharkey toward the door of his office. 'I want to see you, feller,' he jerked over one shoulder at Tucson. Tucson followed him inside the office. Glascow jerked open the door leading to the jail, pushed Sharkey ahead of him. 'Back in a minute,' the deputy growled.

In the jail corridor the clanking of an iron-barred door sounded. A moment later,

Glascow reentered the office, slammed the jail door, righted his desk chair and sat down. 'Well,' harshly, 'what's your story?'

'You can get it from Sharkey. I'll tell the truth in a court of law, when the time comes.'

'Sharkey says you've made a mistake,' Glascow snapped.

'Don't you make the mistake of believing him,' Tucson said gently. 'We caught him red-handed, smashing the lock on the strong box—'

'That stage wa'n't carryin' any money—just mail.'

'That don't lessen the fact that it was a hold-up—to say nothing of murder.'

Glascow's fingers drummed on the desk-top. He decided to attack, 'Look here,' he blustered, 'seems yo're pretty damn sure of yourself—you and your friends. You come ridin' here, makin' accusations. Yo're a stranger to me. I don't see why I should take yore word against Sharkey's. I don't know but what it might be an idea to lock you up until you can be investigated.' He started to rise from his desk.

'Sit down!' Tucson thundered. 'You can't get away with it, Glascow. I don't bluff easy. I've delivered a prisoner to your care. I'm holdin' you responsible for him. Don't let him escape. I'm expectin' to be around Los Potros until this matter is cleaned up, one way or another—'

64

'You resistin' the law?' Glascow bellowed. He had dropped back to his chair, his little eyes red with hate.

'Put it thataway if you like. Now what you aimin' to do about it?'

'Say, who are you anyway?' Glascow snarled. 'You come in here, makin' threats. How do I know you didn't pull this hold-up yourself? Yo're mighty cocky. What's your name?'

'Smith. My friends call me Tucson.'

The color left Glascow's face suddenly, then flowed back. He glared at Tucson, then slowly lowered his eyes. 'All right, Smith,' he growled at last. 'I'll have to ask you to stay around town—'

'I've already stated I'm stayin'. I want to see Sharkey hang. Oh, I won't be leavin' in a hurry, deputy. And remember, I'm holdin' *you* responsible for that prisoner. If he escapes—'

'I don't see why you think he should—'

'I've got reasons for that too,' Tucson smiled thinly. 'Don't let him, that's all. If you do, you'll settle with me—personal.'

Without waiting for a reply, Tucson walked out of the office. At the hitchrack, Stony said, 'Sort of riled for a moment, weren't you?'

'I don't like skunks,' Tucson growled.

'We could hear you talkin' plenty turkey to that hombre.'

Tucson climbed to his saddle. 'Let's get somethin' to eat.'

The three backed their horses away from the hitchrack, then turned toward a building which they had noticed bore a restaurant sign some time before. Stony said, 'Why didn't you ask him if he knew anything about Gaudalupe?'

'I thought of it,' Tucson replied. 'Decided against bringin' the matter up. If the Kid is in town, we'll find him. If he's in a tight, and Glascow is concerned in the business, he'd deny all knowledge of him. We'll let it ride until we see what we can pick up ourselves.' The other two nodded agreement.

'When we goin' to have a look at our new outfit?' Lullaby asked.

Tucson laughed softly. 'Still thinkin' about settlin', eh?'

'If you ask me,' Lullaby drawled, 'there's a heap of things to be settled around this range ... C'mon, let's eat.'

CHAPTER FIVE

BAD MEDICINE BREWIN'

Tucson and his two pardners were nearly through their evening meal at the Kansas City Cafe when a lanky, dour looking man with a long red nose came limping through the doorway. He hung his sombrero on a hook on the hatrack running along one wall and seated himself on one of a long line of stools at the counter. The proprietor of the restaurant sauntered up to take his order.

'Evenin', George, how's the corns this p.m.?'

'Plumb aggravatin',' came the reply. 'It all comes o' wearin' boots is my theory. If the huming race hadn't never took to wearin' leather on their feet, corns an' other sech sim'lar tortures would be a lost art—'

'Listen, Sourdough George Jenkins, what's corns got to do with art?'

'That ain't neither here nor there. Trouble is, if I wa'n't forced to spend so much time on my feet—'

'Yeah, George, I noted you havin' a heap of business with Deputy Glascow past coupla days. Taggin' him around like a houn'-dawg. What's up?'

Sourdough looked startled. 'Oh, me'n Brose has got some private business,' he evaded. 'Do you reckon Brose noted me trailin' him?'

The proprietor nodded. 'He told me this a.m. that if that limpy son didn't quit follerin' him around—'

'What you got to eat this evenin',' Sourdough said hastily.

The proprietor ran quickly through the list of his offerings, accepted Sourdough's order and disappeared in the kitchen at the end of the long counter. Sourdough looked worried. He rested his elbows on the counter, running one hand nervously back and forth over a head that was as devoid of hair as a lizard of fur.

Seated at a table on the opposite side of the room, Tucson had motioned his two companions to silence when Deputy Glascow's name was mentioned.

'Looks like,' Stony commented, 'somebody else had business with Deputy Glascow.'

Tucson nodded and Lullaby put in, 'An' I'd say off-hand it wa'n't friendly business so far as ol' shiny dome is concerned. Might be a good idea to talk to him—'

'That ain't what's interestin' me right now,' Tucson interrupted. 'What did this restaurant man call him?'

'Sourdough somethin' or other?' Lullaby replied. 'I didn't get the rest of the name.'

'I didn't catch none of it,' Stony said. 'Wasn't payin' any attention, until I heard Glascow's name mentioned.'

'To me,' Tucson went on, 'it sounded like he said the name was Sourdough George Jenkins—'

'Wait a minute,' Stony interrupted, 'I've heard the name someplace. Let me see—'

'That option paper!' Lullaby's eyes widened.

Tucson nodded. 'George Jenkins was one of the witnesses. Reckon we'll have to *habla* with him a mite.'

The three rolled cigarettes and sat quietly smoking at their table while Sourdough Jenkins wolfed his food in great gulps, from

68

time to time glancing uneasily through the window that fronted the restaurant. Finally he was finished and ready to leave.

Tucson and his companions rose, paid the proprietor at the counter for their dinners and managed to get through the door before Sourdough left. The street was dark when they stepped outside, only the uneven series of lights from various buildings throwing any illumination along the way. Jenkins came hurrying through the doorway, brushed past Tucson and started west along the street.

Tucson said, 'Just a minute, Jenkins.'

Jenkins jerked nervously around, then slowly came back, suspiciously sizing up the three cowboys. 'Did you speak to me, mister?' he asked.

Tucson nodded. 'Didn't I hear that restaurant man call you Sourdough George?'

'You might of,' noncommittally. 'What about it?'

'Any man called Sourdough,' Tucson said pleasantly, 'is likely to know how to make bread. If he can make bread he's a cook. I'm goin' to be hirin' a cook in the next coupla days. Are you—?'

'So that's it.' Sourdough looked relieved. 'Sorry, gents, I already got a job. That is—' he paused and went on, 'got a job for a coupla days, anyway—'

'Where?' from Tucson.

'I'm workin' for the Tresbarro iron—'

69

'Now we're getting someplace,' Tucson cut in. 'My name is Smith.' He introduced his two pardners.

In the reflected lights along the way, the three could see that Sourdough's eyes were bulging, his mouth hanging open. Finally he found his voice, 'You—your first name Tucson?'

'That's what my friends call me.'

'Cripes Genimity!' Sourdough exploded, grabbing at their hands. 'Why didn't ye say so? I been on the lookout for you three hombres. Should a-recognized ye. Trouble is, my corns been frettin' me so the past few days, I jest can't keep my mind on my work. An' I got other troubles—'

'Why you been on the look-see for us three?' Tucson asked.

'Why, yo're the new owners. Say, don't—'

'That's what I wanted to know,' Tucson said. 'You witnessed an option—'

'Yer rootin'-tootin' I did,' Sourdough exclaimed. 'Never heard o' sech a quick sale or so much biddin' in my life. There I was, a-tryin' to sit easy, bathin' my corns in sody-water, when this young gaffer come ridin' in. Well, one thing and another took place—'

'What young gaffer?' Tucson asked.

'Feller named Jeff Ferguson. Guadalupe Kid he calls—'

Stony said, 'Where's Guadalupe now?'

'That,' Sourdough said, 'is somethin' I

70

can't answer.'

'We're waitin',' Tucson said tersely.

From that point on, Sourdough related the various events that had led up to the killing of Don Manuel and the taking prisoner of Guadalupe.

Stony swore a low oath. 'Me, I'm aimin' to take that deputy apart an' see what makes him tick.'

'Easy, pard, easy,' Tucson said grim-faced. 'Let's get all this story—'

'Mebbe,' Lullaby said, 'Guadalupe was in the jail while we were there—'

'He ain't there,' Sourdough said emphatically. 'That's where I figured Glascow would take him. I come in to Los Potros the day after Glascow took him away, intendin' to see him, but he wa'n't in the jail. Glascow wouldn't say where he was. I been tailin' Glascow around town in hopes I'd get one of these here clues you hear about, but I ain't heard nothin'—'

'You say,' Tucson interrupted, 'that Guadalupe took out the option in our name. Did he say why?'

'Said he knew you were lookin' for an outfit. The Tresbarro was a bargain. Oh, he told us all about you fellers. Says he owes everythin' he is to Tucson. Never saw a boy show such feelin' when he talked about anybody. Shore worships the range you ride on—'

'Ogden warned him he'd never leave the

ranch with that option, eh?' Tucson said quietly.

Sourdough nodded. 'He'd figured to ride to Chancellor the next day and tell you fellers about it. He'd signed that check over to Don Manuel. Don Manuel give it to Car'line Sibley to keep. Car'line was puttin' it between the leaves of a big book where the old Don keeps papers sometimes, when Guadalupe asked her to keep the option with it, until next day—'

'That was the idea,' Tucson said grimly, 'Ogden and Glascow took the Kid away with them, thinkin' he'd have that option on him. Only for luck—but, say, how did the option get mailed to me?'

'I'm gettin' to that part,' Sourdough replied. 'Y'see, Car'line didn't feel safe about havin' that option. Ogden came to the ranch the next day to ask if she knew whether it had been signed or not. Y'see, he wa'n't sure. Anyway, Car'line refused to talk to him, so until yesterday, Ogden didn't know how things stood—'

'What happened yesterday?' Tucson asked.

'Don Manuel was buried. After the funeral, before she came back to the ranch, Car'line decides to mail you that option. She'd kept it in her buzzum all the time. The Kid had told us you expected to wait for him in Chancellor. Anyway, Car'line knew the paper would be safe in the U. S. Mails. Right after she mailed it, Ogden seed her on the street, an' started pesterin' her further about the option. Car'line give him the hoss-laugh an' allows as how it would go to Chancellor in the mail this mornin', when the stage left—but say, I don't see how you got it so soon.'

'We'd left Chancellor,' Tucson told him. 'The stage was held up, strong box opened—'

'By Gawd!' Sourdough struck one fist into the other. 'I'll bet that was Ogden's work. I saw him last night, talkin' earnest to a couple of his plug-uglies. Fellers o' the names of Sharkey and Jeems.'

'I reckon you called the turn, Sourdough,' Tucson said. He gave brief details regarding the hold-up, then said, 'Where's Miss Sibley now?'

'Out to the ranch, takin' care of things until you arrive.'

'Girl out there all alone?' Stony asked.

Sourdough shook his head. 'She hired on a Mex gal to help take care of things.'

'In case of trouble,' Lullaby growled, 'a Mex girl wouldn't be much help. I figure we better get out there, just as soon as we've seen what can be learned about Guadalupe. It's easy to see, there's bad medicine brewin' in this neck of the range. I'm all for findin' that deputy skunk and—'

'Take it easy, pard,' Tucson said quietly. 'The way I figure it, Ogden's the man to see.'

'You're right,' from Sourdough. 'He's king-pin 'round here.'

'Where can we find him?' Tucson asked.

'Usually, this time of night,' Sourdough gave the information, 'he's in his Red Bull Saloon. He likes to keep an eye on the cash drawer. Reckon he don't trust his barkeep over much.'

'We're headin'' for the Red Bull,' Tucson said.

'He might not be there, now,' Sourdough stated. 'Just before supper I saw him and Glascow talkin' plumb serious. Then they jumped hawsses and went someplace. I would have followed but my hawss was 'way t'other end of the street.'

'Why'n't you grab the first pony handy?' Stony asked.

'It's against the law,' Sourdough said solemnly, ''specially when you ain't over popular with the deputy-sheriff, like me.'

'We'll wait in the Red Bull until Ogden shows up,' Tucson said, his jaw setting with determination. 'Then if we don't find Guadalupe, or if he's been harmed—well, Mister Steve Ogden is goin' to find himself on the receiving end of a flock of hot lead capsules. The dose will be bitter as hell, but it'll cure— s'help me, it'll cure!'

CHAPTER SIX

BRAND BLOTTING

The Red Bull Saloon was the distance of a city block from the center of town, on the opposite side of the street from the restaurant in front of which the four men stood talking. They crossed diagonally the dusty thoroughfare and stepped to the raised plank walk stretching in an almost unbroken line, beneath the wooden awnings of stores, from one end of the town to the other.

Loud, boisterous voices floated past the swinging doors that gave entrance to the Red Bull. Tucson and his companions pushed into a long room thronged with cowpunchers and citizens of Los Potros. Smoke floated like a gray pall half way to the ceiling, partially dimming the oil lamps employed for illumination. To the right, as they entered, ran a long bar presided over by a fish-faced individual whose name was Gus Trout. Steve Ogden was nowhere in sight.

At the opposite side of the room were a number of wooden tables at which several men sat playing cards. A faro game was in progress and a roulette wheel whirred. The clicking of poker chips and the droning voice of a dealer sounded an undertone through the various noises of the saloon.

Sourdough Jenkins pushed up to the bar, followed by the three cowboys. After a few minutes, Gus Trout worked his way along the bar to them and asked, 'What'll it be, gents?'

'Where's Ogden?' Sourdough asked.

Trout said, frowning, 'You want to see him?'

'No, Gus I don't *want* to,' Sourdough grunted, 'but it happens to be necessary. My friends got business with him.'

Trout looked swiftly at Tucson and his two companions. 'We-ell,' the barkeep spoke hesitatingly, 'you know Steve is a right busy man, gents. I don't know whether he'll—'

'He'll see us, all right,' Tucson cut in. 'Where is he?'

Trout hesitated again before replying. 'He ain't here right now—'

'We can see that,' Tucson snapped. 'When will he be in?'

Trout's bug-eyes popped angrily, then suddenly dropped before Tucson's steady gaze. 'Reckon he'll be in pretty soon,' he said slowly. 'Stick around. Want a drink while you're waiting?'

'Want a drink?' Sourdough asked the others.

Lullaby said, 'This the only saloon in town?'

Trout cut in to say, 'The Red Bull is the only decent saloon—'

'We weren't talkin' to you, barkeep,' Stony said coldly.

Sourdough said, 'C'mon, I know a better place.'

Ignoring Trout's angry protestations, they pushed outside. On the street Sourdough said, 'We'll head over to the Happy Days. It'll be quieter there too. Happy Hopkins don't get much business these days, if he has got the best location. But you can be sure of his liquor.'

'Howcome he don't get business then?' Tucson asked as the four men recrossed the street.

'Ogden's doin's,' Sourdough said bitterly. 'Ogden sent out word that anybody that patronized the Happy Days wouldn't be in good standin' with Ogden. Hopkins was in business long before Ogden started the Red Bull too.'

'And Los Potros stands for that sort of thing?' Stony asked amazed.

'After ye're here a spell, ye'll see that Ogden has got this town tied into a knot of his own splicin',' Sourdough said bitterly. 'Los Potros has shore gone spineless the past year or so.'

'Ogden's tryin' to run the Happy Days out of business, eh?' Lullaby said.

'Looks thataway. I don't reckon Happy will be able to keep goin' much longer, unless things turn fer the better. Happy don't get many customers. Folks don't like to rile Big Steve Ogden.'

Tucson said shrewdly, 'Reckon the Happy Days had better be our headquarters. We'll have Hopkins on our side to commence with. I'll be interested to see if he has any customers too. Anybody with nerve enough to ignore Ogden's orders, might be a good hombre to connect with. I'd feel in luck if we found any cow-hands there.'

''Tain't likely,' from Sourdough. And a minute later, 'Here we are.'

The Happy Days Saloon was of 'dobe and timber construction. It had a false front and windows on either side of the open-doored entrance. A couple of voices could be heard inside. The men entered. At one side ran a rough board bar. At the opposite side were a couple of square tables and chairs, now unoccupied. The saloon was lighted by oil lamps suspended from brackets about the walls which were ornamented by several pictures of prize-fighters and race-horses.

Happy Hopkins proved to be a jovial, neat individual of comfortable dimensions, with slickly combed hair and a white apron. Four men stood talking quietly at one end of the bar. Tucson noted with something akin to satisfaction that all were in typical cowmen's clothing. It was almost too much to hope that they might be looking for jobs. Sourdough nodded to the cowboys, spoke to the bartender.

Happy Hopkins smiled, 'Evenin', Sourdough. What you havin'?' He glanced at Tucson and his companions as the men lined up at the bar. Sourdough said, 'Happy can give you some cold beer.'

'Don't tell me you got ice.' Tucson looked skeptical.

Happy shook his head. 'I keep it in a tub of water, covered with wet burlap. The evaporation chills it some ... Yep ... Right. Four bottles.'

He dived into a tub at his feet and came up with four dripping bottles, then placed glasses on the bar. The bottles were opened and poured, the contents tested.

'Plumb palatable,' Lullaby commented.

'Right,' Hopkins nodded. 'Comes straight from San Antonio. That's the beer that made Milwaukee jealous.'

Sourdough, introduced Tucson and his companions. Hopkins shook hands. Sourdough, after an approving look from Tucson added, 'It ain't generally known yet, Happy, but ye're shakin' the dew-claws of the new owners of the Tresbarro iron.'

'That so?' Hopkins looked interested. 'This bein' the case, that one's on the house.'

The business of cattle raising was discussed a few minutes. Tucson made a query relative to the whereabouts of the Guadalupe Kid, but Hopkins had never heard of him. At mention of the Tresbarro outfit changing hands, there had been some stir among the four cowmen at the opposite end of the bar. Now, one of the men detached himself from his companions and approached Tucson.

'Wonder if I can cut in a minute?' he asked.

'Muh name's Wing—Bat Wing.'

Bat Wing was a slim-hipped, good-featured, blond youngster with bowed legs and an infectious grin. Tucson liked him and stuck out one hand with the words, 'Name's Smith. Reckon you can cut in on the *habla* if you're inclined. What's on your mind?'

Wing said, a trifle bashfully, 'Well, I didn't mean to listen but I heard some mention to the effect that you and your pals had bought the Tresbarro outfit. I suppose you brought your own crew.'

Tucson grinned widely. 'Don't tell me you're lookin' for a job?'

'Nothin' else but,' Wing replied. 'Happy will vouch for me, if that means anythin'—'

'Him and his pals are okay, Mr Smith,' Happy nodded.

'I'll orate to that effect muhself,' Sourdough nodded. 'I was about to introduce you, Tucson.'

'Don't tell me,' Bat Wing was grinning, 'that you're hiring?'

'You're hired,' Tucson said promptly. 'We'll get together on wages later. It don't happen your pards want jobs, too, does it?'

Bat Wing turned and bawled down the bar, 'Rube, Tex, there is a Santa Claus.'

Two lean, sinewy-jawed, steady-eyed punchers hastened to join the group. Names were passed swiftly around. The newcomers proved to be Rube Phelps and Tex Malcolm.

80

After a few moments the fourth man down the bar joined the group. Tucson and the others hadn't long to wait to learn why this individual was named Ananias Jones.

Ananias Jones was a spare, grizzled man with sweeping white mustaches, sharp blue eyes beneath shaggy eyebrows and a body that resembled in form and durability a length of well-weathered rawhide. Here, Tucson recognized at once, was a typical old-timer of the western ranges, one who had come up through the days of long-horned cattle and cap-and-ball pistols and whose experience would be invaluable on any outfit.

Tucson said, 'You lookin' for a job too?'

Ananias Jones shook his head. 'Nope, me, I'm just ridin' through, vacationin'. Used to work for the Triple-Box-3, hundred miles east from here. Could have stayed there until I died, but, well, it got too peaceful. I sort of caught a bad case of itchin' foot. Couldn't stay put. Kind of like the country hereabouts. Restin' for a few days.'

Happy said to Bat Wing, 'You decided against stayin' with the IXI, eh, Bat?'

Wing frowned. 'Yeah, Tex and Rube and me, we ain't yet reached the stage where we're willin' to wear Steve Ogden's bridle. The job is open. Reckon Ogden thinks we're stayin' on, but we already decided against it, before Mr Smith and his friends come in—'

'My friends call me Tucson.'

81

Bat flushed with pleasure. 'I figure I'm goin' to enjoy bein' on your payroll.'

Tucson said, 'What's this IXI job you mentioned?'

'The IXI,' Wing said, 'is located twenty miles east of here. It was owned by some Easterners, under the name of the Westland Cattle Company. None of the owners ever come out. They left the runnin' of things to the manager, Wilson. A week ago, the Westland Company sold out to Steve Ogden at a bargain price. Ogden plans to merge the outfit with his Box-8 outfit.'

'The rest of the crew stayed on, workin' for Ogden,' Rube Phelps took up the story, 'but us three couldn't stand it. We pulled out.'

'The rest of the crew,' Tex Malcolm drawled, 'already bein' in the Ogden pay, if you ask me, and the manager, Wilson, bein' a first class kitty with a stripe down his back and a bad odor.'

Tucson asked, 'Where's Wilson now?'

'Headed for Kansas City to spend the easy money he got from Ogden,' Bat Wing said bitterly.

'Sold his owners out to Ogden, eh?' Lullaby put in.

Tex Malcolm nodded. 'The IXI got plumb run down. Cattle disappeared like water in a desert. Wilson wrote his employers that it was useless to try to make cattle pay in this country. They took his word. Ogden got the outfit dirt cheap.'

'You got proof of what you're sayin'?' Tucson asked sharply.

Tex Malcolm sniffed. 'Do you think if we'd had proof we'd have put off writing to the owners?'

Tucson said, 'Excuse it, cowboy. I'm just lookin' for info.'

Rube Phelps took up the strain, 'Tex and Bat has just stated how things looked to us. We was waitin' until we got proof before actin'. Then the ranch was sold before we could do anythin'.'

'Y'see,' Bat Wing said, 'Wilson was suspicious of us. We hinted that Ogden might be stealin' IXI cattle, long time back, before we realized Wilson was a skunk. Thereupon and henceforth, us three never did get out on the range. Wilson kept us diggin' corral posts and mendin' harness. Reckon he'd fired us, only he was afraid to.'

Tucson's eyes narrowed. 'You say Ogden brands a Box-8?'

Wing nodded, adding, 'Just a square with an 8 inside.'

'It wouldn't be very difficult,' Tucson said slowly, 'to burn an IXI into a Box-8. Just a matter of extendin' the two I's to make a square and addin' loops at the top and the bottom of the X—'

'By Gawd, you've hit it!' Rube Phelps exclaimed.

'What's the earmarks?' Tucson asked next.

Tex Malcolm supplied, 'The IXI under-split right and left. The Box-8 under-half-crops right and left. By gosh, it—'

Tucson nodded. 'All Ogden had to do was complete his under-half-crop with one slice on each ear. Plumb simple. No wonder the IXI got run down.' He turned to Sourdough, 'Seems like the Tresbarro used to brand a big 3.'

'Still does,' Sourdough nodded, frowning.

'Reckon that was meat for Ogden too,' Tucson said grimly. 'With a runnin' iron it would be plumb easy to change a three to eight, and draw a box around it. How about earmarks?'

'Tresbarro split right and left.'

Tucson's lips twisted to a wry smile. 'Plumb easy to make that earmark fit in with Ogden's too. Just have to crop off the bottom of each ear. No wonder Ogden's been gettin' rich. Probably Don Manuel would have seen that if he wa'n't so trustful.'

'There's a heap of us should have seen these things,' Tex Malcolm said, 'only we didn't, somehow.'

'Reckon we'll have to change our big 3 brand to somethin' else,' Tucson said to Lullaby and Stony. Both nodded emphatically. Tucson continued to the three new hands, 'It's likely to be tough goin' for a spell, waddies. Ogden ain't goin' to like the idea of us comin' into this country. I don't mind tellin' you though that I got certain stories about runnin' an outfit. I'd like to try 'em out. If we do get by in good shape, there's goin' to be a cut on the profits for every man that works for my pards and me.'

'We ain't askin' extra money,' Bat Wing put in quickly, 'but we sure will appreciate buckin' Big Steve Ogden. It's luck—'

'I'm feelin' lucky myself, pickin' up a crew so quick,' Tucson said. He was wishing he could get old Ananias Jones, but the old cowman had made it clear he wasn't seeking employment.

Tucson considered a moment, then said gravely to Ananias, 'Judgin' from your name I suppose you ain't really a cowhand, a-tall.'

'Who, me?' Ananias snorted indignantly. 'Why, mister, I'm the feller that invented cowpunchin' in this country. I've handled cow stuff from Canada to Mexico and from the Mississippi to Californy. Back in the days when it wa'n't necessary to brand. At round-up time we jest whistled and the stock come a-runnin'. Cowhands carried burnin' glasses then, and we used the sun's rays to burn our brands. Then one day I happened to hit on the idea of inventin' the brandin' iron. It took hold like sellin' buffalo robes at the North Pole. I made millions out of the idea. Then lost all my money buildin' a dam across a river not fifteen miles west of the spot where we're standin' now.'

'Was it a big river?' Tex Malcolm

asked innocently.

'Biggest river I ever see,' Ananias said seriously. 'Made the Missouri look like a babblin' brook. Yep, jest fifteen miles west of here—'

'Fifteen miles west,' Bat Wing grinned, 'brings you to the Escabrosa Range. Only water there is Santone Creek—'

'That's how much you know about it, younker,' Ananias said, unabashed. 'In them days the Escabrosa Range was just little dimples, in the ground, what hadn't growed to mountains yet. Yep, just one long valley with this river runnin' through with th' speed of a whirlwind. It was just too swift to dam. My dam held right well for a spell though. The water riz and flooded this whole country. Where there's water, there's fish. I started a fish ranch—'

'A what?' Lullaby grinned.

Ananias said defiantly, 'A fish ranch. We raised sea-cows and done our herdin' in rowboats. That was before the days of steam, natural, but after a time I gets to thinkin' rowboats was purty slow, so I—'

'Don't tell me,' Stony chuckled, 'that you invented the steamboat too?'

Ananias looked suspiciously at the cowboy, then nodded. 'I had a young feller named Fulton workin' for me them days. I give him the steamboat idea to work out, drawed all the plans for him, and everythin'. Well, sir, that boat worked like a charm, but Fulton had gone East with my idea, and I never did get proper credit. He didn't mean to run out on me thataway, but my dam had flooded this whole land. Sudden like my dam burst an' the waters receded, leavin' Fulton an' my brain-boat stranded in a little creek called the Hudson River. Well, that plumb nigh to ruined me. I was all bruk up. Then, one day I got to thinkin' why wouldn't it be a good idea to invent a contraption called the telyphone—'

'That's enough,' Tucson cut in, grinning. 'You've proved your right to the name, Ananias.'

Ananias' blue eyes twinkled. 'But not to bein' a cowhand, eh?'

'There's only one way you can prove that,' Tucson said.

Ananias sighed. 'Looks like I got to go to work just to put yore outfit in plumb efficient shape. If I do, you got to use my patented cow catcher—'

'Never heard of it,' Tucson shook his head.

'By cripes!' Ananias chuckled, 'I thought everybody knew about 'em. They been used on locomotives for years.'

A laugh went up at Tucson's expense. He smiled widely, 'All right, I'll buy a drink on that one. Ananias, we simply got to have you now.'

'Made up my mind to that some time ago,' Ananias said calmly, serious for a moment.

'I'm willin' to throw in with anybody that'll buck Big Steve Ogden. I ain't never had nothin' to do with him, but from what I've heard since hittin' this range, he needs his come-uppance and needs it bad. Tucson, you've hired a hand.'

Drinks were set out. Tucson set down his glass after a minute, said to the others, 'I'm headin' for the Red Bull. Lullaby and Stony can bring you fellows up to date on what's happened so far. I'll be seein' you shortly.'

'Look here,' Lullaby protested, 'you better take me.'

'And me,' from Stony.

Sourdough said, 'Ogden will have a big followin' over there, Tucson—'

'That,' Tucson cut in, 'is just why I don't want you fellows along. If we all go bargin' in there, trouble is li'ble to start poppin'. I'm aimin' to lay my cards on the table. After that, if Ogden gets proddy, well—' Tucson smiled grimly, '—we'll do what's necessary for clarifyin' the situation—with hot lead!'

With a short 'Adios' he turned toward the door and stepped into the street.

CHAPTER SEVEN

'WE'RE HERE TO STAY!'

Leaving the Happy Days, Tucson sauntered back toward the Red Bull, his mind working swiftly over the past three-quarters of an hour. Well, he had a crew, anyway. He laughed. And hadn't even taken possession of his new property yet—his and Lullaby's and Stony's. In fact, he was only barely familiar with the layout of the new holdings. At least, it was a start. Ananias would be an asset, invaluable in keeping up the morale of an outfit when the going was tough. Rube Phelps and Tex Malcolm were the steady, hard-working type, loyal to the man whose money they earned. Bat Wing—Tucson smiled—there was a boy who would require a lot of holding down. Tucson had judged him shrewdly as the sort that is equally ready for fun or a fight.

Now if only the Guadalupe Kid would show up. Tucson didn't think that Ogden would dare harm Guadalupe—not so long as Caroline Sibley and Sourdough knew what had happened. If Ogden had injured the Kid— Tucson's sober face went grim at the thought. Well, he'd soon know, anyway. The Red Bull was only a few steps distant now.

Tucson pushed through the swinging doors

of the saloon. The place was even noisier than before, the smoke thicker. There was considerable heavy drinking going on. Gus Trout was being pushed to the limit of his endurance in attending the demands of his thirsty customers. Without being familiar with Ogden's appearance, Tucson spotted the man at once. No doubt about it, Ogden stood out among the rabble that caroused at the bar. His sombrero was shoved back on his head as he leaned easily against the back-bar. The look on his features was contemptuous as his cold, pale blue eyes played a constant, shifting glance over the customers whose money he was gathering in. A long black thin cigar was clenched at an angle between his teeth, one thumb was hooked in the gun belt that encircled his hips, his sixshooter being concealed beneath the knee-length coat. The coat itself was just thrown back enough to reveal to Tucson a bulge at the left shoulder: Under-arm gun and harness.

Tucson pushed in between two drunks standing at the bar. The two men glared at him a moment, then noting the stern set of his features as he ignored their mumbled protests, grudgingly gave room and went on with their drinking. In a moment, Ogden's eyes met Tucson's. Already warned by Brose Glascow, Ogden had been expecting and was prepared for Tucson's visit. No doubt about it, this must be the man, Smith, Glascow had spoken of.

For the space of a minute the two tall men stared straight into each other's eyes, measuring, calculating, judging. Ogden was trying to glare Tucson down, but it didn't work. Ogden was forced to speak at last, to cover the failure. He said, in a cold voice, 'Well, hombre?'

Tucson said quietly, 'It ain't well, at all, Ogden.'

Ogden forced a thin smile. 'What's the matter, mister, you got a complaint to make about my liquor?'

'You know damn well I ain't, Ogden,' Tucson said easily. 'Don't stall. I know who you are. You're pretending you don't know who I am. I'm Tucson Smith.'

'Yeah,' Ogden sneered. 'What do you want me to do, stand up and give three cheers. I've heard of you—some-place—but that ain't nothing to do with me. You may have a rep as an outlaw buster in some parts of the country, but you're just an ordinary hombre here, see? There's nothing for you to do in this part of the range. We already got law and order.'

Tucson's lips had curved to a slow smile. He didn't say anything. Just stood and looked at Ogden. Ogden's teeth bit harder on the long cigar. Affecting an appearance of carelessness, he half turned away, saying, 'Come in again, when you're passin' through Los Potros. S'long.'

'You all through, Ogden?'

Ogden looked coldly back in Tucson's direction, then faced completely around fighting to meet Tucson's steely gaze. 'I reckon I ain't got anythin' else to say to you, Smith— nor you to me.'

'You already made one mistake, Ogden. Don't make another.'

'Meanin' just what?'

'In pretendin' to think that I'm just passin' through. I'm here—we're here to stay.'

'Who's we?'

'My pards and me. We aim to stay a long time—'

'You won't find any work—'

'On the contrary,' Tucson snapped, 'we find a damn big job—all cut out for us.'

Several men in the vicinity of Tucson had stopped to listen now. Ogden, realizing he was the center of attention said carelessly, 'Said job bein'?'

'The runnin' of the Tresbarro outfit, Ogden. We aim to run it open and aboveboard. We'd like to be neighborly, but—we—don't—like— crooks.'

'Who does?' Ogden asked a trifle hotly.

'You do—apparently.'

'Now, look here, Smith—'

'You've talked your say,' Tucson cut in. 'I'll do the talkin' for a minute—'

'Do you mean to say that you've bought the Tresbarro—?' Ogden commenced. This was news to him; he'd figured that Guadalupe

92

was the—

'I said I'd do the talkin',' Tucson interrupted the man's abstractions. 'I meant exactly what I said. My pards and me have bought the Tresbarro ranch. We're goin' to put it on its feet. I've been gathering an outfit. It lacks just one man.' Tucson's next words came like the crack of a Winchester: 'Ogden, where's the Guadalupe Kid?'

Ogden gave an involuntary start. He had been expecting the question from the moment Tucson entered the Red Bull. Now that it had come, he hadn't been ready for it.

'Who?' he frowned. 'What you talkin' about?'

'Don't lie to me, Ogden,' Tucson said sternly.

'Look here, Smith, you can't talk to me—'

'I'll do more than talk to you in another second. I want an answer.'

The room had suddenly gone quiet. Angry points of light showed in Ogden's pale blue eyes. He glanced away from Tucson, gaze shifting about the room, wondering if Tucson's friends were hidden in the crowd, waiting to make trouble. It didn't seem possible Smith would have come alone to the Red Bull. He finally came back to Tucson, saying,

'Smith, you've got off on the wrong foot.'

'Where's the Guadalupe Kid?'

'I tell you I don't know what—'

Tucson reached to his right holster, drew

93

one gun and laid it gently on the bar before him. 'Maybe,' he said, 'this will refresh your memory, Ogden.'

'What do you mean?' Ogden looked from the gun to Tucson, wondered if Tucson's left hand, hidden by the bar from view, was resting on the left hand gun.

Tucson laughed softly. 'The mate to this gun is in my other holster, Ogden. Unless your memory is refreshed damn sudden, it's goin' to come out—and it won't be laid down on your bar.'

Two spots of angry color burned on the cheekbones in Ogden's dead-white face. He glanced away from Tucson again, an imperceptible signal flashing from his eyes to someone at Tucson's rear. Almost immediately, some sort of altercation broke out a few yards back of Tucson:

Somebody was calling somebody else a liar. There were invitations to 'go fer yore shootin'-iron.' The voices became louder. Ogden's eyes had narrowed. He was waiting...

Tucson snapped. without looking around, 'Tell 'em to quit it, Ogden!' At the same instant one hand closed on the gun on the bar before him, his thumb drawing back the hammer of the forty-five. The muzzle of the gun was bearing on Ogden's mid-section. Tucson repeated, 'Tell 'em to quit it.'

Ogden's eyes shifted nervously. 'It's just a fight, Smith. I can't do anythin'—'

'Dammit!' Tucson lashed out. 'Do as I say.' His eyes bored into Ogden's.

Reluctantly, Ogden raised his voice, 'Decker—Chapman!' he called. 'Leave be.'

Instantly the fight died out. Two hard-bitten cowpunchers, who a minute before had been calling each other vile names, suddenly relaxed and disappeared in the crowd.

Ogden said with a sneer, 'Satisfied?'

'That part's all right,' and Tucson laughed softly.

Ogden felt his temper getting away from him. 'Who's runnin' this place, you or me, Smith?'

'I'm runnin' it right now,' Tucson said promptly. 'I'm tryin' to be patient, Ogden, but don't pull another stunt like that.' He relaxed his grip on the weapon that had been covering Ogden, left it on the bar.

'What do you mean—stunt?' Ogden asked uneasily.

'That fake fight, coyote. If I had turned around to see what was doin', you'd have plugged me. If I didn't turn around, there'd be shootin'. In the shootin' I'd been accidentally shot. My gosh! Don't you know any new ones?'

'You got me all wrong, Smith—' Ogden commenced earnestly.

'*Wrong* is the only way anybody could get you. I'm through talkin', Ogden. Either you produce the Guadalupe Kid plumb pronto, or I'm goin' to take this town to pieces ... And you won't be alive to help put it together. Savvy?'

Tucson's eyes were burning into Ogden's now. Ogden tried to meet that relentless gaze and failed miserably. He started to speak, then the threat on his lips died away. He gulped heavily, forced a smile. 'Now I know who you're talkin' about. Didn't remember at first. The Guadalupe Kid. Sure. Feller named Jeff Ferguson. Yeah. Well, he was took in by Deputy Glascow. He's a suspect in the Tresbarro murder—'

'Where is he now?' Tucson snapped.

Ogden shrugged his shoulders. 'I don't know. In jail, I suppose. That's the deputy's business. I don't see why you came to me—'

'I understand he ain't been in the jail. Ogden, you get him here pronto!'

'But, Smith—'

'Get—him—here—damn—pronto!'

Ogden started to protest again. The hammer of Tucson's left hand gun clicked in the silence of the big room.

'Make up your mind, Ogden,' and Tucson's voice was like a chill breath from the North Pole.

Ogden wanted to refuse. With the whole room hanging on his reply, he knew to send for the Kid would result in lost prestige. For one wild moment he considered trying to beat Tucson to the draw. Then he surrendered.

'Auringer,' he called to one of his henchmen,

96

'go ask Deputy Glascow to bring the Guadalupe Kid here.'

CHAPTER EIGHT

ROARING GUNS

A man at the far side of the room departed hastily. Tucson laughed contemptuously. The whole room was waiting for Ogden's next words. Becoming suddenly aware of the silence, Ogden's face flushed angrily.

'What in hell's wrong with you hombres?' he snarled. 'Get on with whatever you were doin'. You'd think we were holdin' funeral services.'

'We might have been, Ogden,' Tucson laughed softly, 'we might have been.'

Ogden pretended not to hear. 'Gus,' he ordered the barkeep, 'set 'em up for the house.'

'Up to the bar, gents,' Gus Trout bawled. 'Name your sluice juice. The Red Bull is buyin'.'

The voices lifted again. Tucson refused a drink. Ogden came over to Tucson, said low-voiced, 'I reckon you and me got started wrong, Smith.' He forced an ingratiating smile, figuring it best in view of recent events to make it appear to the occupants of the Red Bull that he and Tucson were friendly, thus presenting some sort of palliation for his own shortcomings and, at the same time, lessen the effect of Tucson's actions. 'You see,' Ogden continued, 'I didn't think at first who you meant when you asked about the Guadalupe Kid.'

Tucson smiled dryly. 'I noted you had to have your memory refreshed.'

Ogden's dead-white face flushed. He hurried on, 'You can understand that I'm a busy man. The Tresbarro murder business was being handled by Deputy Glascow. I hadn't paid much attention—'

'No?' Tucson said. 'I understood that Guadalupe had mentioned my name to you, a few days back, at the Tresbarro Ranch. You were there, then, paying quite a bit of attention.'

Ogden looked away for a moment. 'You understand how it is,' he evaded. 'I remember now, that Ferguson hombre did claim to be a friend of yours, but you couldn't expect us to take him seriously.'

'Why not?'

'Deputy Glascow and I talked it over, decided he was lying. You see, you have quite a fine reputation, Smith, throughout the Southwest as an enemy of outlaws—'

'Never mind all that,' Tucson said shortly.

'It's true, nevertheless. Well, in view of the Kid's record—the number of reward bills covering him, and so on, naturally we couldn't believe the great Tucson Smith would have

98

anything to do with a crook—'

'Cut it,' Tucson snapped. 'I didn't ask for any of your sarcasm, Ogden. As for the Kid's record, either you're lying like hell or you're away behind on news. The Kid is all squared up. He never was as black as he was painted. It got so that inefficient law-officers blamed the Kid for crimes, when they couldn't capture the real criminals. Get this, the boy is square with the world, at present. I'm vouching for him—'

'But his record—'

'Any time,' Tucson said coldly, 'that you can boast of a record as clean as the Kid's, I'll be glad to shake your hand. Savvy?'

Ogden said stiffly, 'Am I to understand that you don't want to be friends?'

'That,' Tucson said easily, 'is up to you. We don't want trouble if it can be avoided. On the other hand, we're set to burn powder if anybody interferes with us. That clear? We might as well be frank, Ogden. You don't like me. Well, that goes two ways. But if you play an honest game around here there's no reason why we have to cross guns. Otherwise—'

'I've never played anything but an honest game.'

'I've got my own opinion about that, Ogden. There's been a heap of brand-blotting going on hereabouts—'

'What do you mean?'

Tucson laughed easily. 'Brand blotting,' he stated mockingly, 'is the science of burning new lines over old brands, thus altering the original brand and, apparently, changing the ownership of the animal being brand-blotted—'

'Dammit, cut out the foolishness,' Ogden said impatiently. 'I know what brand blotting is, but you can't—'

'You know too damn well, Ogden, and I certainly do accuse you of bein' plumb proficient in the aforesaid science—'

'By God, Smith, you'll prove that statement!'

'I'm intendin' to do that, Ogden ... Just as an example, how about the changing of the IXI into a Box-8—'

'I own the IXI—'

'You didn't always own it. Do you deny it would be plumb simple to alter the IXI into a Box-8?'

Ogden considered. 'We-ell,' he said slowly, 'it could be done, of course. But that's just a coincidence.'

'I suppose it's another coincidence that the Tresbarro 3 could be changed to an 8 and a box burned around it?'

'Jees! You ain't accusin' me—?'

'I'm suspectin' you, Ogden. I'm figurin' to look for proof—'

'You're crazy!'

'That's something *you'll* have a chance to prove.'

'By God, Smith, you talk like you wanted
100

war,' Ogden said angrily. 'I tried to be peaceable—'

'You're right, I do,' Tucson snapped. 'War to the hilt, Ogden. It's the only way to exterminate this range of skunks. Do I make myself clear?'

Ogden stared a moment at Tucson then jerked away without replying and walked swiftly to the far end of the bar.

Up until the last few moments the conversation had been carried on quietly, but the last few sentences had brought interested glances from those in Tucson's immediate vicinity. A man at Tucson's elbow said, 'You talked mighty straight to Big Steve, stranger.'

Tucson looked at the man. 'You a friend of his?' shortly.

'Just an acquaintance,' the man said warily. 'I run a clothing store down the street. Still and all, it pays to be on Big Steve's friendly side. I'd hate to buck him.'

'That attitude,' Tucson said quietly, 'seems to be a common ailment among them that lack back stiffenin'.'

The man flushed. 'I ain't sayin' you're wrong, but you don't know what conditions have been here.' He cast a cautious look toward the far end of the bar where Ogden stood holding a low-voiced conversation with two men in puncher's togs. 'It may be,' the man continued in a half-scared voice to Tucson, 'that Big Steve is cookin' up somethin'. That's

Fanner Delisle and Nick Barnett he's talkin' to.'

'Meanin' what?' Tucson asked, looking at the two in question. Delisle was a mean-looking, swarthy man with hard eyes; Barnett was bulky-shouldered, unshaven, with a wide loose mouth.

'A word to the wise is sufficient,' the clothing-store man replied. 'I won't say more.'

'Box-8 punchers?' Tucson asked.

The man nodded, added, almost unwillingly, 'They both got a rep for being fast guns ... I—I reckon I'll be pullin' out, mister.'

Tucson said, 'Thanks. In case you ain't through your night's drinkin', let me suggest the Happy Days Saloon. From now on, Hopkins is goin' to get a heap more business.'

But the man was gone with a short nod and no reply. At that moment a voice reached Tucson, 'Tucson—Tucson Smith!' The words shook with joy.

Tucson swung around from the bar. 'Guadalupe! Kid, I'm sure glad to see you.'

The Kid came pushing through the crowd, Deputy Glascow frowning at his shoulder. Tucson held out his hand. The Kid raised his wrists to show handcuffs. Tucson swore, turned savagely on Glascow, 'Unlock these bracelets, Glascow. Quick!'

'Not so fast, Smith,' Glascow growled. 'I want to see Ogden—'

'Unlock 'em!' Tucson's gun was out,

covering the deputy.

Behind Tucson sounded Ogden's suave tones, 'Unlock 'em, Brose.'

The deputy hesitated. 'But look here, Steve. This Smith pulls a gun on me and—'

'Leave be, Brose,' Ogden said curtly. 'Unlock those cuffs. We've made a mistake. Smith, put your gun away, please. We don't want any trouble. The deputy won't start anything.'

Tucson slipped his gun back into holster. Glascow unlocked the handcuffs. Tucson seized the Kid's hand. 'You all right. Kid?'

'Finer'n silk,' the Kid laughed. He indicated a strip of court-plaster above his right ear, 'Got scratched a mite, but it don't mean anythin'. These mugs didn't dare hurt me, with Sourdough and Miss Sibley knowin' that Glascow had taken me away. But they sure searched me plenty and ask more questions than—'

'We made a mistake, Kid,' Ogden smiled silkily. 'We didn't realize you were all square with the world.'

Guadalupe laughed scornfully. 'You mean you didn't realize Tucson Smith would be takin' a hand in the game.'

'Sourdough tells me you weren't in jail, Kid,' Tucson said.

The Kid shook his head. 'This tin-star deputy kept me in a shack out at the edge of town. Him and Ogden just transferred me to

103

the jail about supper time. They were tryin' to learn what had become of an option that I— say, Tucson, have you got an option yet that—'

'I got it.' Tucson laughed openly at the consternation that appeared on Ogden's features, and said coldly, 'Ogden, you didn't know a thing about the Kid's whereabouts, did you?'

'Deputy Glascow,' Ogden said, 'is within his rights keeping prisoners any place he chooses. I've admitted we made a mistake, regarding other happenings. Let's have a drink and drop the subject.'

'Ogden,' the Kid said icily, 'if I ever took a drink with you I'd consider myself a louse ... Tucson, let's get out of here. It's smelling worse every minute. I never did take to skunks. C'mon, I'm achin' to see Lullaby and Stony. Where are they?'

'Not a great distance away,' Tucson smiled. 'Let's get goin'.'

'I want my guns first,' the Kid said. 'Where are they, Glascow? Produce 'em.'

'I ain't got your guns,' the deputy growled.

The Kid looked belligerent. Tucson interrupted him to say, 'Sourdough tells me your guns are out at the ranch, Kid. Glascow never had 'em.'

Ogden had moved away by this time. Glascow sent a look of hate at the Kid and hurried to join his chief. The Kid looked contemptuously after him, then sobered and

104

turned back to Tucson. He said low-voiced, 'Was it all right, takin' out that option in your names?'

'Best thing ever, Kid. But how did you happen to do it?'

'I knew you and Stony and Lullaby wanted a place to call home. I had to work fast. The Tresbarro outfit was a bargain.' Enthusiastically, 'Tucson, wait until you see the layout.'

'I'll pay back the money, Kid. But I don't understand where you got it.'

'You gave it to me.' The Kid flushed. 'Remember, when you gave me a check for that thousand and told me to go straight. I been goin' straight, Tucson. But I didn't want to spend that money. I figured to return it to you someday. You—you see, any damn fool can go straight when he's well-heeled. I wanted to show you, I could play the game square, whether I was broke or not. I—I—'

The Kid broke off, found Tucson reaching for his hand, gripping it hard. The Kid's eyes grew moist. His voice wasn't quite steady when he said, 'Let's—let's get out of here, pard.'

The two pushed through the noisy crowd. They had nearly reached the door when the puncher known as Delisle stepped in front of Tucson, barring the way, 'Just a minute, feller,' he growled.

Tucson and the Kid stopped. Tucson said, 'Well?' coldly.

Delisle rasped, 'I'm Fanner Delisle.'

Tucson laughed softly, 'Well, fan somethin'. What's on your mind?'

Delisle's right thumb was hooked in gun-belt, hand ready for a quick stretch to the butt of his six-gun. From the corner of his eye, Tucson could see the other puncher, known as Nick Barnett, standing a few feet to one side. The plan flashed on Tucson in a minute: Delisle was supposed to start a fight with Tucson and the Kid. It was a matter of two against two. But the Kid was unarmed. Delisle would carry the verbal portion of the argument, leaving Barnett to draw and fire the instant Tucson reached toward holster to draw on Delisle. Delisle, if he drew at all would direct his shot toward the defenceless Kid. The Kid being unfamiliar with Barnett's appearance, wouldn't expect anything from that quarter. Mentally, Tucson was giving thanks for the warning he had had from the clothing store man a short time before.

'You,' Fanner Delisle was saying, 'are right mouthy, mister.'

'That's a disease,' and Tucson smiled, 'that seems plumb contagious in the Red Bull. You had somethin' to fan. Get busy.'

Delisle flushed angrily. 'You made a heap of talk to my boss a spell back, Smith. Big Steve Ogden is a friend of mine as well as bein' my boss. He ain't expected to take notice of small annoyances, but I ain't lettin' you get away

106

with it, see? You got to settle with me.'

Tucson said easily, 'How?'

Delisle glanced meaningly at Tucson's guns. 'You just carryin' that hardware for balance?' He repeated, 'You carryin' that hardware for balance?'

That was the signal! Tucson snapped, 'Take care of Delisle, Kid. Smack him down!'

What happened next occurred in less time than the relating of events require. Not expecting trouble from that quarter, Delisle had made no move toward his gun, and thus was taken off guard as the Kid's body left the floor in a long, low dive, like that of a football player tackling an opponent. The Kid's shoulder struck Delisle's knees like a battering ram, spilling Delisle in an awkward heap on the floor.

At that same instant, Tucson spun on one foot, right arm jerking toward holster. He got it all in a flash as he turned: Nick Barnett's gun was already out, swinging in a short arc to cover Tucson. A burst of savage orange flame exploded at Tucson's hip as he threw himself sidewise, landing on the floor. At the same instant, the roar of Nick Barnett's gun carried a slug high over Tucson's swift-moving form, Barnett having fired as he fell backward.

Catlike, Tucson whirled to his feet. Delisle was just scrambling up, clawing at his six-shooter. It came out, barked savagely. Tucson felt the breeze of a bullet pass his cheek as he thumbed a swift second shot from his forty-five. Delisle spun half around from the impact of the bullet and crashed to the planking.

The Kid after bowling Delisle over had kept going, one hand reaching for Nick Barnett. Barnett had shifted gun to his left hand, as he lay on the floor. The Kid's foot raised in a swift kick that sent the gun spinning from Barnett's grip.

'You all right, Tucson?' the Kid cried anxiously.

Tucson nodded. 'It's over,' he said.

Barnett was in a sitting position on the floor, right arm helpless at his side, the result of Tucson's first shot. All the blood was drained from his features. Delisle was sprawled in a queer, crumpled position, arms outflung on the floor, his eyes already glazing in death.

A hush had fallen over the Red Bull. Somebody broke the silence to say in awed tones, 'By God, that hombre is fast with his gun!' Somebody else added, 'Two of 'em down!'

A circle had formed around Tucson and the Kid and the two men on the floor. Delisle was beyond help. Barnett, his right shoulder smashed, was moaning for a doctor. Tucson and the Kid stood close together.

Tucson said grimly, 'This is Ogden's work. I aim—'

'You better aim to stand right still,' came the vicious tones of Deputy Glascow. 'One move

108

and I pull trigger, Smith.'

At the same instant, Tucson felt the hard, round muzzle of a forty-five jabbed against his spine. Slowly, his arms came into the air, as he shot a word of warning to the Kid not to resist.

CHAPTER NINE

JUST PLAYFUL

'Easy, Kid,' Tucson warned swiftly, 'don't resist. This skunk will let his hammers down on damn little provocation. That's all he's waitin' for.'

'You show good sense, Smith,' Glascow's voice came from the rear. He held a gun in each hand, one covering the Kid, the other boring into Tucson's back.

Ogden's voice sounded at the back of the room. Tucson started to turn, felt the gun press harder against his spine. 'No sudden moves, now,' Glascow grated. 'Big Steve wants to talk to you. Kid, no funny business, y'understand?'

The two turned cautiously toward the bar, behind which stood Steve Ogden, lights of triumph glinting in his pale-blue eyes. The crowd stood back, leaving a clear aisle to the bar. A minute before that same crowd—at least, the bigger proportion of it—had been lost in admiration of Tucson's fast gun-work.

Now, fickle-minded, it had changed with the sudden turn of events. Tucson knew, at the slightest sign of fear, that the men in the Red Bull would turn on him with the savagery of a wolf-pack.

Walking slowly, he and the Kid approached the bar, the deputy, a wide grin on his ugly features, herding them on with sharp prods from his guns.

'Don't like it, eh, Smith?' Ogden was saying. 'It's your own fault. I offered to be friends. But you weren't satisfied. You had to start a fight—you and Guadalupe. Took my men off guard. You're crooks, both of you. Well, you've called the turn for your own finish. Nobody can buck Steve Ogden and get away with it.'

'This game ain't finished yet, Ogden,' Tucson said easily.

'Dependin' on your friends to save you, eh?' Ogden sneered. 'Well, I'll stop them just as I stopped you. We got law and order in this town. Deputy Glascow is putting you under arrest. I aim to hold court here and now.'

'We're entitled to a fair trial,' Tucson protested.

'You'll get it,' Ogden rasped. 'I'll leave it to the crowd in this room what they want done . . . Fellers, do you want strangers comin' in here, shootin' up your friends, or do you want Steve Ogden to run things in a lawful manner?'

'Steve Ogden!' the room thundered.

The sounds died away, while the crowd

waited for Ogden to continue. Somebody mentioned that Fanner Delisle was dead. No one was paying any attention to Nick Barnett who had fainted.

'Seems to me,' Ogden went on, in a triumphant voice, 'that a necktie party is just about what we need to teach—'

'Drop them guns, scut!' ordered a voice at Deputy Glascow's rear. No one had noticed Stony push through the crowd in the hubbub. Stony's tones were stern, unrelenting, 'Drop 'em quick!'

Glascow gasped. His guns clattered to the floor.

'Stick 'em up,' Stony snapped, 'every son in this room!' The deputy lost no time hoisting his arms.

Somebody far behind Stony laughed contemptuously. 'You dang fool,' yelled another voice, 'you can't lick the hull room!'

Ogden shouted, 'Get him—somebody—!'

'Stick 'em up!' came Lullaby Joslin's command from the entrance.

The crowd stopped short, startled.

Then, strange, surprisingly events occurred in rapid succession: in the wall, across the room from the bar, were three windows. From the window nearest the front of the saloon came the sound of shattering glass as a gun-barrel smashed through the pane, then Bat Wing's voice, 'Reach for the ceiling, hombres!'

The second window crashed to the floor. 'Up

111

high, you scuts!' That was Tex Malcolm, his gun swinging in a wide arc that appeared to cover the room.

The pane of the third window cracked, burst inward, and the face and gun of Rube Phelps appeared as though by magic. 'Scourin's, claw for that roof!'

A door at the rear of the barroom banged suddenly inward to admit Ananias Jones and Sourdough, each holding guns, 'Stretch 'em high, coyotes. We're achin' to burn powder!'

The stern commands came with such smooth rapidity and precision that they might have been the result of long rehearsing. Silence fell as the crowd frantically stretched its arms skyward. Ogden glanced nervously at his backbar as though expecting some hitherto unknown opening to present still further guns and hard-voiced orders to oppose his wishes. For the moment all the wind was taken out of his sails.

There was a moment's silence, broken by Tucson's soft laughter. He turned to Ogden, 'How do you like it?'

Ogden's dead-white face had gone purple. He started to speak, but could only gulp heavily.

Even the Guadalupe Kid looked startled, 'My gosh, Tucson, where did they come from?'

'This is our crew, Kid,' Tucson chuckled.

From Stony and Lullaby, 'Hello, Kid. Greetin's, Guadalupe.'

'Sure glad to see you hombres,' the Kid replied joyfully.

Deputy Glascow started to protest. 'Look here, a joke's a joke, but this has gone too far.'

Tucson wheeled on the deputy. 'Speakin' of jokes, you ain't gone far enough, Glascow. Take my advice and leave this town as fast as your hawss will take you.'

'I'm hopin' he'll stay,' Stony grinned. 'Bet we could have a heap of fun with this deputy hombre. He looks plumb susceptible—'

'Look here, you—' Glascow commenced angrily.

Stony shoved one gun in holster, reached out suddenly and seizing the brim of Glascow's sombrero, yanked the hat down over the man's eyes, then gave him a quick shove into the crowd. Glascow tugged at the hat, managed to clear his vision after a moment and gave vent to a squeal of rage. 'You're under arrest—' he started.

Stony laughed, 'All right, deputy, take me up.'

Glascow started forward, then stopped. From the doorway Lullaby said, 'Tucson, any orders?'

Tucson shook his head, then turned to Ogden, 'We'll be leavin', now, Ogden. Nobody's goin' to try and stop us. I could settle things, here and now, but I'm aimin' to give you a chance to think the situation over. There's a heap of misguided hombres in this

113

town that think you're running things. You're not. From this moment, you're on the downgrade and movin' fast. Take my advice and get out of town. Or stay, just as you like. If you do stay, watch your moves. You wanted war. Now you're goin' to get it. This is only a taste of what's comin' your way, unless you change a heap.'

Ogden's face was a study in suppressed violence. He cursed long and fluently, ending with, 'I'm stayin', see? I'll make you and your crew so sick of war that—that—' His wrath choked him and he couldn't go on.

Tucson smiled, 'Plumb sorry your windows got busted. You see, my outfit's plumb playful at times. You know how cowboys are. Send me a bill for the damages. I sure hope,' and the words were sarcastic, 'they don't get any more playful than they are. It'd be just your luck to have your whole buildin' took down sometime—piece by piece. And you with it.'

He turned suddenly away. 'All right, fellers. We'll meet you in front.'

Guns and faces at doors and windows disappeared. Stony, Guadalupe and Tucson started for the doorway, the crowd falling back before their advance. Just as the swinging doors were reached, Ogden found his voice,

'You, Smith,' he snarled, 'there's more to this. You ain't had the last say.'

Tucson turned back, laughed coolly. 'I shore hope I ain't,' he drawled. 'Ogden, there's a

114

heap more I aim to orate in your direction. Get your ears—and hardware—ready.'

With that he passed through the door, Guadalupe and Stony just ahead of him. As the swinging doors swung to a stop at their backs, a long sigh of relief ascended from the crowd.

'I reckon,' Tucson laughed, as Lullaby showed up before him, 'that's a lesson that Ogden won't forget for a long spell. Gosh, how did you fellers do it?'

'It was Lullaby's idea,' Stony said. 'The minute we heard the shots we left the Happy Days. Lullaby and me looked in the door of the Red Bull. Glascow was just herdin' you and the Kid up to the bar. We could have stopped proceedings then, but Lullaby thought it might be more effective to do the way we did—'

The Kid chuckled gleefully. 'My gosh, I never saw so many heads and guns poppin' into sight in my life. No wonder the Red Bull got a scare.' He was pumping the hands of Lullaby and Stony.

The rest of Tucson's crew was gathered around now. There was more shaking of hands as Tucson mentioned names to the Kid. The men moved away from the Red Bull. Looking back over his shoulder, Tucson noticed quite a few of the Red Bull's crowd standing before the saloon, gazing after him and his companions.

Tucson said, 'There's no place for spreadin' news like a saloon. I suggest we all head for the Happy Days and tell Hopkins what happened.

News of this doin's will get around town. There ain't no better way to let folks learn that Steve Ogden has lost a round in his latest fight. You see, there'll be quite a heap of hombres start drinkin' at Happy's place again.'

'Good idea,' Lullaby nodded.

The group moved across to Happy Hopkins' place. Happy looked relieved when he saw them enter. 'Sure glad to see you gents, again,' he smiled. 'Didn't know but what I'd lost my new customers 'bout as soon as I found 'em.'

'You better get ready for additional business, too, Happy,' Tucson said. 'I got a hunch there'll be quite a few curious hombres anxious to get acquainted with the gang that's challenged Steve Ogden's right to run rough-shod over Los Potros.'

Tucson was right. By twos and threes somewhat shamefaced individuals commenced to straggle into the Happy Days. Several of these newcomers Tucson recognized as having been in the Red Bull a short time before. Business for the Happy Days was on the increase. Hopkins, perspiring and smiling, moved from group to group. Cigars were passed out, a toast offered the new owners of the Tresbarro outfit. More men entered the Happy Days. The bar was thronged.

Finally Tucson suggested leaving. His crew gathered about him. Guadalupe mentioned his lack of a horse. 'That night Glascow and Ogden dragged me away,' he was saying, 'they'd brought an extra hawss with 'em. They knew what they intended to do, all right.'

'I'm surprised at you, Guadalupe,' Stony chided the Kid, 'lettin' them two bums kidnap you.'

The Kid grinned, motioned toward the strip of court-plaster at one side of his head, 'Cowboy, I was too groggy to know what was goin' on.'

Tucson and his companions stepped into the street, after saying good-night to the occupants of the saloon. Bat Wing, Rube Phelps and Tex Malcolm climbed into saddles at the hitchrack. The three mesquiteers left to get their mounts which still waited before the restaurant at which supper had been eaten. Sourdough's mount was found at a hitchrack not far distant. Ananias Jones' pony was at the local livery, and here the Guadalupe Kid hired a saddle and mount.

Fifteen minutes after their departure from the Happy Days, Tucson and his men were riding west out of town on the trail that led to the Tresbarro Ranch. The horses moved at an easy lope, the Kid riding ahead with Tucson to show the way, though the road was plain to follow under the full moon that sailed the night sky.

Behind Tucson and the Kid were Stony, Lullaby and Sourdough, riding near. The new members of the crew were bunched closely at their backs. Four miles from town found the

117

riders guiding their mounts along the floor of the canyon that cut through the Little Escabrosa Range, the thudding of ponies' hoofs sending echoes rattling along the high canyon walls.

The Kid was talking about the ranch layout. 'You see,' he was saying, loud enough for Lullaby and Stony to follow his words, 'the west boundary of your spread lies along the ridge of the Escabrosa Range. The Little Escabrosa Range juts off in a northeasterly direction from the southern end of the Big Escabrosas. The two ranges form a triangle, and the Tresbarro—your—spread lies right in that triangle.'

'How big an outfit is it?' Lullaby wanted to know.

The Kid replied, 'As I said before, it's in the shape of a big triangle, with the point toward Mexico. The west boundary line is about twenty-four miles long. Your north boundary—the inverted base of the triangle—runs about twelve miles. I don't know the length of the remainin' boundary. It's an irregular shaped triangle. Anyway, you get an idea.'

Stony did some quick mental calculating, then exclaimed, 'My gosh, Kid, that's quite a spread. We must be buyin' in the neighborhood of ninety thousand acres—'

'It's that anyway,' Sourdough called from the rear. 'I heard Don Manuel say, once, but I

118

forget the figures.'

'Wait until you see it, waddies,' the Kid said enthusiastically. 'It's got everythin'—pasture lands, alfalfa, water the year 'round from Santone Creek—' He stopped suddenly, his voice continuing in a more subdued tone, 'Gosh, I hope you like it. I'm sort of runnin' off at the head—'

'Sure, we'll like it, Kid.' Tucson said. 'Don't you worry.'

'There'll be the last taxes to pay,' the Kid said, 'and things are pretty well run down. There'll be repairs and paintin' to do. And don't expect too much of the stock. Don Manuel told me—damn his killers, anyway— that he didn't think there was more than about fifteen hundred head. There's somethin' queer there. I saw his tally book, and it ain't possible for a herd to depreciate that fast. You see, there should have been accordin' to his last tally, 'bout three thousand head at present.'

'We'll go into the stock end of it later,' Tucson said. 'I aim to have a look at some of the Box-8 cows, as soon as possible, and see if there's any evidence of blottin'.'

'One thing you ought to do,' the Kid proposed, 'is start usin' a stamp iron in brandin', Tucson. Don Manuel never used anythin' but a big runnin' iron to burn his 3 brand.'

'We'll get stamp irons,' Tucson nodded. 'Lullaby, Stony, I been thinkin' we ought to change our brand too, when we take over.'

'What'll we change it to?' Stony asked, grinning. 'The Bar-O-Soap?'

'How about Bar-B-Q?' from Lullaby.

'Barbecue?' Stony said. 'Gosh, Lullaby, can't you keep your mind off food?'

'I ain't no worse than you,' Lullaby retorted. 'You're always thinkin' about drinks. It was you wanted to use a "bar" in the brand.'

'Same old Lullaby and Stony,' the Kid laughed. 'Always scrappin'. I been thinkin'—'

Tucson broke in to say, 'I'd sort of like to keep the old 3 brand, only for our own good, we got to get somethin' different.'

'I've been thinkin' it over,' Guadalupe stated. 'Listen, how does this sound to you: you already got a 3. Why not add a "bar" and an "O"?'

'Three-Bar-O,' Stony said slowly. 'It sounds all right, but does it mean anythin'?'

'Three-Bar-O,' Lullaby echoed. 'Tresbarro. They sound somethin' alike, rannies.'

'Look,' Stony said, 'in Spanish, "*tres*" means 3. Three-barro. It sounds good.'

'I'm gettin' to it,' the Kid said, somewhat excitedly. 'Look, fellers, it can't be anythin' but 3-Bar-O. Let me name the outfit, will you?'

Tucson said, laughing, 'You've gone to a heap of trouble on our part, Kid. I reckon you got that right.' Lullaby and Stony agreed. 'But why,' Tucson continued, 'are you so eager to have it 3-Bar-O?'

'It—it describes you three so well,' the Kid laughed joyously. 'O means nothin'. Three-Bar-Nothin'. Get it? I never knew you three to bar anythin'. You're always ready to take on anythin'. Gosh, fellers, it—well, it's just got to be 3-Bar-O. You three bar nothin'!'

A sudden cheer went up from those in the rear. 'Three yips for the 3-Bar-O!' Bat Wing yelled. The yells were given.

The three mesquiteers consented, laughing. And thus the 3-Bar-O, the fame of which grew with the years, gained its name. 'We'll get it registered in the State's Brand Book just as soon as possible,' Tucson nodded, adding, 'provided there ain't no other outfit of that brand.'

'Never heard of one in this state,' Sourdough said.

The horses were out of the pass through the Little Escabrosas now, the trail running in a northwesterly direction across rolling, grass-covered hills. During the conversation the horses had slowed gait somewhat. Spurs were employed to again send the animals along at a swift, ground-covering pace. Gradually, Tucson and the Kid drew a little apart from the others. The Kid said once, 'We'll be there in a little while.'

'Figured it would be farther,' Tucson said.

The Kid shook his head, 'The ranch house is just about twelve miles from Los Potros. That's another convenience.'

121

Tucson nodded, remained silent a moment while the horses' hoofs drummed across the range under the bright moonlight. Finally, he spurred closer to Guadalupe, asking, 'Where does this Miss Sibley fit into the picture with Don Manuel dead, Kid?'

'She's his heir,' the Kid replied. 'Gets anythin' he has to leave. I saw the will, that afternoon, before those skunks raided the ranch. Of course, the whole business will have to go through the courts, but you and Lullaby and Stony will pay the money to her.'

'What kind of a girl is she?'

'Well,' the Kid blushed, 'she was callin' me "Jeff" an hour after I'd met her. Gosh, Tucson, she's pretty.' He frowned, 'I sure been wishin' I didn't have such a record behind me.'

'You forget that record, Kid,' Tucson said. 'Just call yourself lucky that it's *behind* you. We're backin' you from start to finish.'

The kid nodded, didn't reply. The riders drummed on.

A half hour later the horses were pulled to a halt before the house. At the sounds of their arrival, a light in the ranch house was abruptly extinguished. Then came the sound of a door opening and Caroline Sibley's voice: 'Who's there?' The tones sounded shaky.

'It's all right, Caroline,' Guadalupe called.

'It's us, Car'line,' Sourdough hastened to assure the girl.

'Oh, Jeff!' Tucson didn't miss the note of

122

gladness in the girl's voice.

The men were dismounting. Stony said, 'Jeff?' Lullaby said, 'Caroline?' The two looked at each other and grinned. Stony whispered, 'The Kid works fast.'

Sourdough said to Tucson and his two pardners, 'You fellers go into the house. We'll make to put your horses up, all right.'

Lamps had been relighted in the ranch house by this time. Guadalupe pushed Tucson ahead of him into the big main room. 'Caroline,' the Kid said, with the air of one presenting a god, 'this is Tucson Smith—the great Tucson—'

'Chuck it, Kid,' Tucson blushed as he reached for the girl's hand. And to Caroline Sibley, 'The Kid's got an exaggerated opinion of my importance in his bringin' up. Don't believe a word he says.' And presenting Lullaby and Stony, 'Here's a pair that's had just as much as I have to do with the Kid.'

'Oh, I've heard about all of you.' The girl's right hand went out to the other two.

'Just so long as you ain't heard *all* about me,' Stony grinned, 'it's all right, Miss Sibley.'

'And Tucson has gathered a crew already,' the Kid was saying. 'Things is sure goin' to pop around this neck of the woods. But wait, Caroline, until you hear what happened tonight, and—and—'

'Looks to me,' Caroline laughed, 'as though we were all in for a long spell of talking.' She turned to a round-faced Mexican girl hovering on the edge of the group, ''Cellia, you go find Sourdough, tell him and the others to hurry up with those horses and then make a big pot of coffee.' The Mexican girl hurried away. Caroline continued, 'And there are some cigars and some old brandy of Don Manuel's here. I'll get them.' At mention of the old Spaniard's name, the girl's eyes moistened. 'Please excuse me a minute.' She hurried from the room.

The Kid swung enthusiastically to Tucson and the other two. 'How's she look to you?'

Tucson grinned and said, 'You talkin' about Miss Sibley or this layout?'

The Kid flushed crimson, 'Dang your hide, Tucson, you knew I was referrin' to the ranch ... Sit down, hombres.'

'Oh, I get you.' Tucson sobered. 'Kid, it looks like home.'

'We're settlin' down at last,' Lullaby said fervently.

Stony snorted, 'Considerin' recent past events, I'm oratin' to the effect that the 3-Bar-O won't do easy settlin' for some time to come. We got a fight on our hands, waddies.'

Tucson nodded seriously. 'Stony speaks truth. A heap of powdersmoke is due to cloud this range before things is settled. Howsomever, we're in it with both feet. The 3-Bar-O has come to stay.'

CHAPTER TEN

THE PRICE OF A LIFE

In a small office partitioned off in one corner of the Red Bull, Steve Ogden sat talking to his ranch foreman, Jake Elliot. Elliot was a bull-dog jawed man with a paunch and wispy straw-colored hair, about forty years of age. He was noted for a mean disposition and an abnormal capacity for red liquor. It was only a trifle past mid-morning, but already the bottle on the table between the two men was half empty. Ogden had, so far, taken only one small drink. The door leading into the saloon was closed.

Ogden reached into a small drawer in the table, produced a box of long black cigars, offered one to Elliot and lighted one himself. The two men drew meditatively on their smokes a moment before Ogden said impatiently,

'It's all right with me, Jake. Hire what Mexes you need to work the stock. Our regular crew may be necessary for other—well, what I mean is, I'd like 'em to stick around town more or less. With the IXI in our hands, I knew you'd have to take on several new *vaqueros*. I didn't expect you to carry on twice the work with the Box-8 crew alone. So far as our regular men are concerned, they'll get their orders from me—

through you, of course.'

Elliot exposed tobacco-stained fangs in a nasty grin, 'Work such as brand-blottin' or lead slingin', eh?'

Ogden frowned. 'I didn't say that.'

'It's all right, chief. I was only judgin' from past performances—'

'I'll do all the judgin' that's necessary,' Ogden cut in curtly. 'I'm payin' you for results, Jake, not for tryin' to use your brain. Nearly two weeks ago I gave certain orders. What is there to report?'

'I've had four men out, spyin' and listenin',' Elliot stated. 'Auringer, Merker, Knight, and Chapman—'

'Never mind who they are,' Ogden said impatiently. 'What did they learn?'

'Plenty,' Elliot replied. 'You can't get away from it, boss. This Smith hombre works fast and he gets results. In less than two weeks they've made the Tresbarro place look like a new outfit. My men report that paintin' and repairs have been rushed from dawn 'til sundown—and don't forget that there's only been a coupla men workin' around the buildin's. The rest been ridin', gatherin' stock. I reckon Smith is makin' a complete tally before he starts—'

'How many cows did they pick up?'

'As near as Knight and Merker could guess—spyin' from a bluff where they was hid out—around eighteen hundred head.'

Ogden considered, said absent-mindedly, 'We haven't done so bad, at that. Still, I didn't think we'd left that many—'

'Cripes, those Smith hombres been combin' the brush and hills, gettin' animals that we never bothered to go after. There was only about twelve hundred head on the open range. By the way, Smith and his pals are usin' stamp irons—brandin' a 3-Bar-O. The bar and O bein' under the three. Chapman tells me around Los Potros they're bein' spoken of as the Three-Bar-Nothin' outfit—'

Ogden nodded shortly. 'Yeah, I've heard that. But you don't mean to tell me that Smith is rebrandin' all that eighteen hundred head?'

Elliot shook his head. 'Nope—just some young stuff that we'd missed—'

'I don't pay you money to miss anythin', Jake,' Ogden snapped.

'Hell, we never did comb the brush. Wa'n't necessary,' Elliot defended, and went on, 'They're puttin' the iron on some old mavericks that's never been out of the brush, too. Oh, they been gettin' a gatherin', all right.'

Ogden gazed meditatively out of the small window that gave light to his office. Finally he looked back to Elliot, 'All right, Jake, you boys keep after the cows that still wear the old 3 brand. Oh yes, and if any of the crew could do a little dry-gulchin' of the 3-Bar-O hands—well, you know I pay a bonus for such work.'

Elliot nodded. 'They ain't dared get near

enough for anythin' like that, yet. Those 3-Bar-O waddies been travelin' in pairs too. It's been too risky to come close enough for a shot. Howsomever—'

Ogden's clenched fist came angrily down on the table top. 'Dammit. Jake,' he exclaimed, 'what do those lazy dogs think I pay double wages for. They'll have to take risks if they keep on my payroll. And that goes for you too.'

Elliot said meekly, 'Yes, chief.' He poured another drink, said, 'Here's regards,' and downed the liquor. Then, 'Anythin' else?'

'That's all I can think of right now.'

Elliot said 's'long' and opened the door. Ogden didn't reply. The door closed on Elliot's heels. A few minutes later it opened again to admit Deputy Glascow. Glascow looked worried as he slammed the door behind him and dropped into the chair recently vacated by Jake Elliot. Without speaking he poured a drink into Elliot's glass and downed it.

Ogden said sarcastically, 'You sure look cheerful this mornin', Brose.'

'You would too,' Glascow growled, 'if you knew what I know.'

'The same bein'?'

Glascow swore a lurid string of oaths, ending with, 'Steve, we're due to have trouble with Fin Sharkey.'

'What's the matter with Sharkey?' Ogden queried coldly.

'He's almighty cocky, for one thing,' from

128

Glascow. 'Says he's sick of layin' in jail.'

'Been treatin' him all right, ain't you?'

'Givin' him anythin' he wants but his freedom.'

'Tell the fool he can't have that until his trial comes.'

'Oh, hell, I've told him all that. But he don't feel sure about gettin' off. He's afraid you'll let him hang.'

'Maybe I will,' Ogden said calmly. 'The dang fool—'

'You think so, do you?' Glascow glowered at Ogden. 'And what's goin' to happen to us, then? Sharkey says he'll spill everythin'.'

Ogden's eyes narrowed. 'Look here,' he said finally, 'make it clear to Sharkey that we'll see that he gets off.'

Glascow laughed humorlessly. 'I'd like to know, myself, just how you aim to accomplish that. Tucson Smith and his two pals were right there when the stage was held up, and old Panzer rubbed out.'

'We'll bring a dozen witnesses to swear that Sharkey was someplace else at that moment.'

'Findin' that dozen witnesses will be easy enough,' Glascow said, shaking his head, 'makin' a jury disregard the words of Smith and his pals is somethin' else. Don't forget that Smith has a good rep in this country. He's pretty wide known.'

'Don't forget,' Ogden lashed out impatiently, 'that it's a ten to one shot that

129

Smith won't be alive when that trial comes off. And we'll handle Joslin and Brooke too.'

Glascow said uncomfortably, 'I shore wish we could be shore of that, Steve. I've tried to tell Fin Sharkey that he ain't no cause to worry, but he's plumb proddy these days. You know, Steve, if Fin ever spilled what he knows about you and me, it would be—'

'Never mind,' Ogden cut in harshly. 'I know what it would mean. You're right, Brose, Sharkey mustn't come to trial.'

'What's the answer?'

Ogden considered, then said slowly, 'How'd it be, Brose, if you gave Sharkey a saw—one capable of sawin' through steel bars?'

'You mean, let him escape?'

'What did you think the saw was for, to amuse himself?'

Glascow shook his head. 'I don't like it—'

Ogden swore at the deputy. 'Dammit, Brose, I pay you money to do things my way in Los Potros—and elsewhere. What you like doesn't enter into the matter.'

'Now, wait a minute, Steve, don't get proddy,' the deputy said placatingly. 'Lettin' him escape won't clear the atmosphere. He'll still know too much. You know, he's sore. You never paid him for that hold-up. He claims he's due for Puma Jeems' share too.'

'I don't pay for failures,' Ogden said shortly. 'You give Sharkey that saw, Brose. If it will make you feel any better I'll offer a reward for

130

his apprehension after he escapes.'

Glascow's face lighted up. 'That reward payable to me?'

Ogden nodded, then smiled thinly, 'We won't even mention it to anybody else, Brose.'

Glascow breathed a long sigh of relief. 'That's settled then. Sharkey gets a saw this afternoon, with instructions to use it tonight.'

'Better make it late,' Ogden said thoughtfully. He changed the subject, 'What's new around town?'

Glascow frowned. 'It's just like I told you yesterday, Steve. This town's commencin' to turn against you some. You ain't got it scared like before. The Happy Days is gettin' a heap of your old business. I dropped in there—'

'I ain't bothered about that. The worms in this town will come back to the Red Bull on the run after I've settled things.'

'When'll that be?'

Ogden shrugged his shoulders. 'Not very long now, Brose. You heard whether Smith and his pals have taken up that option yet—or tried to?'

The two men exchanged smiles. Glascow said, 'Nope, he ain't made a move in that direction yet. You ought to know damn well he can't—'

'I was just wonderin',' Ogden said idly. 'He'll have a surprise comin'. Where'd you hear it?'

''Course, I can't say for sure,' Glascow continued, 'but one of the Bridle-Bit hands

131

said he was talkin' to Sourdough Jenkins yesterday, when Jenkins come in town for supplies. Anyway, this Bridle-Bit hombre states that the 3-Bar-O is too busy gatherin' stock and makin' repairs to get that ownership settled.'

The Bridle-Bit was a small ranch located about thirty-five miles north of Los Potros and operated by a cowman named Hartigan.

Ogden nodded. 'You keep on droppin' into the Happy Days,' he said. 'Can't tell what you may pick up in the way of news. Most of the Bridle-Bit hands spendin' their money there now, eh?'

'All of 'em,' Glascow said.

Ogden nodded slowly. 'In case of a range war, who'd the Hartigan outfit side with—the Box-8 or the 3-Bar-O?'

'The 3-Bar-O,' Glascow said promptly. 'You might as well face the facts, Steve. Hartigan spent his money in the Red Bull just so long as he was afraid of you. Now that you're gettin' some opposition, he's ready to swing to Smith. Hartigan's always been too small to buck you alone.'

'I'd figured it that way,' Ogden said, frowning. 'Well, we'll finish this Hartigan hombre after Smith is out of the way. I always intended to take care of him after I'd done with the Tresbarro business. Yep, Mister Hartigan's finish is just postponed a spell. How about Reece's Rocking-R outfit?'

132

Glascow swore and said, 'You don't need to worry about him. Right now, Reece is on the fence. He'll jump to the biggest bidder. His outfit bein' south of here is surrounded with desert country—'

'I know all that,' impatiently. 'I've seen his cows—ganted up like a pile of bones—'

'That's the point I'm makin',' Glascow pursued. 'You promise Reece some grazin' and water for his stock and you can have anythin' he's got. His outfit is on its last legs now. He's a spineless sort of critter. Part of his time he comes here, part to the Happy Days.'

'You see him, Brose. Flatter him some. Tell him I want to be neighborly and he can throw his stock over on IXI range if he cares to.'

'I'll do that, chief—'

A knock came at the door. Ogden said, 'Who is it?'

'Me, Gus Trout.'

'C'mon.'

The bartender of the Red Bull entered, said, 'Steve, there's a hombre out here wants to see you. Name of Sundown Saunders.'

Ogden's face lighted. 'Good.'

Glascow frowned. 'Sundown Saunders,' he said slowly. 'Cripes! Steve, that's—'

'The fastest gun in the Southwest,' Ogden finished with a thin smile. 'His guns are for hire. I knew it. I wrote a letter, sent for him nearly two weeks ago, after—' he hesitated lamely, '—after the 3-Bar-O smashed

133

my windows.'

Glasgow nodded comprehendingly. 'You ain't so dumb, chief.'

'Wisest move I ever made,' Ogden nodded. 'This Saunders has been in dozens of gun fights. Sheriffs of tough towns have hired him. He's been used in range wars. More speed than a strikin' rattler and just as mean, from what I hear. He did a term in the penitentiary and it sort of soured his disposition. They say he ain't got any friends. Reckon the only good thing I ever heard about him is the fact that he always keeps his word.'

'Yo're usin' him on Smith, eh?'

'Don't talk so much, Brose.' Then to Gus Trout, 'Send Saunders in here, Gus.'

The bartender left. A minute later the door opened slowly, cautiously and a pair of narrowed dark eyes surveyed Ogden and the deputy. There were too many men after Sundown Saunders' scalp for him to enter a strange room in any other manner. After a moment he relaxed, slammed the door quickly behind him.

'Which one is Ogden?' he said harshly.

'I'm Steve Ogden.'

'How am I to know that?'

Ogden said carelessly, 'The deputy will tell you.' And added, 'Don't you trust to my word?'

Cold laughter met the question. Saunders said, 'I don't trust anybody.' He was gazing warily at the badge on Glascow's vest.

'Shore—this is Steve Ogden,' Glascow put in.

Saunders didn't say anything for a minute as his sharp eyes studied the two. He wasn't more than twenty-two or three, and of medium height with slim hips encircled with criss-crossed, well-worn cartridge belts to which were suspended holstered six-shooters. His features were hard, embittered, his manner suspicious. He wore corduroy trousers tucked into knee boots. Rawhide thongs held his holsters firmly to thighs. A dark woolen shirt, red bandanna, and black sombrero completed his attire.

After a moment Saunders nodded, said to the deputy, 'All right. My business is with the other one. You get out.'

Glascow flushed hotly. 'Look here, you, I'm the peace-officer in this town. You can't order me around—'

'Get out!' The words stung like the flick of a whip lash.

Glascow felt a chill course his spine. He tried to meet the cold eyes that bored into his and, realizing he was looking into the eyes of a professional killer, failed miserably. Gathering the fleeting remnants of self-respect he commenced to bluster anew.

'Leave be, Brose,' Ogden cut in curtly, and echoed, 'Get out.'

Glascow started for the door. Saunders

135

backed one pace, his suspicious glance following every move until the deputy had left and closed the door behind him.

Ogden said, 'Sit down. Have a drink,' motioning toward the bottle and glass on the table.

Saunders said coldly, shaking his head, 'Gun-play and liquor don't mix ... Man I know sent me word you had a job. What's the proposition?'

The cold manner had somewhat unsettled Ogden. 'It's this way,' he commenced, 'I'll hire you on as a hand on my Box-8 spread and then—'

'I don't sign up to any man's outfit,' came the cold interruption. 'What's the job?'

'Lone wolf, eh?' Ogden sneered.

Sundown Saunders' upper lip drew back in a snarl. 'One job at a time,' he stated. 'When you asked to hire my guns, that's what you get. If that don't suit you—' He broke off, started to rise.

'Sit still,' hastily. 'I understand you're the fastest gun in the Southwest country.'

'Nobody's ever proved different.' Saunders' tones were positively chilling.

'You'll have a chance to back up your rep. There's a feller recent come into this country named Smith. He's stealin' cattle right and left. Bein' he's pretty good with his guns, us peaceful cattle owners have to take what he hands out. We don't like it, but there's no other way out. I'll warn you, he's fast—'

'Dammit, get on with your story.'

'He and his crew come in here one night and busted all my windows. They're runnin' this town ragged. I talked it over with the peace-officer you saw here. He don't like the idea of violence, but we don't see any other way of gettin' rid of this trouble-making hombre. Once he's out of the way, his organization will fall apart.'

'How about his pals?'

Ogden shrugged careless shoulders. 'There might be one or two of 'em raise a rumpus. If so, well, you'll get a chance to earn more money—'

'You're hirin' me to put this hombre out of the runnin'?'

Ogden nodded. 'It's up to you. But no back shootin'—'

Saunders swore a low oath. 'Don't say that again,' he warned. 'I don't dry-gulch. I'll take care of him. My price is twenty-five hundred, cash on the spot.'

'Pretty high, ain't you, Saunders?'

'Killin' comes high, Ogden,' Saunders said tonelessly. 'Take it or leave it.'

'But, look here—'

'Cash on the spot,' Saunders said harshly.

'Look here, Saunders, I'll give you five hundred now and—'

Saunders rose to his feet, eyes contemptuous. 'I didn't come two hundred miles to argue with a cheap skate.'

'Sit down, we'll get this worked out. But how am I to know that you won't get the money and then disappear?'

Saunders remained standing. 'How do you know,' he sneered, 'that I won't take your money and then run to the other fellow and get more for tellin' what I know. Don't be a fool. I've never yet broke my word to anybody. If I say I'll get this hombre, I'll do my damdest to earn your money. But, cash on the spot. I don't know anythin' about you. How do I know you'd keep the rest of your bargain if I trusted you. Nope, I don't trust anybody.'

Ogden surrendered. 'Damn if I know how you expect to manage to carry twenty-five hundred silver. Will you take a check?'

'Cash on the spot,' Saunders repeated. 'Bills is pretty plentiful in this country now. If you ain't got 'em, you can get 'em. Big bills.'

Ogden sighed. Murder came high. 'All right, wait a minute.'

He rose from his chair, turned a dial on the small safe that stood in the corner at his rear. The iron door swung open. There were several packets of bills inside the safe. Ogden believed in keeping plenty of money on hand. He counted out twenty-five hundred dollars, in large bills, and handed a small roll to the gunman.

Saunders counted the money, thrust it into a trousers' pocket.

138

'Suppose you fail—' Ogden commenced.

Saunders didn't reply. Just sneered confidently, contemptuously. It was his regular attitude toward those who lacked the nerve to do their own killing.

'You seem pretty sure,' Ogden said a trifle lamely.

Saunders ignored that too. 'What did you say this hombre's name was.'

'Smith—Tucson Smith he's called—'

Ogden halted suddenly. The tiniest flick of surprise had momentarily appeared in Saunders' cold eyes. His face hardened, grew more cruel, as he stared steadily at Steve Ogden. Ogden again dropped into his chair, trying to avoid that steely glance.

Saunders nodded slowly at last. 'You louse,' he said contemptuously.

'Why—why, what do you mean?'

'You tricked me, Ogden. What's this Tucson Smith look like.'

Ogden gave Tucson's description, ending, 'Why, what's the matter?'

'You know damn well what's the matter. I've heard of Tucson Smith. He ain't the kind to come raidin' other men's property. You lied to me, you cheap rat—'

'Now look here,' Ogden commenced, 'I won't stand—'

'You'll stand for everythin' I want to say. You're lower than a snake's belly, Ogden. I know now that Smith has got your nerve.

139

You're afraid to face him, yourself. He's got your number, got the Indian sign on you.'

'You meanin',' Ogden tried to gain hold of the situation, 'that you've lost your nerve, eh? Afraid to go up against Tucson Smith, afraid he's faster'n you.'

Saunders laughed harshly. 'I ain't lost my nerve, and I'm bettin' my life he ain't faster'n me. How do you like that?'

'You—you mean,' Ogden stammered eagerly, 'you're going through with it, just the same.'

'Ain't never broke my word yet—even to a skunk. I took your money, didn't I? I'll earn it, too. That satisfy you?'

'Good, Saunders. Think how it will add to your rep to rub Smith out. You'll get more jobs, you'll—'

Saunders looked steadily at Ogden. Ogden fell silent, then put a weak question, 'How you aimin' to do it?'

'That's part of my job,' Saunders said harshly. 'I'll work it out. Here in town.'

He turned toward the door, jerked it open, and passed into the saloon. Ogden watched the disappearing form, saw it leave the barroom and step into the street. Only then did Ogden discover that his forehead was beaded with tiny drops of cold perspiration.

'Whew!' he muttered his relief. 'I'm glad I ain't due to face that—that—My God! He ain't human.' A smile slowly formed on Ogden's

140

face. 'Reckon it's been worth it. I won't be bothered with Smith much longer.'

CHAPTER ELEVEN

MISSING RECORDS

The following morning after breakfast in the mess shanty, the 3-Bar-O crew rose and left the building to carry out certain orders which Tucson had outlined as the day's work. Only Lullaby and Stony remained seated. Sourdough George came in and commenced clearing off the long table. Tucson started to roll a cigarette.

'But I don't see why it's necessary for me and Stony to go into Los Potros with you and Miss Sibley,' Lullaby was saying. 'Why can't you and the girl clean up all them legal documents without us? Can't you act for us, Tucson?'

'Sure, I could,' Tucson smiled, 'if you two wanted to give me a power of attorney, but such a paper would have to be notarized. You'd have to go into town anyway. So you might just as well come along, and we'll get this transfer of the property all taken care of and give Miss Sibley her money—or at least put it to her credit so when the deal—the will and so on—finally goes through, everythin' will be in proper order.'

141

'Dang it,' Lullaby grumbled, 'here we're just commencin' to get settled and you go draggin' me off to town. How do you know the bank will have the papers in order—?'

'I saw Orcham about that a week ago. It's best that everything goes through the proper channels—'

'Who's Orcham?' Stony asked.

'The banker in Los Potros.'

Lullaby persisted, 'Mebbe our money won't be there yet.'

'It ought to be,' Tucson said. 'Accordin' to that letter Sourdough brought from town, day before yesterday, the money had been sent. There's another reason why you'll have to go to Los Potros. We'll have to decide whether we want a joint account, or if you fellers want—'

'What sort of joint you figurin' to open?' Stony grinned.

'Anyway,' Tucson smiled, 'you fellers will have to give the bank your signatures.'

'C'mon, pard, we might as well go,' Stony said. 'Mebbe we'll find some excitement in town.'

'Not much chance in Los Potros,' Lullaby said.

'Can't tell,' from Stony. 'Mebbe Steve Ogden will have some new ideas in trouble-makin'.'

Tucson frowned. 'Ogden has been takin' things altogether too quiet, the past coupla weeks. I don't like it.'

'The calm before the storm, eh?' Lullaby grunted.

Tucson said, 'Somethin' like that. I'll feel a heap better when this deal has gone through and everythin' is settled.'

The three men rose and went to the bunkhouse to get ready for the trip to Los Potros. Although Caroline had insisted that the new owners stay at the ranch house, the three mesquiteers had declared that they wouldn't feel at home sleeping any place but the bunkhouse with the rest of the crew, so the only occupants of the ranch house were Caroline and the Mexican girl, Moncellia.

Tucson left it to Lullaby and Stony to saddle horses and went up to the house to see Caroline. The girl met him at the back door, an expression of worry on her attractive features. 'I was just coming to find you,' she said.

Tucson smiled. 'That's sure flatterin'. We're just about ready. The boys are saddlin' up now. Your little black mare seems to have gone lame, but—'

'Jeff will probably saddle the chestnut for me. He's going, isn't he?'

'Sure, sure,' Tucson replied promptly. As a matter of fact, the Kid hadn't been included in the trip. Now, looking into the girl's eyes, Tucson suddenly realized that it was very important that the Kid go to Los Potros. He said gravely, 'I come to ask you if you'd mind ridin' in the buckboard with Guadalupe. You see, we got to get some supplies.' A bald-faced lie if there ever was one.

'Not at all,' Caroline replied brightly. 'That'll be fine.'

'Be back in a minute,' Tucson said, swinging around. He hastened toward the corral where he found Guadalupe, Stony and Lullaby saddling ponies.

'Nev' mind Miss Sibley's chestnut, Kid,' Tucson said. 'Throw a coupla horses on the buckboard. Miss Sibley don't feel like ridin' a saddle this mornin'. You'll have to drive her, Kid.' And added, 'Besides we got some supplies to get.'

The Kid's face brightened, then dropped, 'Caroline sick?'

'No, you dumb rannie,' from Tucson, 'but you know how it is, she wants to put on nice clothes, goin' to the bank an' all. She'd mebbe get all rumpled straddlin' a saddle.'

Stony said suspiciously, 'I thought Sourdough got all the supplies needed day before yesterday.'

'Forgot a lot of things,' Tucson said gravely. 'Rather it was my fault. I forgot to tell him. I remember now, Ananias mentioned that we'd need some more whitewash and some paint. There's a coupla spades required and— and—oh, shucks, we need plenty canned goods too.'

Lullaby was saddling up near the corral fence. He put one booted foot against the

144

pony's side, pulled the cinch tight, and looked over his shoulder with a wink at Tucson. 'You, Tucson,' he said, low-voiced, 'are sure gettin' to be one awful liar.'

Tucson nodded, grinning, 'Ain't it the truth. But, you know, Caroline said somethin' about makin' a visit East to see some relations, after she gets her money. Well, I figure the Kid ought to have a chance to see her as much as possible.'

Lullaby said, 'You sentimental slob.'

Tucson's grin widened. 'Yep, me, I'm just Cupid's little helpmate.' He turned, frowning, and yelled at Guadalupe, 'Hurry it up will you, Kid? We want to get there by the time the bank opens.'

'Be right with you,' Guadalupe called back.

Tucson retraced his steps toward the house, entered by the back door, nodded to Moncellia who was washing dishes, and passed on into the main room of the ranch house. From a bedroom, Caroline called, 'I won't keep you waiting a minute. I was just changing from riding skirt to—'

The rest of the sentence was lost on Tucson. In a minute the girl appeared, the frown of worry still creasing her forehead.

Tucson said, 'That's a right pretty dress, Miss Sibley. Green is plumb becomin' to you.'

'Thanks, Tucson. I wish you'd remember my name is Caroline—you and the rest of the boys.'

'I'll tell 'em about it—and keep it in mind

145

myself. Say, what's the idea of screwin' your forehead into a frown this mornin'?'

The girl was standing near the table. Now she looked up suddenly, 'Tucson, I'm bothered.'

'By what?'

'Tucson, I can't find the deed to this property.'

Tucson said quietly, 'No? You mislaid it?'

'I—I don't think so.'

'Where you been in the habit of keeping it?'

The girl crossed to a book shelf on one wall, took down a big heavy volume printed in Spanish, brought it back and placed it on the table. 'It was right in here. Don Manuel always kept valuable papers between the leaves of this book.'

'Suppose there'd been a fire,' Tucson said.

'Don Manuel was careless,' Caroline admitted. 'But he trusted everybody. Never figured that he'd have any trouble. But you see, everything else is here—the will, and his *documentos*—'

'Banker Orcham told me he had a copy of the will.'

The girl nodded. 'It's just the deed that's gone.'

Tucson examined the *documentos* which granted, to the original Tresbarro, ownership of the property. They were on parchment, yellow with age, and covered with quaint writings in Spanish, one issued direct from the

Spanish throne, and the other, at a later date, signed by a Governor of Mexico. A third saffron-colored sheet, known as a *diseño*, gave a crude map of the Tresbarro holdings. There were several other parchments covered with legal verbiage in Spanish.

'You see,' Caroline was saying, worriedly, 'after this country became part of the United States another paper was issued to Don Manuel to show that he owned the ranch in the United States. It was his deed to prove that under U. S. Government—'

'In other words,' Tucson said gravely, his eyes narrowed, 'you haven't one thing to prove that Don Manuel held this land, after it came under the government of the United States. Up until that time, the Tresbarro family could prove ownership—'

'But he did have the deed. I've seen it,' Caroline said anxiously. 'I've asked 'Cellia, but she doesn't know a thing—'

'Why should she?'

'I had her cleaning in here, when she first came. I thought she might have moved the book and the paper fell out. But she doesn't remember anything of the kind—'

'When did you see the deed last?'

'The evening that those murderers raided the ranch and shot Don Manuel. Oh, if we could only prove Steve Ogden was back of that, I'd—'

'We'll catch up with Ogden one of these

days,' Tucson said grimly. 'Let's get this deed business finished. Have you been away from this house for any length of time since then?'

Caroline considered. 'The only time the place has been absolutely deserted, was the afternoon of Don Manuel's burial. For several hours there wasn't a soul here.'

'Anybody else know that Don Manuel kept his papers there—I mean, in this book?'

'He's never made any secret of it. Wait! I remember once—it's several months back— Deputy Glascow happened to be riding past and he dropped off for supper. Don Manuel never liked him, but he always treated the deputy courteously. Anyway, the conversation turned to old Spanish Grants. I remember Don Manuel getting down this book and showing his *documentos* to Glascow.'

'Hmm,' Tucson smiled dryly. 'Glascow happened to be passing by, the talk turned to Spanish Grants. By the way, did Glascow attend the Don's funeral?'

Caroline's eyes narrowed. 'Now that you mention it, I don't remember seeing him.'

From the front of the house came the creak of saddle leather. A buckboard rolled to a stop before the gallery.

'But—but what are we to do?' Caroline asked.

'I reckon we don't need to worry—yet,' Tucson said easily. 'The deed is probably registered at the courthouse in Chancellor.

They'll issue a copy—'

Caroline looked relieved. 'I know it is registered at the county seat. Well, that's that. I've had my worry for nothing.'

Tucson didn't say anything, beyond, 'They're waitin' for us, Caroline. Let's get moving. Better bring those *documentos* with you. We'll see what Orcham says.'

They left the house. Tucson swung up to the saddle of the waiting horse. Guadalupe descended to help the girl up to the seat of the buckboard. Stony and Lullaby looking at Tucson's sober features sensed that something was wrong. Stony said, 'We won't get to the bank before opening time now.'

'Reckon we won't,' Tucson agreed. 'Howsomever, *that* won't make much difference.'

The buckboard swung out of the ranch yard with a flourish of Guadalupe's whip and started off at a smart gait. Tucson and his pardners swung their ponies a short distance to the rear to avoid the dust of the wagon.

As briefly as possible, Tucson acquainted Stony and Lullaby with the disappearance of the Tresbarro deed. For a few minutes after he had concluded nothing was heard except the steady pounding of ponies' hoofs and the rattle of the buckboard fifty yards ahead.

Finally Stony raised his voice: 'Glascow?'

Tucson nodded. 'Looks thataway to me. 'Course, we can't be sure.'

149

'That bein' the case,' Lullaby asked, 'what happens?'

'If the deed is registered at the county seat, it won't make any difference.' Tucson replied. 'Otherwise, we may have to save the ranch for Caroline before we can buy it.'

'Save it—how?' Lullaby wanted to know.

Tucson shrugged lean shoulders. 'You tell me and I'll tell you,' he said. 'We can't lay plans until we know just where we're at.'

Stony frowned, 'Seems I heard that the courthouse at Chancellor burned down coupla months back.'

'You heard correct,' Tucson answered, 'but as I understand it, most of the records were saved.'

'We better hope so,' Lullaby said.

Conversation was dropped. The riders loped steadily along the trail. Up ahead, Guadalupe and Caroline were sitting close together on the seat of the buckboard, with never a backward glance. Before long, horses and wagons were entering the pass that cut through the Little Escabrosa Range. Half of the distance to town had been covered.

Tucson and his friends arrived in Los Potros shortly after ten o'clock. Already the morning sun was sending down rays of heat. There weren't many horses nor pedestrians along the street. Here and there, men lounged in the deep shadows beneath wooden awnings.

Tucson led the way straight to the Los

150

Potros Savings Bank. Here, Guadalupe drew the buckboard to a halt, assisted Caroline to descend to the plank sidewalk and then turned the wagon to go to the general store with a hastily compiled list of required supplies which Tucson had furnished him.

The Los Potros Bank was a small brick building with one wide window and an entrance in the front. The interior was partitioned off, a third of the way back, by a wooden counter topped with glass and a cashier's wicket. At one end of the partition, near the right hand wall, was a low, waist-high gate giving access to the rear of the bank where were located a couple of desks, a steel vault and the private office of Dan Orcham, who was an attorney as well as head of the bank.

Orcham was a tall, stoop-shouldered man, with thin graying hair and shrewd eyes behind the spectacles resting on his thin-nostriled nose. He wore a neat gray suit of conservative cut. Seated at his desk, he could see through the open door of his private office, past the gate in the partition and through the doorway that fronted on the street.

By the time Tucson and Caroline had entered the bank, with Lullaby and Stony at their heels, Orcham was on his feet, one hand extended across the partition gateway. He said good-morning, held the gate wide that the four might pass through to his private office, entered behind them and closed the door.

Chairs were found for Tucson and his friends.

Tucson opened the conversation with 'Did our money arrive yet, Mr Orcham?'

Orcham nodded. 'A draft arrived from the First National of El Paso, yesterday, to the order of Smith, Joslin and Brooke. If you'll tell me just what disposition—'

Tucson interrupted Orcham to say, 'We've talked that over—my pardners and me—and decided to leave the money right here in your care, and draw on it as needed.'

Orcham looked pleased. 'That will mean a lot to the Los Potros Savings Bank, gentlemen, knowing you have faith in us. We don't get many large accounts. Steve Ogden, for instance, prefers to do his banking at Chancellor, though I understand he always keeps a considerable sum of money on hand. Now and then he does business through this bank, but—well, you understand how it is, a bank is never any stronger than its depositors make it. We're small, we admit, but Los Potros needs a bank and we hope to grow with the town.'

While Lullaby and Stony fidgeted uncomfortably the banker talked for several minutes. Finally details were settled, the signatures of Tucson, Lullaby and Stony put on record, then Tucson asked,

'How about the papers transferrin' the Tresbarro property to the 3-Bar-O? I realize it can't all be done at once, but once papers are all signed, and so on. I'd like for Caroline to have her money as soon as possible.'

Orcham nodded. 'As you know, I'm handling the matter of Don Manuel's will—in fact, I drew it up for him. That is all taken care of. There'll be no hitches in that direction. So far as the papers covering the selling of the property is concerned, well, I've gone just about as far as I can until—' He hesitated.

Caroline who had thus far remained silent said, 'Is anything wrong—?'

'You see,' Tucson cut in at the same time, 'we wanted to take up our option. What's up?'

'A rather queer situation has come up,' Orcham explained. 'At the Registry of Deeds Office, in Chancellor, no record of Don Manuel's ownership can be found—'

The words were interrupted by an exclamation from Tucson: 'You mean, the deed was never recorded—?'

'We don't know,' Orcham frowned. 'The book in which the Tresbarro property should be registered has disappeared—'

'Disappeared?' blankly from Caroline.

'You mean,' Tucson said, 'that the deed book was lost in the fire when the court house burned two months back?'

Orcham shrugged his shoulders. 'I don't know what to think, folks. At the time of the fire it was thought that, though a good many valuable records were lost, all of the books in which deeds were registered had been saved.

Now there seems to be one missing. Of course, Miss Sibley has the deed so—'

'But I haven't,' Caroline said.

Orcham looked startled. Tucson explained the situation.

A concerned frown ridged Orcham's forehead. 'I don't like the looks of this, at all,' he said slowly. 'The disappearance of the deed will complicate matters. That deed and the registry book constitute the only proof—'

'But look here,' Tucson put in. 'The disappearance of the book will affect a heap of people—'

'Not so much as you think,' Orcham shook his head. 'Owners of property registered in that book will undoubtedly be able to produce their deeds and thus prove ownership.' He turned to Caroline, 'You are sure you haven't any idea where the paper is?' Tucson's suspicions concerning Deputy Glascow hadn't been mentioned.

Caroline shook her head. 'I'll look through the house from top to bottom when I get back. Maybe it will show up.'

'It may be the registry book will put in an appearance, too,' Orcham said soothingly. 'You see, the present court house offices are installed in an old warehouse, in Chancellor, until a new court house can be erected. Naturally, affairs are pretty much in a muddle. The offices are crowded. There seems to be very little system. I'm in hopes the book will be found. I'm having a search made—'

'Look here,' Tucson said, 'when this range was taken over from Mexico, some sort of an Act of Congress must have been necessary to make it part of the United States. I'm just wondering if there'd be any record at Washington.'

Orcham shook his head. 'Washington would have nothing but a blanket record, covering the whole county. We did things a little differently in Tresbarro County: the county issued deeds to individuals. A few other counties did the same—'

'Then,' Tucson said soberly, 'unless the deed or the registry book shows up, clear title to the Tresbarro property can't be had.'

Orcham shook his head. 'That's the situation.'

Tucson pursued, 'Suppose those records never show up, what happens?'

'The Tresbarro property reverts, in that case, to the public domain. Anyone can settle and homestead—'

Caroline wailed, 'Everybody knew Don Manuel owned the land—'

Orcham smiled dryly. 'They couldn't prove it in court though, Miss Sibley. Now don't you worry; I have hopes this will all come out the right way. That registry book is bound to show up, or you'll find the deed.'

Orcham didn't feel so sure of this in his heart, but the words calmed Caroline. Tucson and the banker exchanged understanding glances. Tucson said finally, 'Well, anyway, Mr Orcham, you can have the papers all ready for signatures. Meanwhile, just transfer the necessary amount of money to Miss Sibley's account and make it payable the instant the deal goes through.'

And thus the situation stood when Tucson and his friends had left the bank. Caroline said, worriedly, 'Do you think there'll be any trouble about the matter, Tucson?'

Tucson smiled gravely, shook his head, and lied cheerfully, 'Not a bit, Caroline. This thing will be all ironed out before you know it. Fact is, I'm not so anxious for it to be settled. You see, we don't want to lose you. So long as things stand at present, we insist on having you at the ranch.'

Caroline smiled, talked a few minutes more then hastened away to the General Store to find Guadalupe. Tucson, Lullaby and Stony headed for the Happy Days Saloon.

CHAPTER TWELVE

'COME A-SHOOTIN'!'

On the way to the Happy Days, Tucson said soberly, 'I don't like the looks of things, cowhands.'

156

'Why can't we grab Glascow, hawgtie him,' Stony proposed, 'and then make him tell us what he done with that deed?'

Lullaby said, 'Don't forget, rannie, that we ain't got proof he took the deed. If we did that, we might never locate that paper.'

'Lullaby is right,' Tucson nodded. 'Best thing we can do is stand pat for a spell, until we see whether the court house record shows up.'

'Bet it don't,' Lullaby growled.

Tucson nodded. 'I feel the same way. Somehow, it's all too damn pat—that book and paper disappearin' simultaneous.'

It was just about noon when the three mesquiteers entered the Happy Days. Hartigan, owner of the Bridle-Bit spread stood at the bar drinking with one of his hands. A group of the town's citizens was shaking dice for cigars at another portion of the bar. A bulky shouldered young fellow in denims was talking to Happy Hopkins.

Tucson had met Hartigan the previous week. He nodded and the Bridle-Bit owner smiled cordially. The young fellow in overalls turned around, spoke to Tucson. Tucson recognized him as Taggert, the former stock tender at the Wagon Springs stage station.

Tucson smiled, 'Decided not to leave this section eh, Taggert?'

Taggert grinned sheepishly. 'I couldn't see bein' run out of the county just for tellin' the truth about a few hombres in this town. You said somethin' about stickin' around and gettin' a job. I came on the stage this mornin'. You still feelin' the same way?'

'Reckon I am,' Tucson nodded. 'We can use another hand.'

'Look here,' Taggert said, 'I'm no cowman. Never roped a calf in my life and I can't bust broncs—that is, I never tried. The only thing I know is takin' care of horses. I could mebbe save you money on veterinary bills. I've done some blacksmithin' too.'

'Now I know we can use you,' Tucson said quietly. 'You're hired. What's your first name?'

'Well,' Taggert crimsoned, 'my name's Aloysius, but my friends call me Bud.'

'You'll go on the payroll as Bud,' Tucson nodded.

'Thanks, Mr Smith.'

'Cut the "mister",' Tucson smiled. 'We're known as Tucson, Lullaby and Stony.'

Happy Hopkins said, 'Heard the news, Tucson?'

'What news you mentionin'?'

'About Deputy Glascow doin' his duty.'

'By gosh, that would be news,' Stony cut in, 'but I don't believe it.'

'It's a fact,' Taggert nodded. 'He killed Fin Sharkey at two o'clock this mornin', while Sharkey was makin' an escape from jail. Sharkey had sawed his bars. Glascow happened to be there and filled him full of lead as he was crawlin' through the cell window. By cripes! I didn't think Glascow had it in him.'

Tucson was silent for a moment. 'I still don't,' he said slowly.

Lullaby said, 'I'd figure that deputy to be sleepin' at two in the mornin'.'

'And ain't it dang funny,' Stony put in, 'how Glascow *happened* to be on the job?'

Hartigan pushed down the bar to Tucson's side. 'You know,' Hartigan said slowly, 'I couldn't understand, myself, Deputy Glascow bein' on the job at that hour.'

'The whole thing smells to me,' Tucson said.

'In what way?' Taggert wanted to know.

Tucson said quietly, 'Ever hear of killin' off evidence?'

Taggert whistled softly. He didn't say anything.

Hartigan said, 'You think that Sharkey was workin' for Glascow—or somebody else—in that hold-up?'

'If by "somebody else", Hartigan,' Tucson said directly, 'you mean Steve Ogden, the answer is yes.'

Hartigan looked uncomfortable. 'Me, I'd be a mite wary namin' names. I'll admit frank, though, I admire your spirit, Smith.'

'Thanks,' dryly. 'Me'n Ogden got a lot of bones to pick over, one of these days, right soon, Hartigan. How you standin'?'

'What do you mean?'

'In case of a range war, you backin' me or Ogden?'

159

Hartigan said slowly, 'I'd hate to see a war break out on this range, but I'm sayin' frank, Smith, that the 3-Bar-O gets my backin'—such as it is.'

Tucson nodded. 'Good. You can count on the 3-Bar-O from now on too.'

Stony said slowly, still thinking about Deputy Glascow, 'I wonder who gave Fin Sharkey that saw.'

Lullaby drawled, 'Why don't you ask Glascow?'

'Speakin' about Sharkey and Glascow,' Taggert put in, 'I reckon Sharkey must have told Glascow how I shot off my mouth regardin' the law enforcement in this town. You know, that day at Wagon Springs, when I quit my job.'

Tucson said, 'Why, Glascow been ridin' you since you come to Los Potros?'

Taggert shook his head. 'Not today—haven't seen him today. But a week or so back, I run across him over to Chancellor. I was in the court house—or rather that big barn of a buildin' they're usin' for a court house—payin' some taxes on a little lot I got at the county seat. Well, Glascow clouds up like a thunderstorm, when he sees me and announces that he understands I been callin' him names. Said he had a notion to arrest me.'

'So what?' Tucson said interestedly.

'Well, I didn't want no trouble,' Taggert continued. 'On the other hand I wasn't aimin' to let him run roughshod over me, so I told him to go ahead. Glascow allowed as how he had business in the court house, but that if I hadn't left town by the time his business was finished, he'd take me up. Well, I bluffed some and told him I'd be waitin' outside the courthouse when his business was done, and we'd take the matter up with Sheriff Morgan who was in town.'

'Did you?' Tucson asked.

Taggert shook his head. 'Glascow blustered and swore some and brushed past me. Figurin' I had called his bluff I thought I'd rub it in some. So I waited in front of the buildin' until quittin' time, but he didn't come out. Reckon he must have left by another door.'

Tucson laughed softly. 'Didn't see him again, eh?'

'Not right away. I got tired of waitin' around and went to eat supper. It was about dark when I caught sight of him ridin' out of town. I reckon he figured I couldn't be bluffed—'

'What was he carryin' when he left town?' Tucson said quietly. 'I mean, how large a package?'

Taggert measured certain dimensions in the air with his hands, 'Oh, 'bout so large—say a foot by two feet—mebbe three inches thick. It was done up in paper so I—' He broke off, suddenly, eyes widening, 'Say, how did you know he was carryin' a package? Was you in Chancellor—?'

'Just guessed it,' Tucson smiled lazily. 'Did it look like a box, or a ledger or—'

'Ledger?' from Taggert.

'Yeah, you know, a big book like records are written in.'

Taggert considered. 'We-ell, it might have been. You see, it was wrapped in paper. I couldn't tell rightly.'

Tucson said, 'Uh-huh, it doesn't matter.' Apparently he had lost interest in the subject, but he exchanged glances with Lullaby and Stony. Hartigan and Taggert looked puzzled, but neither said anything. Tucson changed the subject. Drinks were set out by Happy Hopkins, at Tucson's request.

Sundown Saunders abruptly slipped through the entrance and approached the bar; his shifty eyes glanced quickly over the room. Hopkins nodded to him, went to take his order. Tucson glanced at Saunders, noted the gunman's bleak features and dark hostile manner.

'So long as I'm settin' 'em up, Happy,' he called down the bar, 'you might as well invite the gent to come in on this.'

'I'll do that, Tucson,' Hopkins nodded, and to Saunders, 'Tucson Smith is settin' 'em up. What's yours?'

Saunders turned slowly and surveyed Tucson with narrowed eyes. 'Me, I prefer to pay for my own,' he said coldly. 'I'm particular as hell who I drink with.'

Stony swore and started down the bar. Tucson caught his arm and pulled him back, at the same time hushing the words of his other friends. 'Right, stranger,' Tucson said easily, 'it's up to you.'

'I ain't askin' your permission for that either,' Saunders said harshly.

Lullaby drawled, 'Want I should go down there and tie a knot in that youngster's tail.'

Tucson shook his head. 'Leave him alone. He's probably got a hangover.'

'Not on that drink he don't get hangovers,' Taggert put in. 'Happy's servin' him sarsaparilla.'

Hopkins returned to Tucson, looking unhappy. 'Know who that is, Tucson?'

'An unmannerly brat if you ask me,' Tucson laughed easily.

'Ever hear of Sundown Saunders?' Hopkins continued.

Tucson's eyes narrowed, he cast another glance at Saunders. 'So that's the fastest gun in the Border Country, eh? Sure, I've heard of him. What's he doin' here?'

Hopkins shrugged fat shoulders. 'Nobody knows. He's been in and out of the Red Bull several times, I understand, but he ain't friendly with anybody there so far as I can learn. Mean as a skin-sheddin' rattler, 'pears like. He's been in and out of here a lot. Refuses to talk or get friendly with anybody. Hasn't started any gun fights though, as I've

163

heard of—'

He broke off suddenly as Sundown Saunders came sauntering down the bar to join the group. He tossed a dollar on the bar, said coldly, 'Whisky, barkeep.'

Hopkins' hand trembled as he set out a bottle and clean glass. Saunders poured with a steady hand, replaced the bottle and rested both hands on the edge of the bar. He turned his head to look at Tucson.

'So you're the great Tucson Smith, eh?' he sneered.

Tucson said quietly, 'You can leave off the "great", Saunders.'

The room had suddenly gone tense, so quiet a pin could have been heard to drop. The rest had backed away a trifle, leaving a cleared space between Tucson and Saunders. Realizing something unusual was in the air, Lullaby and Stony stood waiting.

Saunders' upper lip curled back in a snarl. 'You've heard of me, eh, Smith?'

'Never anythin' good,' Tucson said quietly.

A flush darkened Saunders' embittered face. 'I never heard anythin' else about you, 'ceptin' you was good,' he said harshly. 'Did you come here to start a Sunday School Class? I'm sick of you damn' Bible backs. Always preachin' an' pretendin' to be so good. Cripes! You give me a pain.'

'I figured you wa'n't feelin' well,' Tucson said. He lounged against the bar, right elbow resting on the edge of the counter. Saunders stood as before, both hands still in plain view on the bar, near the untouched glass of liquor.

Tucson said quietly, 'You lookin' to cut another notch in your gun, Saunders?'

Saunders' short laugh wasn't nice to hear. 'Notches, cripes! The only time I figure to notch walnut is when I've made a miss.' He hesitated to let that sink in, then continued, 'I ain't never cut any notches yet.'

Something of the deadly, vicious personality of the gunman was permeating the barroom. Lullaby and Stony were pale, tense. It was like being in close proximity to some horrible, evil monster. Only Tucson stood steady as a rock, conversing with Saunders.

'I understand you think you're pretty good with a six-gun,' Saunders lashed out.

'I've never said that,' Tucson denied.

'You're a liar!' Saunders sneered. 'You go 'round boastin'—'

Tucson said, level-voiced, 'You better get out your iron and go to work, Saunders.'

Saunders' hands remained on the bar. 'You must be in a hurry to die, Smith.' Even in that moment, Saunders realized Tucson was waiting for him to make the first move. Unconsciously, a certain respect for this tall red-haired puncher crept into the gunman's mind. He rushed on, 'Think you're a better gun than me, eh?'

'I didn't say that, either.'

'I'm goin' to give you the chance to prove it, Smith. Either that, or leave Los Potros by sundown.'

Tucson said, still in the same level voice, 'You're forcin' a fight, Saunders. Why? Who's payin' you?'

Saunders swore. 'I'm sick of this palaverin',' he snarled. One hand reached to the glass of whisky, jerked the fiery contents toward Tucson's face. Tucson's right hand blocked the glass, his left hand flashed to holstered gun. Then he stopped, noticing that Saunders had made no effort to reach for his six-shooter.

The guns of Lullaby and Stony were already covering Saunders. They had expected the old trick of blinding an opponent with whisky and thus gaining the advantage, but Saunders hadn't even placed his hands on gun-butts. They were still in plain view on the bar. He turned slowly and surveyed Tucson's partners, said insultingly, 'Put 'em away, hombres. I ain't drawin'.'

Tucson said, 'You've got to draw pretty damn quick, Saunders. Either that, or get out of Los Potros, yourself.'

Saunders nodded eagerly. 'Got the idea, eh, Smith? Good! This town ain't big enough for both of us. I'll be expectin' you, 'bout sundown. I'll leave the Red Bull. You can start any place you like. But—come a-shootin'.'

He turned his back on the room and walked

166

swiftly toward the street with never a backward glance.

CHAPTER THIRTEEN

RATTLESNAKE MEAN

There was a long silence when Sundown Saunders had left, broken only by several deep sighs of relief. Tucson spoke first, smiling grimly, 'Looks like I'm in for somethin'.'

Lullaby and Stony swore. The others remained silent. Hartigan said at last, 'What you aimin' to do about it?'

Tucson said slowly, 'What would you do, Hartigan?'

Hartigan said, spacing his words evenly, 'Make my will and wait for sundown.'

Tucson said, as slowly as before, 'I'll be waitin' for sundown.'

The Bridle-Bit hand with Hartigan said, 'Meanin' you don't figure it necessary to make a will, Mr Smith?'

Tucson smiled wryly. 'All I own is in a joint account with my pards. It ain't necessary to make a will. They'll get—'

'Dammit!' Lullaby's voice sounded hoarse, strained. 'Don't talk thataway, Tucson. Let me handle this damn snake—'

'I'll take the job of killin' Saunders and welcome,' Stony snapped.

167

'You two figure you're faster'n I am?' Tucson asked quietly.

Both shook their heads, 'But you see—' Lullaby commenced.

'Reckon, from what I've heard,' Hopkins interrupted gloomily, 'there ain't nobody faster than Saunders—' He stopped suddenly, looked ashamed.

Tucson said, 'That's all right, Happy. I might as well know the worst. Know anythin' else about him?'

'You know how he gets his name,' Hopkins said. 'I understand he works by formula. With his rep, he figures the waitin' gets to a feller's nerve. Same with his throwin' that whisky at you. Lots of times that stunt has been worked, then a shot fired while the whisky-blinded victim is scramblin' for his gun. But that ain't Saunders' way. He figures to make it clear that he could have drawed on you, but didn't, because he feels so confident of beatin' you to the shot, later, when you get an even break—if anybody could be said to get an even break against speed like his. Anyway, that's meant to shake your nerve too, so when you do meet him, face to face, you're too shaky to shoot straight.'

'In other words,' Tucson said grimly, 'he outsmarts 'em as well as outshoots 'em.'

Several of the customers in the Happy Days left to break the news of the impending fight to their friends. Now, in addition to Happy

168

Hopkins, only Tucson and his pards, Taggert, Hartigan and the Bridle-Bit hand were in the saloon.

Again Lullaby and Stony offered to take the fight off Tucson's hands, but Tucson silenced the words almost before they had commenced. 'No use of that, pards,' he said quietly. 'You know I wouldn't stand for that. You might just as well save your breath. The thing for me to do is find out all I can about Saunders. It's my guess, of course, that Ogden has brought him here to kill me. Guess we're all agreed on that.'

The others nodded soberly. 'S'help me,' Lullaby burst out, 'I aim to kill me a few skunks—'

'Save your breath, cowboy,' Tucson advised again. 'We got to meet this situation, one thing at a time.' He turned to Hopkins, 'Anythin' else you know about Saunders, Happy?'

Hopkins said, 'Reckon that's all, Tucson, and that's just on hearsay. He served a term in the penitentiary once. He's meaner'n the meanest snake you can think of. Hates everybody and everything. Kills to live and lives to kill. He don't trust anybody—not even his own mother, I reckon, though come to think of it, I've heard that he never knew who his father and mother was. Guess the only decent thing I ever heard about him is that he never broke his word to anybody—friend or enemy. And I never heard of him havin' any friends.'

The Guadalupe Kid abruptly burst through the doorway, his face working with emotion. 'It—it ain't true, is it, Tucson?'

Tucson smiled gravely. 'What you talkin' about, Guadalupe?'

'There's talk around town that you're aimin' to cross guns with Sundown Saunders.'

Tucson nodded. 'How much chance have I got, Guadalupe?'

'Not a dawg's chance—!' the Kid exclaimed, then halted and finished, lamely, 'I mean Saunders ain't got a chance.' His eyes didn't meet Tucson's.

'It's all right, Kid,' Tucson said gently. One arm went around the Kid's shoulders. 'I reckon Saunders is plenty fast—'

The Kid jerked away, 'I'm takin' this fight off your hands.'

'No, you're not, Kid.'

'I am!'

'Think you're faster'n he is, Kid?'

Guadalupe fell silent. Tucson went on quietly, 'One nice thing about a situation like this is learnin' how many friends a feller has who are willin' to bear his burdens ... Listen, Kid, what do you know about Saunders?'

'I used to know him,' the Kid said reluctantly, 'back in the old days, you know, when—'

'Ever seen him in action?'

'Three times. I've talked to men who have seen him shoot, too. Never heard that he killed anybody that didn't need killin', at that. He's one mean hombre, Tucson—'

'I've heard that too. But he's fast, eh, awful fast?'

The Kid nodded. 'He won't make a move to draw until you do, though. He'll give you that break, damn him, knowin' he can pull faster'n anythin' that ever jerked iron. I saw three fellers try to outnerve him. It was always the same. He'd give 'em until sundown to leave town, knowin' they wouldn't. Each time he met 'em in the open street, the two walkin' toward each other. Each of those three worked out the same plan for beatin' Saunders, the plan bein' to approach so close to Saunders that the guns on both sides *couldn't* miss. You see, they figured to shake Saunders' nerve, but it couldn't be done. One feller got within five yards of Saunders before pullin' his gun—'

'And then?' Tucson asked.

Guadalupe laughed humorlessly, 'Saunders had a forty-five slug in him, before he could jerk his muzzle clear of leather.'

Tucson's lips tightened. 'You any knowledge of how fast he can empty his gun, Guadalupe—I mean, just how—'

'I see what you mean—' The Kid hesitated, reluctantly.

'Go ahead, Kid,' Tucson urged.

'Well,' the Kid declared, 'once we were shootin' at a mark, and I saw Saunders pull his gun and throw five slugs—oh, cripes, Tucson,

171

it's no use. You wouldn't believe me if I told you how fast he slung them slugs.'

'Shootin' at a mark and at a man are two different things,' Tucson pointed out.

Guadalupe shook his head. 'Not to Sundown Saunders it ain't. He's got nerves of chilled steel. You can't outnerve him. He ain't human. If you're thinkin' of some way to get his nerve, you better give the idea up right now. The best thing I can say for him is—he's one ornery killer. He ain't got a heart. He's just a lightnin' fast shootin' device—'

'You're makin' it pretty clear to me, Kid,' Tucson said gravely. 'I've seen a heap of killers and gunmen in my time, but most of 'em had some good points, unless there—'

'There's a reason for Saunders, all right,' said the Guadalupe Kid. 'He was raised, as a button, to run with the wild bunch. At the age of sixteen he was framed for a murder. He spent four years in the pen, before the real murderer was turned up and Saunders pardoned. But it was too late to change him then. He'd been an incorrigible in prison. They'd beaten him, starved him, tortured him, tryin' to break his spirit. He came out of the pen hatin' the whole world and with the idea of makin' the whole world pay. That four years in the pen warped his mind, or somethin'—'

He broke off and started away. Tucson caught his arm, 'Where you headin'?'

The Kid said savagely, 'I'm goin' to kill

Saunders if I have to shoot him in the back. I'll stop this. It ain't right for you to face him in a fight. It wouldn't be a fight. It'd be murder!'

'Just a minute, Kid,' Tucson said firmly. 'You can't do this. In the first place, nobody's takin' this fight off'n my hands. In the second place, even if you did shoot Saunders in the back, would you feel like facin' Caroline?'

The Kid didn't reply for a moment. He averted his eyes, then, 'What's Caroline got to do with this?'

'I'm leavin' that answer to you, Kid,' Tucson said gently.

The Kid didn't answer that.

Tucson went on, 'In the first place, we've got to get Caroline out of town before—by the way, where did you leave her?'

The Kid said, 'Down at the General Store. She was looking at dress goods or somethin'.'

Tucson considered sending the Guadalupe Kid back to the ranch with Caroline, and realized instantly the Kid wouldn't leave him now. Tucson turned suddenly to Taggert, said, 'Guadalupe, here's Bud Taggert. He's our new hand. Remember, I told you about him bein' at Wagon Springs that day ...'

Taggert and the Kid shook hands. Tucson continued, 'Bud, it's up to you to take Miss Sibley back to the ranch. Don't mention this fight a-tall. Guadalupe, you go find Caroline. Bud'll go with you. Tell Caroline we're all going over to Chancellor to see about those papers, instead of goin' back to the ranch tonight. Don't let her see that anythin' is wrong.'

The Kid said, 'That's an idea.'

'Anythin' you say, Tucson,' reluctantly from Taggert, 'only—only I was figurin' I better stay in town to help you, in case—' He broke off, unable to continue.

Tucson shook his head, said a trifle wearily, 'Thanks just the same, Bud, but I reckon nobody can help me. This is my problem.'

There was some further talk. Bud and Guadalupe departed. Ten minutes later, Lullaby, standing in the doorway of the Happy Days announced that Caroline and Taggert had just passed in the buckboard. A half hour passed. Guadalupe hadn't returned.

After a time, Tucson said quietly, 'Reckon I'll go see what's become of the Kid.'

'We'll go with you,' Stony said. He and Lullaby started forward.

Tucson shook his head. 'I don't want you. No tellin' what the Kid might get in his mind. He's upset about this Saunders business. If I get him alone, I can talk him out of things. His pride won't let him be bossed when you two are around—'

'But look here, Tucson,' Lullaby protested, 'you might get into some trouble.'

'I don't reckon,' Tucson shook his head. 'Any trouble I got comin' is postponed until sundown. You two ain't had your dinner yet.

You better go eat—'

'Good God!' Stony burst out. 'Do you suppose we can eat at a time like this? What in—?'

'I'm intendin' to,' Tucson smiled gravely. 'I ain't dead yet. And there's no use you two actin' like a coupla old women. Me, I got some thinkin' to do and if I got to nurse along a pair of worried old hens I certainly can't—'

'C'mon, Stony,' Lullaby growled.

'I'll find you at the restaurant when you've finished,' Tucson said.

Reluctantly, the two departed. Tucson nodded to the men in the saloon and stepped out to the sidewalk. Here he stopped and started to roll a brown paper cigarette. Stony and Lullaby sauntered on, without looking back or speaking another word. The pair realized that Tucson wanted to be left to his own thoughts that he might lay plans, dig deep into old memories for sound tactics of gun-fighting, and otherwise prepare himself for the meeting with Sundown Saunders.

CHAPTER FOURTEEN

GUADALUPE FAILS

Forcing a smile he didn't feel, the Guadalupe Kid had sent Caroline Sibley on her way in Bud

Taggert's care. Once the buckboard had rolled down the street, the Kid's smile vanished to be replaced by a look of dogged determination. Crossing the street diagonally, he headed for the Red Bull Saloon.

There was quite a crowd in the barroom when the Kid stepped through the swinging doors, most of the men being engrossed in a discussion of the coming fight between Tucson Smith and Sundown Saunders. Evidently, Ogden had impressed Saunders' reputation on his customers: several men were trying to get bets on Saunders' winning the duel, but, even with odds offered, there were no takers.

Ogden stood behind his bar, talking to Deputy Brose Glascow. As Guadalupe entered, Ogden looked up, frowned. He said, 'You ain't welcome here, Ferguson.'

'That,' the Kid snapped, 'works two ways. I ain't here to buy and I don't want to see you, Ogden. Leastwise, now now. Where's Sundown Saunders?'

'Why ask me?'

'You brought him to Los Potros, didn't you?'

'Can't say I did,' Ogden lied.

'Where is he?' Guadalupe persisted.

'You come here to beg off for Smith?' Ogden sneered.

'You know damn well I didn't.'

'I ain't so sure.' Ogden smiled triumphantly, indicated Deputy Glascow. 'Mebbe you come to appeal to the law to stop the fight.'

'Your tin-horn deputy,' Guadalupe stated coldly, 'ain't got the guts to try. He couldn't stop a fly less'n it buzzed right into his mouth which is open most of the time. An' then I don't think he'd have enough sense to close it—'

'You look here, Ferguson,' Glascow bristled. 'You can't—'

'Shut up!' Guadalupe snarled. 'Ogden, where's Saunders?'

Ogden started to deny knowledge of Saunders' whereabouts, then stopped. Perhaps Ferguson had come to take up Smith's fight. In that case—Ogden smiled. Well, Saunders could take care of Ferguson as well as Smith. Two birds for the price of one. Ogden said, 'Last I saw of Saunders he was sittin' out back, hatin' the world and everyone in it.'

Guadalupe jerked around, pushed past several men, reached the rear of the barroom and stepped through the back door. Sundown Saunders was seated, smoking a cigarette, on a box, resting against the rear wall of the Red Bull.

One hand shifted quickly to six-shooter as Guadalupe stepped outside. Guadalupe said quietly, 'No need to pull, Sundown.'

Saunders scowled up at the Kid. 'H'are you, Guadalupe?' he said coldly, more from force of habit than from any interest in the Kid's welfare. 'Heard a feller of your name was in town. Figured it might be you. You on

Ogden's payroll?'

'No. You are though.'

Saunders considered that. 'I didn't say so.'

'That ain't necessary. We know. But I ain't askin' you to violate any business confidences between you and your employer. That's your business. When you throw wartalk at Tucson Smith, that's my business.'

Saunders' eyes narrowed. 'Howcome? You ridin' the straight trail these days, Kid?'

'Ain't rode nothin' else for some time.'

Saunders laughed harshly. 'All right, pull your prayer-book and start in. Owin' to the fact that I knew you 'way back, before you went soft, I'll try an' listen without laughin'.'

The Kid asked, 'Did you ever laugh, Sundown, I mean a real laugh that you enjoyed?'

Saunders appeared to be thinking. Finally he said, 'Now that you speak of it, I don't believe I ever did, Kid. Never found anythin' to laugh about.'

Guadalupe nodded. 'I used to feel that way. I've changed my mind. It's a damn nice feelin', Sundown.'

'What you leadin' up to,' Saunders asked impatiently, 'you takin' Smith's fight on your own shoulders?'

The Kid shook his head.

Saunders said, 'I didn't think you was that kind of a fool.'

Guadalupe moved around in front of

178

Saunders. Grudgingly, Saunders made room on the box. The Kid sat down.

'I offered to take on Tucson's fight—'

'The more fool you—'

'—but he just laughed at me. Sundown, I want to give you some advice.'

Saunders sighed wearily, settled his back against the building with an air of resignation. 'Shoot,' he invited in bored accents.

Guadalupe said, 'You go saddle up your horse and ride as fast as it'll carry you out of Los Potros. If you don't, Tucson Smith will blast you from hell to breakfast.'

Saunders emitted another long sigh. 'Kid, you ought to know better than to try that bluff on me. It's been tried too many times.'

'But you don't realize how fast Tucson is—'

'Cripes,' impatiently, 'I don't care, either. Save your breath, Kid. I know damn well he can't match me—and you do too. Hell! Does he put in hours, every day, year in, year out, practisin' drawin' and shootin'? No, Kid, it don't go down. Smith is as good as dead, this minute, and you know it. Smith send you here to try and bluff me into leaving?'

'If you knew Tucson you wouldn't say that. What you got against him?' The Kid's voice sounded weary, full of failure.

'That's my business.'

The back door of the Red Bull swung open. Ogden looked out. Saunders said icily, 'We didn't invite you into this conversation, Ogden.'

Ogden rasped, 'I'm just makin' sure I don't get double-crossed.'

Saunders flushed darkly. 'You repeat that statement, Ogden, and nobody will ever double-cross *you* anytime.'

Ogden hastily drew inside.

Guadalupe forced a thin smile. 'Still a man of your word, eh?'

'I don't know what you mean,' coldly.

'Why deny it? Ogden's hired you to get Smith. He as much as give the show away with that talk about double-crossin'.'

'That's your opinion. I ain't sayin' anythin'.'

The two men rolled cigarettes in silence. Saunders struck a match, lighted his smoke and tossed the flaming bit of wood to one side, forcing Guadalupe to light his own cigarette. Guadalupe said, after a deep inhale, 'So you don't believe me when I say Smith will beat you to the draw?'

'Lay off that, will you?' Saunders snarled. 'No, I don't believe you. Me, I don't believe anybody.' And nodded, 'All's I believe is what my senses tell me, and I know damn well that Smith ain't got one-half my speed.'

The Kid felt beaten. His bluff had failed miserably. He said flatly, 'I suppose you realize you'll have me to face—if anything happens to Tucson.'

Saunders shrugged his shoulders, looked bleakly at the Kid, said, 'That's just your hard luck.'

'I reckon. But after me will come Tucson's pards.'

'That's their hard luck.'

'One of 'em will get you eventually.'

'I doubt it, but what if that happens? Life ain't such a sweet proposition, anyway. A matter of three squares a day, forty winks, and a lot of powdersmoke.'

'You're wrong, Sundown, damnably wrong.'

'I'd like to see it proved otherwise.'

The Kid's voice became earnest, 'I ain't bluffin', now, Sundown. It's been proved otherwise to me. You knew me, back in the days when I was ridin' trails with the wild bunch. Pretty mean and ornery, I was—'

'I liked you better than anybody else in the crowd just for that reason,' Saunders admitted.

The Kid said bitterly, 'It's a hell of a thing to be popular for. Only for Tucson Smith—Look, you've wondered why I'm talkin' this way. I'll tell you what Tucson has done for me. First, he saved my life, after I'd tried to take his. He gave me a new start, backed me against all comers. Even talked turkey to the law, and made his words stick. He squared my accounts—'

Saunders' harsh, unbelieving laugh interrupted the words, 'It's a right pretty fairy tale, Kid. You made up any details for my entertainment?'

'I'll give you details—plenty details,' the Kid

181

said fiercely. 'You listen to me.'

For ten minutes he talked in a steady voice. Once Saunders broke in dryly to say, ''Pears like you've found a new religion, Kid.'

'I'm tellin' you,' Guadalupe snapped. 'There never was a man like Tucson.' He talked on, relating the various events that had brought, and held, him and Tucson together. Mostly he talked about Tucson, of the deeds Tucson had accomplished with the help of Lullaby and Stony. The cold look of unconcern was slowly erased from the icy mask that was Saunders' face as he said quietly, 'I didn't think men like that lived, except in story books, Kid.'

'I'm tellin' you,' the Kid repeated. He went on and on, talking himself out in the vain effort to save his friend.

Saunders finally held up one hand for silence. 'That's enough, Kid. I'm sorry. You almost persuaded me, but your talk ain't altered matters. You believe all this now, but your mind is runnin' in circles. You come to me to see if I'd call off this fight, didn't you?'

Reluctantly, the Kid admitted the truth of the statement.

'You've put on a good show to save the life of a pard,' Saunders said coldly. 'It wasn't quite good enough though. You're hipped on this Tucson Smith. Because of that, I'd be almost willin' to do somethin' for a friend—' he caught himself suddenly, '—if you were a friend of mine. But you're not. You'll get over

182

this hero-worshippin' idea that's got you hawgtied. A year from now you'll even forget where you buried Smith.'

The Kid turned suddenly. His right fist crashed into Saunders' face. Saunders' right hand flashed to gun butt, then he relaxed, smiled thinly and wiped a tiny trickle of blood from his lips. 'I'll overlook that,' he said coldly. 'You ain't right in your mind, just now. It proves what I've said, you can't trust anybody, even a feller you're sittin' talkin' peaceful to.'

Guadalupe was standing before Saunders now. His voice shook a trifle. 'I'm plumb sorry about that, Sundown. Lost my head for a minute. You can have satisfaction—anytime.'

'I thought that was already arranged,' Saunders said coldly, 'to come off after I've finished with Smith.'

'You're goin' ahead with the fight—'

'Ever know me to break my word, Kid?'

'Not that I ever heard of.'

'All right. I've took money for crossin' guns with Smith—'

'Hell, you could return the money—' Guadalupe commenced eagerly.

'The money's gone. One of Ogden's faro dealers took it last night—'

'I'll get the money and lend it to you—'

'I've passed my word, Kid. Money or no money, I've passed my word. I'll be waitin' for Smith at sundown—'

'I'll be waitin' for you right after—'

'Anytime, Kid, anytime,' Saunders said coldly, and added, 'You might tell Smith I ain't ever notched my guns, but he'll deserve a notch. It'll be somethin' to be proud of.'

The Kid didn't answer. He swallowed heavily and walked quickly around the corner of the building.

Saunders sat back against the wall, his eyes blank. 'Crazy as a loon,' he muttered. 'It must be like a religion, or takin' dope or somethin', to have faith in a hombre like that. The Kid'll wake up some day and realize I'm right. Reckon I'm gettin' soft, feelin' this way. I'm sort of goin' to hate to kill him...'

CHAPTER FIFTEEN

TUCSON'S BAD JUDGMENT

A sudden silence descended on the Red Bull Saloon as Tucson Smith entered the place. Gradually, men fell back from the bar. Glasses were set down. Deputy Glascow straightened suddenly from his lounging position at the long counter and spoke to Steve Ogden. Ogden looked surprised, then uneasy. He nodded to Tucson, forced a cold laugh,

'I should think you'd be home sayin' your prayers, Smith, or makin' a will—'

'There's a heap of folks think that,' Tucson

184

said easily, 'but I got other things to occupy my mind.'

Glascow guffawed, 'I'll say you have, Smith.'

Ogden was wondering what had brought Tucson to the Red Bull. The owner of the Box-8 didn't know whether to keep his gun-hand ready for trouble or not. He said, 'What can we do for you, Smith?'

Tucson said, 'I'm lookin' for Guadalupe Ferguson.'

'Why come here?' Ogden sneered. 'You know me'n the Kid ain't on friendly terms.'

'I figured he might have come lookin' for Sundown Saunders.'

'Oh, you want Saunders too?'

Tucson shook his head.

'Damn right he don't,' growled a man in the background, named Chap Bell. 'He'll see Saunders soon enough.' Bell was a Box-8 puncher, a hard-bitten individual with hard eyes and a bad reputation.

'Soon enough,' Glascow jeered. 'Too soon, you mean.'

Tucson disregarded the conversation, his eyes boring into Ogden's. 'You ain't seen Guadalupe?'

Ogden shook his head, his gaze falling before Tucson's steady glance.

Tucson said, 'I think you're a liar, Ogden.'

Ogden flushed, said, 'Up until sundown this evenin', you're entitled to think all you want,

185

Smith, or anythin' you want. If you had the sense you're credited with, I'd think you'd be gettin' your affairs in order.'

'You referrin' to any affairs in particular?' Tucson asked.

Ogden shrugged his shoulders carelessly. 'You ought to know your business. Ain't been havin' any trouble gettin' clear title to the Tresbarro property, have you?' Ogden hadn't been able to resist the temptation to ask that.

Tucson standing a few feet from the bar, said, 'Nope, no trouble. There's a coupla papers missin', but we know who took 'em—'

'What do you mean?' Glascow interrupted.

'You know what I mean,' Tucson snapped.

Glascow paled, looked anxiously at Ogden, but didn't say anything.

Ogden affected carelessness, 'He means, Brose, that the book deeds are recorded in has disappeared.'

Tucson said quietly, 'You got your nerve to admit it, Ogden.'

Ogden looked surprised. 'Why shouldn't I admit it? I was in Chancellor, yesterday afternoon, at the court house. One of the clerks happened to mention that particular book was missin'. That's tough, Smith. Until that book is found, the 3-Bar-O is likely to be open grazin' for anybody that wants to range cattle—'

'Don't you try it, Ogden,' Tucson said sternly.

Ogden laughed triumphantly. 'My Box-8

and IXI cows will be needing water pretty soon. You ought to be neighborly, Smith—oh, I forgot, you won't be here to have anythin' to say about it. Well, mebbe your pals will be neighborly. Excuse it, they may not be here either—'

'Damn right they won't,' Chap Bell cut in with a loud laugh. 'The whole 3-Bar-O crew is due for trouble if—'

'Shut that loud mouth up, Ogden,' Tucson snapped, glancing over his shoulder at Bell who stood some distance away, near the back door. 'We're wastin' time.'

'It was your idea,' Ogden sneered. 'I didn't ask you to come here ... Bell, leave be.'

Chap Bell shut up. Ogden went on. 'You can leave any time.'

'I'm askin' where Guadalupe Ferguson is,' Tucson said coldly. 'He was seen to come in here. Where is he?'

Ogden swore. 'How do I know where that ...' The name he called the Kid was vile.

Tucson's mouth straightened to a tight line. 'You're takin' that back now, Ogden. Quick! Or pullin' your gun. Make up your mind!'

Ogden started to laugh, suddenly sobered. Tucson's cold eyes sent chills coursing his spine. Tucson felt Ogden knew something of the Kid's whereabouts, sensed that the man was lying.

'Take it back, or jerk your iron,' Tucson went on.

Ogden gulped, then nodded, 'All right, I didn't mean nothin'.'

With a laugh of contempt, Tucson turned away from the bar. Ogden momentarily lost his head because of the humiliation Tucson had put upon him. His right hand swept down, brushed back his long coat, closed on the six-shooter at his thigh. And then he halted:

Tucson had whirled completely around to face Ogden again, and this time he held in his hand a leveled forty-five. Tucson laughed softly, 'Want to complete that draw, Ogden?'

Ogden's dead-white face turned a sick, sallow color. He flung his arms high in the air, lost his head completely. 'Get him, somebody!' Ogden screamed. 'A hundred dollars to the man who downs Smith!'

Tucson's other gun was out now, covering Brose Glascow. He didn't dare turn. Behind him he heard a rustle of quick movement.

Chap Bell reached for his six-shooter. At that moment Sundown Saunders stepped into the barroom through the back door, his eyes taking in the situation in an instant. Saunders' right gun flashed out. Chap Bell's gun muzzle was free of holster now, lifting swiftly toward Tucson.

Saunders' gun barrel described a short savage arc through the air and terminated against the side of Bell's head. Bell went down like a poled ox.

'Put them guns away!' Saunders' words

trembled with rage. 'I'm drillin' the first man to burn powder. Quick, put 'em away!'

A dozen hands that had dropped to gun-butts were quickly held far out from sides. Chap Bell groaned, rolled on his face, but didn't get up.

Saunders snarled, 'You lousy back-shootin' skunks. Smith, your guns are still in sight. Put 'em away!' Tucson slipped his guns back into holsters. Saunders continued, 'Nobody's throwin' down on you, Smith, not while I'm here.'

Tucson turned to face the gunman. 'Much obliged, Saunders.'

'You needn't thank me,' Saunders spat savagely. 'I'm just savin' you for tonight—at sundown.'

'I'll be meetin' you,' Tucson said coldly.

'What you want here?' Saunders snapped.

'I'm lookin' for Guadalupe—'

'He left a few minutes back. He's all right. We were—'

'Ogden said he hadn't seen him.'

'Ogden's a liar. He knew we were talkin' out back. You better get out now, Smith—'

'You can't call me a liar, Saunders,' Ogden's features writhed angrily.

'I'm doin' it!'

'You're facing trouble, Saunders,' Ogden continued. 'You may be able to outshoot me, but you can't run rough-shod over this whole town. I'll see that—'

189

'You'll see that what?' Tucson cut in, his voice like chilled steel. 'So help me God, Ogden, if you do anythin' so Saunders can't meet me this evenin', I'll come here and blast your hide so full of holes—'

'You've said enough, Smith,' Saunders cut in harshly. 'Get out. Nobody'll throw down on you when you're leavin'. An' nobody's goin' to stop me from killin' you at sundown.' An involuntary look of admiration for Tucson had crept into Saunders' bleak eyes. 'I ain't savin' your skin because I like you, see? No, it's because you're my meat, and I don't stand for anybody else cuttin' in on my game.'

'Right, Saunders,' Tucson nodded coldly. 'See you this evenin'.'

He turned and stepped quickly out of the Red Bull.

Ogden had cooled down somewhat. 'You missed your best chance there, Saunders.'

Saunders swore. 'I don't back-shoot, Ogden. I don't have to. Cripes! You're lower'n a rattler's belly.'

He turned and stalked angrily through the rear doorway.

Ogden said hotly to Glascow, 'That cuss is too cocky. After tonight we'll see what's what. But we'll let him finish Smith first.'

* * *

Tucson, after leaving the Red Bull had headed

for the Kansas City Cafe where he expected to find Lullaby and Stony. The two were there, seated moodily in the shadow of the restaurant's wooden awning. Lullaby said, 'Seen Guadalupe?' Tucson shook his head.

'He's lookin' for you,' from Stony.

'I was lookin' for him,' Tucson replied. 'I got sort of worried—but he was all right.'

'Where you been doin' your lookin'?' Stony asked.

'Red Bull.'

'T'hell you say,' from Lullaby. 'See Saunders?'

Tucson nodded, smiled dryly, 'Yeah, he's got his points. He just saved my life.'

Exclamations of astonishment greeted the statement. 'Yep,' Tucson said grimly, 'Ogden was all set to get me rubbed out, then and there, when Saunders come in the back door and put a quietus on the whole business. I told him much obliged and he nearly snapped my head off. Gosh, he's one savage hombre.' Tucson went on and related briefly all the details of the encounter.

When he had finished, Lullaby shook his head in perplexity. 'Damn' if I ever saw such a situation. You and Saunders due to shoot it out at sundown, Saunders savin' your life so you'll meet him, and you threatenin' to take Ogden apart if anythin' happens to Saunders. It ain't accordin' to Hoyle.'

Tucson said ruefully, 'It'll be accordin' to

Hoyle in about three more hours, hombre. Make no mistake, Saunders is out to fill me so full of lead that I'll be weighted down, whether I fall or not. God, he's mean. Ain't a charitable streak in him.'

'But what you aimin' to do, Tucson?' It was almost a wail from Stony.

Tucson said, 'I been thinkin' it over. I got to get me some guns.'

'Guns?' blankly from Lullaby. 'What's the matter with your forty-fives?'

Tucson shook his head impatiently. 'Don't talk. I know what I'm doin'.' He added grimly, after a moment, 'I *think* I know what I'm doin'.'

He led the way to a store bearing a sign that said GUNSMITH—GUNS BOUGHT, SOLD and REPAIRED. Lullaby and Stony followed close, their features expressing bewilderment.

The shop was filled with guns of various kinds in all stages of condition. The proprietor, a little grizzled man of sixty, was engaged in cleaning a shotgun when the cowboys entered. He rose and approached them.

Tucson said, 'Do you happen to have a Colt's single-action, .32-20, on a forty-five frame.'

The proprietor said he had one six-shooter of the type asked for. Tucson said he wanted two.

Stony cut in, 'What in time are you up

to, Tucson?'

Tucson said, 'Don't worry, hombres, I know what I'm doin'.'

The proprietor of the shop said suddenly, 'You want two .32-20s, eh? I have a pair of second-hand guns that might do.'

'Trot 'em out,' Tucson said. 'If they're in good condition, I'd sooner have used weapons. They'll be broke in.'

The proprietor went to the back of his shop, returned with two six-shooters in holsters, with belts attached. Tucson examined the guns, tried them for balance, and so on. 'Sweet pair of lead-slingers,' he murmured. Finally he removed his own belts and forty-fives, strapped on the brace of new weapons, handed the old guns to Lullaby. 'I'm keepin' these,' he announced. 'Let me have a couple of boxes of ca'tridges too.'

Guns and loads were paid for. While the gunshop proprietor was making change he commented, 'Looks like there'd be some lead-slingin' around town this evenin'.'

'So I hear,' Tucson replied calmly.

'Saunders was in, early this mornin', gettin' his guns adjusted and looked over,' the proprietor volunteered. 'There wasn't a thing wrong with 'em, but he wanted to be sure. I reckon he'll beat this Smith man to the shot.'

'They tell me he's fast,' Tucson smiled dryly.

'So I hear. He's a mean customer. I don't know Smith to see him, do you?'

'I'm slight acquainted with him,' Tucson admitted. He pocketed his change, thanked the proprietor and departed, wearing the recently acquired guns.

Outside, Lullaby grumbled, 'What's the idea of them new weapons?'

Tucson said, 'Sundown Saunders.'

Lullaby and Stony looked aghast. Stony exclaimed, 'You ain't intendin' to use them guns when you meet Saunders?'

Tucson nodded, 'Somethin' like that.'

'My God, have you gone crazy, pard?' Stony exclaimed.

Lullaby was dumbfounded. 'You really intend to use a .32-20 load against Saunders, instead of a .45?'

'A .32-20 on a forty-five frame makes a right nice weapon,' Tucson pointed out.

'I ain't denyin' that,' Lullaby grumbled, 'but it shore ain't got the stoppin' ability of your old forty-fives. You hit Saunders with a 250 grain slug, Tucson, an' he's done, whether you strike him plumb center or high up. But with a .32-20—aw, shucks, pard, you must be crazy usin' a lighter load.'

'Mebbe I am,' Tucson admitted. His face was stern, his thoughts far away.

Stony shook his head. 'Dam'd if I understand what you're up to. You lay aside your old guns, that you're plumb familiar with usin', and get two strange hawg-laigs throwin' a lighter load. Why, one of them .32-20s is

194

likely to pass right through Saunders an' he won't notice it until after—' Stony broke off, unable to continue the argument.

'But I've shot this .32-20 on a forty-five frame before,' Tucson pointed out. 'I know what I'm tryin' to do—'

'Yeah?' Lullaby grumbled. 'You've used that damn pea-shooter caliber about once to every hundred times you've thrun lead from your regular guns. What's got into you, Tucson? You ain't showin' good sense. Passin' up guns you're used to for—for somethin' that won't feel right in your hand when you grab for it—'

'Let's not argue the question,' Tucson said wearily. 'Mebbe my idea will work out, mebbe it won't. I'm aimin' to pull out of town for a spell—no, right now, and you two ain't goin' with me.'

'What you aimin' to do?' Lullaby asked, suspiciously.

'Ruin a heap of ammunition. I want to get used to these new guns—'

First sensible thing you've said,' Stony jerked out nervously.

Tucson nodded. 'I want to get myself familiar with the hang and the draw and the balance. After I've shot these guns a spell, I may find out they need some workin' over—though they seem pretty good right now.'

'Where'll we see you?'

'I'll be back at the Happy Days plenty before

195

sundown. If I started practisin' around town, there'd be a crowd collectin'. I want to be alone for a spell. I'll go back in the hills a coupla miles. Meantime, you two go find Guadalupe. Keep him out of trouble.' Tucson's voice grew stern, 'I don't want nobody—nobody, understand?—interferin' between me and Saunders. *Adios*.'

He walked quickly away to find his pony, climbed into the saddle a short distance down the street and rode out of Los Potros.

Lullaby looked glumly after his retreating form. 'God knows what's got into Tucson,' he complained to Stony. 'I don't like this business of changin' guns at the last minute. There's somethin' a-heap wrong.'

'You ain't tellin' me anythin' new,' Stony snapped irritably. 'If I didn't know Tucson I'd say he was plumb insane. As it is, well, I hate to admit it, but Tucson's made a mistake—a mistake that you and me are due to rectify, Lullaby. We'll toss for first chance at Saunders.'

'Toss be damned!' Lullaby swore. 'I already got my mind set on pluggin' Saunders plenty, just as soon as he downs Tucson—'

'Don't talk that way, Lullaby.' Stony's voice was hoarse, strained, something of terror in the tones. 'Don't talk that way.'

Lullaby swallowed hard. He didn't say anything as the two went in search of Guadalupe.

CHAPTER SIXTEEN

GUNS AT SUNDOWN

It lacked three-quarters of an hour to sundown when Tucson stepped quietly into the Happy Days Saloon. Guadalupe, Lullaby and Stony stood at the bar. Hopkins sat on a stool behind his counter. No one else was present. There wasn't any drinking going on. The men looked soberly at Tucson. There wasn't a word spoken for a minute.

Tucson strove to make his voice light, 'What is this, a Lodge of Sorrow you're holdin'?'

Hopkins explained in a voice that wasn't quite steady, 'I give out word I ain't servin' anybody. Figured you'd want to be alone with your pards now that—now that—' He gulped and failed to go on. Lullaby said awkwardly, 'How'd the new guns work out, pard?'

Tucson said quietly, 'Couldn't find any fault with 'em.'

'Except,' Stony said bitterly, 'that they're .32-20s, I agree.'

'Tucson,' Guadalupe's face was white, 'you can't afford to fool with Saunders. I talked to him today. He's set to kill you.'

'That ain't news to me,' Tucson said flatly.

'You shouldn't have gone to the Red Bull lookin' for me,' Guadalupe continued. 'You shouldn't have risked it—'

Tucson smiled dryly, 'What, with a friend like Saunders to save me from bein' shot up?'

'Savin' you,' Guadalupe swallowed hard, 'so nothing could prevent him killin' you—*tryin'* to kill you—'

'Let it ride as is, Kid,' Tucson advised. 'Forget it.'

'But, look, Tucson,' the Kid pleaded, motioning to Tucson's forty-fives and belts on a nearby table, 'put your regular guns on. That way, you'll have some chance. But with strange weapons, you're givin' *all* the advantage to Saunders.'

Tucson shook his head, said stubbornly, 'Let's have no more talk about these new guns. My mind is made up, cowboys.'

The others fell silent. No one spoke for five minutes. A big clock, back of the bar, ticked monotonously in the quiet. Long shadows commenced to creep across the barroom floor. Tucson looked at Guadalupe. The Kid's eyes were brimming with tears.

Tucson forced a soft laugh he was far from feeling. 'Happy,' he said, 'I reckon you better set out the drinks. There's no use makin' a undertaker's parlor out of your place.'

Lullaby growled, 'Quit talkin' about such places.'

Hopkins nodded and groped around in a cupboard back of his bar. Finally he came up holding a bottle dusty with age. He tried to

198

hold his voice natural, 'I can vouch for this bourbon bein' twenty-five years old,' he stated. 'It ought to be plumb velvety.'

The cork was pulled, glasses were set out. The bottle passed in silence from hand to hand. Hopkins poured a drink for himself. 'Been savin' this bottle for some special occasion,' he announced. 'We'll drink to the damnation of Sundown Saunders.'

Tucson barely tasted his drink. After a time he said, 'Right smooth liquor, Happy.'

Hopkins nodded. No one else mentioned the quality of the bourbon.

Outside, a hush had traveled along the street. All activity appeared to have stopped while Los Potros awaited the outcome of the impending duel. The sun dropped lower. Almost it was touching the highest peaks of the Escabrosa Range now.

Only a few ponies remained at hitchracks along the thoroughfare. Wagons had been taken off the street. Doors and windows were thronged with humanity awaiting the expected gun-fight. Now and then a voice broke shrilly through the silence offering to lay a bet on Sundown Saunders. There weren't any takers, though had they been within hearing distance, Tucson's pards, through sheer loyalty, would have leaped at the opportunity.

Inside the Happy Days, Hopkins was saying, 'How about another drink?'

Tucson shook his head, 'Thanks, no.' The

others didn't reply.

One by one, Tucson removed his new guns from holsters, spun the cylinders to see that all was in good mechanical condition, then replaced them. Lullaby and Stony looked reproachfully at the .32-20s, but didn't reopen the argument.

Tucson finally said, 'I reckon you fellers know what to do, if I don't come back—'

'Don't talk that way, Tucson!' Guadalupe's voice was shrill with strain, his features contorted until he looked half insane.

'We know what to do, all right,' Lullaby growled. 'We'll throw a heap of lead—'

Tucson cut in quietly, 'I mean about the ranch.'

'T'hell with the ranch,' Stony half-snarled. 'I wish we'd never come to this damn range.'

Tucson smiled, 'Thought you were lookin' for some *real* excitement, Stony. And Lullaby wanted to settle down.'

Stony and Lullaby looked at each other a moment, swallowed hard. Tucson had been trying to get them started on one of their old arguments, but the effort failed. He sighed wearily. The tension in the barroom increased. Hopkins cleared his throat, and Stony jumped as though a cannon had been exploded near his ear.

The time was drawing near, the sun dropping lower and lower. From the street came a rustle of expectancy. A chill shiver ran through Tucson's being.

He held his voice steady, 'Reckon I better get goin'. Wouldn't want to keep Saunders waitin'.'

Something like a sob broke from the Guadalupe Kid. Stony and Lullaby pressed close, their faces ashen, their hands groping for Tucson's. Hopkins came around the end of the bar, his knees strangely weak, one hand reaching to grip Tucson's. He said something; Tucson didn't catch the words.

Lullaby appeared reluctant to release Tucson's hand. Tucson said, his throat dry and constricted, 'Don't squeeze that paw too hard, pard. I may need it.' He tried to smile. His lips felt parched as though they might crack at any moment.

'Good luck, pard,' Lullaby muttered brokenly.

Stony said, 'Take him, Tucson. We know you can do it. It'll be easy.' The words refused to sound convincing.

Tears were running openly, unashamedly, down Guadalupe's face, now. He tried to speak. Words failed him.

Tucson turned toward the door, quickly stepped to the plank sidewalk. His friends followed a few paces behind, then halted at the edge of the street. Tucson moved out to the center of the road.

The sun was nearly gone now, its dying rays bathing the empty street with a blood-red light that reflected strangely in Tucson's set features and touched with crimson fire the top-most ridges of the Escabrosas. Purple shadows were in the draws and canyons of the mountains and between the buildings along the street. Another five minutes and such light as there was would be gone.

At Tucson's appearance, a man yelled, 'There's Smith!' The name ran swiftly from lip to lip and carried to Sundown Saunders waiting in the Red Bull, a block and a half away from the Happy Days Saloon. Saunders turned away from the bar, stepped outside, and waited, leaning against an upright that supported the wooden awning before the Red Bull. After a moment he saw Tucson step to the center of the road.

The street was lined with men, their nerves tense for the first sound of a shot. Something of fear tinged Tucson's spirit now. His legs felt strangely numb and lifeless as they plodded steadily along the dusty street. His arms swung loosely at his sides, finger-tips just brushing holsters as he walked. A myriad thoughts coursed his mind. Was this the end? What of Lullaby and Stony—afterward? Had he been right after all in changing to guns carrying lighter loads?

Long shadows commenced to stretch across the street. There wasn't a sound to be heard now. Tucson plodded steadily on and on, appreciably lessening the distance between

202

himself and the Red Bull. Half consciously he noted the dying light, making accurate shooting difficult. Thoughts were piling swiftly into his brain now. He could feel his muscles growing tense. Hell! He'd have to loosen up some. Yes, he'd been in gun fights before, but never in one where he had faced a cold-blooded killing machine like Sundown Saunders. And all this was an old, old story, too oft repeated, to Saunders. The gunman was sure to carry the advantage.

'Dammit,' Tucson mused, 'I got to shake off this feelin'.' He could feel cold beads of perspiration dotting his forehead. Steadily, he strode on and on.

Saunders, waiting carelessly before the Red Bull, saw the crowd part before him. Back of him, he heard Steve Ogden say hoarsely, 'He's your meat, Saunders. Finish him.'

Saunders snarled something unintelligible over his shoulder and stepped out to the center of the street, dropping into a half crouch, arms hanging loosely at his sides. He stepped lightly, swiftly, on the balls of his feet. Almost, he seemed to be gliding along the thoroughfare to meet Tucson, so smoothly did he proceed.

Yes, this was an old story to Saunders. Thoughts were milling in his mind, too: this Smith was a brainy cuss, he'd try to outnerve Saunders, not make a move toward his guns until he was up close. Yeah, that'd been tried before. It had never worked though. Cripes!

They all come pretty close. They had to at sundown when the light was failing. A harsh laugh parted Saunders' lips. What a dumb hombre this Smith was provin' to be. Just like all the rest. Saunders sneered. The Guadalupe Kid sure went soft when he fell for Smith's ways. Saunders was experiencing a feeling of boredom for this old story.

Not more than a hundred yards separated the two men now. There wasn't any hesitancy in Tucson's manner as he walked on and on, closing the distance. If anything, he quickened his pace. There was Saunders, before him, lessening the intervening yards with every step, his moving form standing out against the shadow-barred, deserted roadway of dusty-white.

'Figurin',' Tucson muttered grimly, 'waitin' for me to come closer and closer. He wants to make sure, wants me close enough so he can almost reach out and touch me with his gun barrel.'

Only eighty yards separated the men now. Then seventy-five. Seventy. Five more steps. Abruptly Tucson's arms flashed downward. His guns came out in one swift, eye-defying movement.

Fast as he was, Saunders was faster. Saunders' right hand gun had belched lead and flame even before Tucson thumbed his first shot. A bullet whined close to Tucson's head as a lance of white flame leaped from Tucson's left gun. Then Tucson's right gun barked, but in the interval between his shots, two more of Saunders' slugs had come dangerously close.

Hot lead streamed from Tucson's .32-20s. Saunders staggered, twisted sidewise and slumped to the earth. Even as he dropped he discharged two more shots at Tucson. Both flew high.

Saunders struggled to a sitting position in the dust, raised one gun. Tucson was closing in at a swift run now, crimson flame darting from his weapons in a mad blur of sound. Abruptly he held his fire. Saunders had collapsed, face down, in the dusty roadway!

The reports echoed flatly along the street to be submerged in the wild yell that sounded throughout Los Potros. A gray haze of drifting powdersmoke thinned out, disappeared. Men swarmed into the roadway, shouting, cursing, many of them speechless. Steve Ogden, swearing disappointed oaths, had turned back into the Red Bull.

Tucson's pardners, wild with joy, came sprinting up behind Tucson as he broke through the surrounding crowd and dropped at Saunders' side. An incoherent Lullaby reached for Tucson's hand, but Tucson shook him off with, 'Wait a minute,' and turned Saunders on his back. Wonderingly, Lullaby, Stony and the Kid stood to one side, noting the steady flow of crimson that seeped into the dust beneath the form of the vanquished gunman.

Saunders' features were ashen. After a moment he opened his eyes, glared up at Tucson. 'You done it,' he muttered. 'Took me by ... surprise ... shootin' at that distance. How'd you know ... I wa'n't accurate ... over fifty yards? I never told anybody...'

'Your name, Sundown,' Tucson said gently. 'You always planned your fights the same way, always at a time when the light was bad. You had to get 'em up close to you.'

'Outsmarted me, by God,' Saunders muttered bitterly. 'You're right fast, at that, Smith.' His eyes closed, Tucson noted the crimson stain on Saunders' breast and one arm. He said to Lullaby, 'Get a doctor, pard.'

Lullaby's jaw dropped. He stammered, 'There's one right here, waitin'.'

Tucson smiled grimly, 'You mean—you had one ready—for me?'

Shamefacedly, Lullaby and Stony nodded. They couldn't speak for joy. A professional-looking little man with gray hair pushed through the crowd, nodded to Tucson, then knelt by Saunders' side. He ripped Saunders' shirt wide open, then turned to open the black bag he carried.

Something was said about 'air.' Tucson rose and ordered back the encircling crowd of curious men. The doctor made a hasty examination. Tucson again dropped at Saunders' side.

'How about it, Doc?' he asked.

The doctor shook his head. 'I don't know. Three of these wounds look serious. You know the kind of a hole a forty-five slug makes.'

'I was usin' a .32-20, Doc.'

The doctor glanced quizzically at Tucson. 'That,' he said shortly, 'might make a difference. We'll see. Got to get him to my office. I can take care of him there.'

Tucson nodded. 'Lullaby, grab his heels. I'll take—'

'Your friends have already arranged a wagon and blankets,' the doctor cut in. 'It's waiting behind this building—just a few steps away. It seems somebody was mistaken.'

Tucson said dryly, 'I reckon they was.' Lullaby and Stony didn't meet his gaze. The crowd parted as Saunders was picked up. The gunman opened his eyes, 'Now what?' he muttered.

Tucson said gently, 'We're aimin' to try and patch you up, Sundown.'

Saunders looked steadily at Tucson for a minute and sneered, 'Aw, rats.' His eyes closed and he fainted.

Guadalupe said, 'Nice disposition, eh?'

Tucson was carrying the gunman's shoulders. Lullaby was at the feet. Stony said curiously, walking at Tucson's side, 'Say, what was the advantage of usin' a .32-20?'

Tucson crimsoned a trifle. 'I knew I'd have to let him have it. A forty-five would have been sure to kill him.'

Stony's eyes widened, he let out a wild yell, then in lower tones asked, 'You mean, you didn't want to kill him?'

'You get it,' Tucson said steadily. 'From all I hear, Saunders never has had a chance. I aim to give him one.'

'Oh, you utter unmitigated fool!' Stony exclaimed. 'Lullaby, did you hear that?'

They were passing between two buildings now, the wagon just a few more steps away. The crowd of curious had been left behind.

Lullaby said, 'I heard it. Me, I ain't sayin' a thing. I've already accused Tucson of makin' one mistake. From now on I shut my trap. I'm satisfied with the way things come out—more than satisfied, cowboy. We ain't got a kick in the world!'

*

CHAPTER SEVENTEEN

THE NEW DEPUTY

Three mornings later the 3-Bar-O crew was sitting down to breakfast having replied a few minutes before to Sourdough Jenkins' cry of 'Come and git it, or I'll throw it away.' The long table in the mess shanty was loaded with steaming platters of food. On one side of the table were seated Rube Phelps, Stony and Bud Taggert. Across from them sat Ananias Jones,

Guadalupe and Lullaby. The upper end of the table was vacant, having been reserved by common consent for Tucson who wasn't present. At the lower end sat Hartigan, owner of the Bridle-Bit outfit.

Bat Wing and Tex Malcolm were out with the herd, waiting to be relieved after their night's vigil, this last being a wise precaution of Tucson's. Not knowing just what course Ogden's next plans might take he had deemed it safest to always keep a couple of hands near the cattle that any raid, or rustling, might at once be made known at the ranch house.

Hartigan had arrived at the 3-Bar-O the previous evening to make a neighborly call, and, finding Tucson had gone to Chancellor on business, had been persuaded to stay and take a seat in the nightly 3-Bar-O poker game. The game had broken up late, with Hartigan some twenty dollars ahead, and it hadn't been difficult to induce him to remain for the remainder of the night.

Lullaby heaped his plate with food, 'My gosh,' he grumbled, cocking one wary eye toward the doorway into the kitchen, 'we ought to get a new cook. Same old fodder, beans and bacon, bacon and beans.'

Sourdough emerged through the doorway bearing a huge coffee pot which he slammed down on the table. 'I heard that, Lullaby,' he snorted, 'I been hearin' the same complaint for nigh on thuty years. Th' Cowboy's Lament, I

209

calls it. You cowhands is all the same. Always kickin'. You don't realize what a cinch you got. If'n you had my corns a-pesterin' you all the time, ye'd know what trouble is.'

'We got you an' your corns both,' Stony snickered, 'an' if that ain't a trial and a trib'lation, I never saw—'

'You'd have plenty trials,' Sourdough snapped, 'if you had your dues, said trials bein' in a court room an' bein' held for your benefit.'

Rube Phelps grinned with a mouthful of food, 'Don't forget, Sourdough, you're talkin' to one of the owners.'

Sourdough bristled in the manner of all ranch cooks, 'And what of it? I don't have to work here—'

'Certain you don't,' Lullaby put in, 'we realize you can starve if you want to.'

'You meanin', Lullaby Joslin,' Sourdough demanded indignantly, 'that I couldn't cook for no other outfit.'

'No, sweetheart,' Lullaby chuckled, ''cause we wouldn't let you go. C'mon, pour us some Java, will you?'

Somewhat placated, Sourdough filled the coffee cups and retreated to the kitchen to fill fresh platters at the iron range.

Stony said in warning tones, 'Hey, Sourdough, be careful. Don't get too near that hot stove.'

Sourdough moved quickly back from the range, stuck an inquiring face through the doorway, 'Why not?'

'Your corns might pop,' Stony snickered.

'Cripes Genimity!' Sourdough said disgustedly. 'Will you cowhands quit actin' foolish? Ever since Tucson downed Saunders you ain't had a serious thought.'

Taggert said, 'I'm admittin' I feel right well about that myself.'

'We all are,' Guadalupe nodded. He started to get to his feet.

Lullaby suddenly became extremely solicitous, 'Look here, Kid,' he said seriously, 'you ain't et half enough. You better have more coffee, too.'

Stony raised his voice, 'Hey, Sourdough, bring on some more biscuits. Guadalupe's hungry—'

'I ain't, Sourdough,' Guadalupe protested. 'I'm all through. Sure, fellers, I had enough. Don't want any more. I got some work to 'tend to outside.'

'Same sort of work that kept you out lookin' for the moon last night?' Lullaby asked interestedly.

'Tell her 'good-mornin' for us too,' Stony grinned.

Guadalupe flushed and backed away from the table. At the doorway he donned his sombrero with an air of nonchalance that didn't quite come off.

Lullaby asked innocently, 'When you aimin' to get married, Kid?'

Guadalupe flushed hotly. He shook his head, stammered, 'Me, I ain't ever goin' to get married.'

'I've heard a heap of fellers make that same statement,' Lullaby drawled, 'but I note they keep right on buildin' school-houses.'

But Guadalupe had fled hurriedly. Hartigan laughed, 'Weren't ridin' the Kid, were you?'

Stony grinned. 'It's the same way every meal, when he ain't got any immediate work. He rushes right up to talk to Caroline. Won't hardly wait to finish his eatin'.'

'How's he makin' it?' Hartigan wanted to know.

'He don't talk and she don't let on,' Ananias Jones spoke through a mouthful of biscuit and coffee, 'but we all got eyes. She allows when she gets the money for this ranch, she's headin' East to visit relatives. If you ask me, I think it's got the Kid worried.'

'I understand from what Tucson told me,' Hartigan said, 'that the deal can't go through until certain papers turn up.'

'That's the how of it,' Lullaby nodded. 'Howsomever everythin' else is ready. We've signed all the papers necessary; now if this record business can only be cleared up, Caroline will get her money.'

Sourdough entered to place more food on the table and carry away empty plates. 'After a time,' Sourdough announced, 'when things get settled down here, we'll be able to have fish for

212

breakfast now and then.'

'Fish!' Lullaby exclaimed. 'Where you aim to get fish?'

'Out of water, of course, idjit,' Stony grinned.

'Sometimes they come out of cans,' Lullaby said dryly.

Sourdough explained, 'There's trout in the upper reaches of Santone Creek. We used to have fish right along when we had plenty time to go catch 'em.'

'Gosh,' Lullaby said enthusiastically, 'I'd sure like to go fishin' sometime. What do you catch 'em on?'

'Hooks, simpleton,' Stony cut in. 'What did you think?'

'Can't tell,' Lullaby retorted, 'some suckers will bite on anythin'.'

Stony reddened. Sourdough continued, 'If you mean what do I use for bait, well, sometimes I use worms an' sometimes little minnies—'

'Little Minnie's what—?' Lullaby asked blankly.

'Minnies—minnies,' Sourdough sputtered. 'You know what grows into big fish—'

'Oh, minnows,' Hartigan said gravely. 'You mean minnows—'

'Now, don't you try to ride me, Hartigan,' Sourdough bridled. 'I don't mean min-o. I said minnie. That's the word. A small fish to be used for bait.'

Lullaby winked at Hartigan. 'Your trout must be right skinny if you have to feed 'em little fish to make 'em big enough to eat. Nope, all this sounds to me, Sourdough.'

Sourdough said hotly, 'Oh, you be damned!' and flung off to his kitchen. The others burst into laughter. When the noise had died down, Ananias Jones said quietly, 'Me, I'd like to fish again.'

'Ever do much fishin'?' Hartigan asked.

'Fishin'? Me?' Ananias smiled confidently. 'Back in my younger days I held the champeenship for catchin' the biggest fish, down in the Gulf of Mexico.'

Hartigan was all interest now. The others cast sly looks at each other and grinned furtively. Hartigan wasn't very well acquainted with Ananias. He said gravely, 'I never been down in the Gulf, but I've heard the fish run pretty big in those waters.'

'Big?' Ananias said scornfully, 'Mister Hartigan, until you've ketched fish in the Gulf, you don't know what fishin' is. Even see a tarpon?'

Hartigan's eyes widened. 'My gosh! Did you ever catch those in the Gulf? I saw one in a museum, once, stuffed.' He stretched his arms apart as far as he could reach, 'It was this long.'

Ananias nodded disparagingly. 'Yeah, I've seen plenty of them little ones. That size we use to throw back when they got to tanglin' our hooks. Undersize. Game warden wouldn't let us take 'em due to bein' under the legal limits.'

Hartigan exclaimed, 'I've heard how they catch big fish in the Gulf, but I didn't reckon it was anythin' like you say. What's the biggest fish you ever caught?'

Lullaby leaned over and whispered to Stony, 'He's sure askin' for it.'

Stony nodded, 'Ananias will let him have both barrels, see if he don't—'

Stony broke off suddenly, noting that Bud Taggert was listening, open-mouthed, drinking in every word of the conversation. He remembered then that Taggert hadn't encountered Ananias either. Rube Phelps on Hartigan's left could scarcely keep his face straight.

Ananias was saying earnestly, 'The biggest fish I ever caught? Well, lemme see. I ketched so many big ones that it's sort of hard to tell. I reckon the biggest—yep, that's it, the one I hooked off Matagorda Island that time.' He broke off to explain, 'Matagorda is a sizable island a few miles off'n the Texas Coast. I wa'n't workin' cows them days, bein' as I was vacationin'. I rented me a little boat named the *Scaly Ann*. Fishin' boat it was—'

'Sure it wasn't *Sally Ann*?' Lullaby interrupted.

'Ain't I told you,' Ananias said impatiently, 'it was a fishin' boat? The *Scaly Ann*, the Ann bein' short for anabas—'

Lullaby whistled softly. 'You sure
215

overreached yourself that time, Ananias.'

'Ana-what?' Stony frowned.

'Anabas,' Ananias snapped angrily, 'an anabas bein' a fish what can travel overland an' climb trees. If you don't believe me, look it up in the dictionary. What difference does it make? The name of the boat was called the *Scaly Ann*. You or me tellin' this story?'

'You are,' Stony said meekly. Hartigan was frowning at the interruption.

'All right,' Ananias said gruffly. 'I don't know why you allus have to be so skeptical when I tell a story—'

'How about the big fish?' Hartigan reminded.

'Well,' Ananias continued, 'I loaded up the *Scaly Ann* with two days' fodder, tackle, a jug o' red-eye and other bait, and sets sail for Matagordas Island. 'Bout noon I reaches a likely spot to drop anchor, two miles off'n the coast of Matagordas. I takes a good slug of likker out of my jug and baits up. To make a long story short, I sits there a coupla hours without gettin' a strike, but I knowed there must be fish in them waters, 'cause the gulls was a-screamin' around and—'

Lullaby said innocently, 'You didn't mention that you had girls aboard. What made 'em scream? It sounds plumb brutal.'

'Not girls—gulls!' Ananias grew red. 'Sea gulls. Birds. I don't expect *you* to understand, though. Anyway,' he continued to Hartigan, 'there was them girls—gulls, dammit!—a flyin' around and screamin' over my head, when all of a sudden I felt somethin' strike—'

'Damn them gulls, anyway,' Stony snickered.

'—somethin' strike my line,' Ananias went on with a defiant glance at Stony. 'By Cripes! The pole was nigh jerked out of my hand. I takes a swig out of my jug and sets myself for a battle, bracin' both feet against th' buckboard—'

'Thought you was in a boat,' Lullaby said.

Ananias glared at the cowboy. 'I always made it a rule to have a buckboard in my boats, for just such purposes as I'm tellin' about now. Anyway, here I was fightin' to hold onto this critter I'd hooked, when sudden he turned and made a run straight for my boat. Didn't hit me though. But he dashes back an' forth like a mad steer, an' my pole was bendin' double an' wig-waggin' like a flag in a gale. It gets so bad finally I has to let go my jug an' use both hands—'

'What was it—what kind of fish?' Bud Taggert was listening, bug-eyed.

Ananias shook his head. 'He hadn't bruk water yit so I couldn't tell. Every arm in my bone-sockets was tremblin' from the strain of fightin' that critter. Finally I thinks, just as he makes a mad dash out to sea, that I better cut my line before boat an' all gets swamped. Here that dang fish was pullin' like a locymotive in one direction an' my anchor rope was stretched tight in the other. Them two lines was singin' in the breeze like fiddle strings playin' the *Chisholm Trail*. Well, sir, before I could cut that fish loose, I felt my boat movin'. Next think I knowed, my anchor had been jerked out of its moorin'. Then I see we was goin' to travel. The anchor come loose with such a jerk that it was yanked clean out of the water. I looks up an' sees it sailin' over my head—'

'An' the fish got away,' Taggert burst out.

'Got away nothin',' Ananias said convincingly. 'When that anchor come down, it struck that fish that was tryin' to get away. Yep, hooked it squar back of th' gills. Then I knowed I was in for it, with a double-hooked fish. But by that time I was bein' hauled all over th' Gulf. It was just like a merry-go-around. Three times me an' th' fish an' th' boat circled Matagordas Island, and the scenery was movin' fast just like a blur with stars an' sky an' clouds all mixed up.'

'Stars?' Hartigan said. 'Do you mean you were still fighting that fish when night come?'

'All night long I fit him,' Ananias nodded solemnly. 'By this time I was mad. I'd made up my mind that I'd land that fish if it took all my life. Well, come dawn, he'd weakened some, but my boat, the good old *Scaly Ann*, was leakin'. My plankin' had sprung under the strain. I knowed I had to work fast. Gradually my line slacked, an' I figured that fish was just about through. I took another drink from my jug an' drifted up silent to see could I gaff him into my boat, or would I have to tow him. Then, I got the surprise of my life.'

'What was that?' Hartigan queried tensely.

'Lookin' over the side of my boat, I see I'd drifted right over the monster. There was that huge dark shadow floatin' down below the surface and I could see fins a-wavin' slow. Big? Mister, I never see anythin' like it. That black shadow, layin' under my boat, stretched as far as I could see in all directions. It was huge!'

'By Gawd,' Hartigan exclaimed, 'it must have been a whale!'

'Hell's bells, mister!' Ananias stated, 'I was baited with a whale!'

Hartigan suddenly choked. He eyed Ananias sternly, then commenced to smile in sickly fashion.

Bud Taggert was on the edge of his chair. But hadn't caught on yet, so great was his interest and his ignorance of fishing, 'But—but,' he gasped, 'what sort of a fish did you catch?'

Ananias said solemnly, 'I never learned, Bud. There was still a heap of fight in that fish. When I started to throw the gaff into him, he started to run with me again. Towed me miles and miles out to sea. I couldn't stop him. My jug was empty, my food gone. What happened, nobody knows.' Dramatically, Ananias made as though to wipe away a tear, as he concluded,

219

'I was never seen again.'

Taggert's face crimsoned. For a moment he couldn't talk. Then he sputtered, 'Why—why, you cantankerous ol' liar!'

A roar of laughter went up that shook the mess house. Stony and Lullaby were rolling on the table. Rube Phelps was pounding one hand on his knee in sheer joy. Even Hartigan was laughing now.

Lullaby choked out, 'Was somethin' said about landin' fish?'

'I just happened to remember,' Hartigan said sheepishly, 'what Ananias means. Next time we're all in town, I'll buy a drink—'

'You'll buy a whole flock of drinks on that one,' Stony roared.

Ananias was smiling beatifically. 'There's other big fish down there, too. Mebbe you'd like to hear about the time I tamed the pair of sword-fish an' taught 'em to fight duels?'

Hartigan abruptly gained his feet. 'Or the sawfish that helped you in your carpenter work, I suppose,' he sneered genially.

'Nope,' Ananias said unabashed, 'That was my hammer-headed shark. And then there was the dogfish that chased the cat-fish up the tree.'

'I got to get air,' Hartigan said abruptly.

'And us cowhands better think about draggin' it,' Lullaby said, his face sobering. 'I figured Tucson would be back by now.'

'Clear out all of you,' Sourdough ordered. 'I got a mess to clean up.'

Hartigan at the doorway, said, 'Here comes Tucson, now.'

Tucson entered the mess house with Guadalupe at his back. 'Hi-yuh, crew,' he smiled. 'What's new? Hey, cookie, do I get killed if I asked for a mite of breakfast.'

Sourdough, with the independence of all ranch cooks, looked dourly at Tucson, said, 'Well, *you* can get away with that, but I ain't establishin' no precedents for the rest of these saddle-bums.'

'Fine,' Tucson smiled. He sat down. 'Glad to see you here, Hartigan. You ride over this mornin'?'

Hartigan shook his head. 'Dropped around last night to say "hello" and see how your outfit was shapin' up. Your crew inveigled me into takin' a few lessons at stud.'

'Said crew,' Bud Taggert said bitterly, 'payin' for the lessons.'

Tucson laughed heartily. 'Sorry I missed the game.'

Sourdough set food and coffee in front of Tucson. Lullaby asked, 'What did you learn in Chancellor, pard?'

Tucson said, 'That missin' record book ain't turned up.' He grinned at the sudden look of relief that came into Guadalupe's features. 'That good news, Kid?'

The Kid blushed. 'Hell, no. I'm anxious to see the deal go through so Caroline can have her money an' go visit them relatives she wants to see so bad.'

'Yes, you are,' Stony scoffed, 'in a pig's ear.'

'I talked to Sheriff Morgan,' Tucson went on, 'told him just how things stood in Los Potros. He'd heard of me, so I made my *habla* carry some weight. He was plumb surprised, but says he don't dare ask for Glascow's resignation, unless we can produce actual proof, in writin', that Glascow is workin' under Ogden's orders.'

'You sure Morgan is on the level?' Lullaby asked.

Tucson nodded. 'Not a doubt of it. He was considerable surprised to hear we were havin' trouble. All reports he had had from Glascow said everythin' was runnin' smooth. Howsomever, Morgan maintains he can't do much about it, his hands bein' tied by county politics. It was Ogden money that put Glascow in office—'

'So we're up against a brick wall, eh?' Stony said angrily. 'With the sheriff of the county refusin' to take a hand—'

'Wait a minute,' Tucson interrupted, 'don't blame Sheriff Morgan. He's give us a break. While he couldn't force Glascow to resign, he done somethin' better, the same bein' the swearin' in of one Tucson Smith as a special deputy in Tresbarro County, accountable only to Sheriff Morgan.'

Lullaby said enthusiastically, 'Gosh, that's fine, pard.'

Tucson drew from his pocket a deputy-sheriff's badge, displayed it, then thrust it out of sight again.

'Why don't you pin it on?' Stony asked.

Tucson shook his head. 'Not yet, I'd like to spring a surprise on Glascow. Morgan ain't goin' to notify Glascow there's a new deputy in the county.'

'You didn't see Glascow when you come through Los Potros then?' Guadalupe said.

'Didn't see Glascow or Ogden. The barkeep in the Red Bull admitted with some reluctance that Ogden left for his Box-8 spread right after I had my fight with Saunders. Ain't been in town since. I don't know where Glascow was. He wa'n't in his office. The jail didn't have any prisoners. Wouldn't be surprised if Glascow was out to the Bar-8.'

Stony asked, 'That badge give you as much authority as Glascow?'

Tucson smiled, 'I rank Glascow. It's a sort of special under-sheriff job that Morgan give me.'

Lullaby said, 'Did you see Saunders?'

Tucson nodded. 'I dropped in at the doctor's. Doc Benson says Sundown will recover. His fever has left and unless complications set in—'

'Then what?' Hartigan asked.

'I aim to have him brought out here, when he can be moved,' Tucson replied. 'I want to get acquainted with him, see if we can't change his viewpoint on life—'

223

'You can't tame a wildcat,' Lullaby growled.

'Anyway, I can try,' Tucson smiled. 'I didn't talk to Sundown. He's too weak to do much but sleep and take a mite of nourishment. But I reckon Doc Benson will pull him through. Nick Barnett is coming along good too.'

'Nick Barnett?' Hartigan asked.

Tucson explained, 'Barnett and a feller named Fanner Delisle started to make trouble in the Red Bull the first night I hit Los Potros, Delisle was buried the next day. One of my slugs smashed Barnett's shoulder—'

'Sure, sure,' Hartigan interrupted. 'I heard about that. I'd forgotten.'

'I talked to Barnett some at Doc Benson's. He's right sore at Ogden. Ogden has refused to pay for medical care and board at the doctor's. I got a hunch that if I can tie a knot in Ogden's tail, and throw a prison-term threat at Barnett, Barnett will tell everythin' he knows about Ogden's activities.'

The men sat around the mess-shanty while Tucson ate. Finally he finished his coffee, set down the cup, spoke to Rube Phelps, 'Rube, you and Guadalupe better saddle up and go relieve Bat Wing and Tex Malcolm. Those rannies will be gettin' hungry—'

He stopped suddenly as a thudding of swift hoofs was heard outside. Bud Taggert, standing near a window, exclaimed, 'Here's Bat now! Somethin' wrong. His face is all blood!'

There came a rush for the doorway. The 3-Bar-O pushed outside just as Bat Wing pulled his horse to a stop in a scattering of dust and gravel.

Bat leaped down from the foam-flecked, panting pony and turned a sweaty, blood-smeared countenance toward his friends.

'Tucson,' he cried, 'there's hell to pay! Ogden has shoved cattle over on 3-Bar-O holdin's, claimin' it's open range and he's goin' to have our water. Tex is tryin' to hold 'em off...'

The boy swayed. Tucson caught his arm. 'This,' Tucson said grimly, 'is the show-down!'

CHAPTER EIGHTEEN

RANGE WAR

There came a sudden rush toward the corral to get horses.

'Wait a minute,' Tucson called sharply. 'We ain't all goin'.' He stilled the clamor of protests that rose, as the men came back, 'No use runnin' off at the head,' he said quietly. 'We got to see where we're at ... Bat, you hurt bad?'

Bat Wing had caught his balance by this time. He smiled sheepishly through the blood and grime. 'I'm all right. Slug nicked my arm, lost a mite of blood, but just as soon as

225

you tie it up—'

'But your face,' Tucson protested. 'It's all blood—'

Bat looked blank. 'Nothin' wrong with my face. Reckon mebbe I smeared the blood when it run down on my hand. I'll be ready to ride in a minute—'

'Tell us about it,' Tucson cut in.

'Jake Elliot's headin' 'em,' Bat said swiftly, 'you know, Ogden foreman—'

'Ogden or Glascow with 'em?'

'Nary one. Didn't see 'em anyway. Tex and me sighted the cows about dawn and rode up to see what was doin'. Elliot announces he has the right to graze on open range, and the Box-8 water-holes peterin' out, he intends to turn the stock onto Santone Creek. Tex give him an argument, warns 'em not to come no farther. Jake Elliot tells us to get out of the way, or take the consequences. He orders his men to start the cattle again. The herd and the punchers starts comin'. Me'n Tex pulled our irons and plugged two of the cows. Elliot takes a shot at me. That's when I got it in the arm. Somebody back with the cows cuts loose at Tex. Tex replied and nicked his man. By this time Elliot was headin' back, away from me and Tex. We see we was outnumbered, so we wheeled our horses and run for a group of rocks. Been holed up there since. Finally, a spell back, I gets back on my bronc and lines out for the ranch—'

'Tex hurt?'

226

'Wasn't when I left. He had his rifle and they're keepin' away from him. Puttin' all their time to drivin' the cows—'

'How far away—'

''Bout eight miles. Over near Santone Creek—'

Tucson turned swiftly to the others. 'Taggert, Ananias, and Bat will stay here. The rest of you saddle up. Quick!'

'Aw, Tucson,' Bat pleaded, 'let me go—'

'Don't know why I should stay—' Ananias growled.

Taggert said, 'I'd shore like to go—'

'Let's not argue about this,' Tucson said quietly. 'You fellers will have to stay with Sourdough. That's the best way, with Caroline here. No tellin' what Ogden's got in mind. He may come ridin' and—' Tucson broke off, 'How many hands did Elliot have with him, Bat?'

'Ten or twelve. I ain't sure. Reece is with 'em—'

'You mean Reece that runs the Rocking-R?'

'Yeah, that skunk. Some of the cows is his. He's got probably two punchers. Lemme see, that's three, Elliot is four. Then there was four Box-8 hands—Knight, Merker, Chapman, Decker. Couple Mex *vaqueros* too, but they didn't take no part in the fight—'

Caroline's voice was heard calling from the back door of the ranch house.

Stony said, 'Go tell her about it, Guadalupe.

I'll saddle up for you.'

The Kid said gratefully, 'Thanks, cowpoke,' and sprinted toward the house.

Sourdough appeared with water and bandages and commenced to administer to Bat's wound, which the boy was insisting was 'only a scratch.' Tucson gave quick orders, 'Ananias, you break out cartridges and rifles for us. I reckon there's only four rifles here, at that. Make sure there's plenty ammunition left, in case trouble comes here ... Bud, you drift down and saddle my horse—'

'Look here, Tucson,' Hartigan cut in, 'don't forget me.'

'This ain't your fight, Hartigan. This is 3-Bar-O business.'

'It'll be my fight, if Ogden ain't licked plumb pronto. I'll make a hand. If things get too warm, I'll ride on and rouse out my own crew. If Ogden once gets the upper hand, this thing will spread like wildfire. We'll all have to hire gun fighters to exist—'

'Right,' Tucson said shortly. 'We're glad to have you.'

Hartigan dashed away to saddle up. Bat Wing was taken, protesting, into the mess shanty and seated on a chair. The boy had lost quite a bit of blood, but refused to give up. In a few minutes Guadalupe arrived from the ranch house. Whatever had passed between himself and Caroline certainly hadn't dampened his spirits any.

There came a rush of hoofs as horses arrived.

Lullaby led Guadalupe's pony. Taggert had Tucson's horse. Tucson climbed into the saddle. Taggert said, 'I wonder if there's a gun here that I could use, Tucson. I don't happen to own one and if trouble came—'

'Those .32-20s are hangin' in the bunkhouse.' Tucson declared hurriedly. 'I ain't no more use for 'em. I'll make you a present of 'em.'

Taggert's words of thanks were lost in the rush of dust and noise as the riders got under way. Bat Wing was still protesting it was his right to accompany them, but was being held back by Sourdough and Ananias. From the ranch house floated a long cry from Caroline. Only Guadalupe appeared to know what she said.

The riders were clear of the ranch yard, now, Tucson, Lullaby and Stony riding at the head. Behind them, Guadalupe and Hartigan plunged spurs into their ponies to keep the pace. Rube Phelps was riding low, at one side, to avoid the dust of the leaders.

For three-quarters of an hour the men pushed their ponies to the utmost. There was little talk. Words were lost in the swift rush of wind that beat into faces and whipped back flecks of foam from the jaws of the distance-devouring ponies. The grey-green landscape of hills and grass and sage and cactus rushed by in a swiftly moving blur. Behind the riders a thin haze of dust spread over the earth.

Suddenly, as the tired ponies were fighting their way up a long grassy slope, Tucson flung up one hand as a signal to halt. The riders came to a quick stop.

'Thought I heard shots,' Tucson snapped. 'Wait here.'

He pushed his pony more cautiously up the slope. Nearing the top, he stopped again, dismounted, dropped reins over his horse's head and crept forward cautiously on foot. Reaching the crest of the hill, he dropped on his stomach and wiggled forward for the next three yards.

There, screened by tall grass, the scene spread out before him. From this point on, the hill sloped gradually down to the line of cottonwoods that denoted Santone Creek. A half mile from the creek, was a broad, level stretch of sandy gravel, dotted with heaps of tumbled boulders and granite outcroppings. A ragged volley of shots sounded while Tucson watched. He saw puffs of smoke emerge from a rock barrier, a quarter mile distant. Then, some distance farther on, came the sharp crack of a rifle. Tucson caught a momentary glimpse of Tex Malcolm's sombrero among a nest of rocks.

'Good ol' Tex,' Tucson muttered, 'he's holdin' 'em off.'

Tucson started to edge back, then, far off to the left he saw a moving bunch of about one hundred cows. Several riders accompanied the stock.

Tucson laughed grimly. 'The damn fools have split forces. Reckon they figured four or five was enough to handle Tex.'

Suddenly he leaped to his feet, turned toward the waiting riders. 'Bring 'em up!' he yelled.

The riders got under way, came sweeping up the slope, Lullaby leading Tucson's horse. Tucson yelled further words as they approached. The horses swerved to one side. Tucson caught at his pony's bridle, leaped, the swift motion carrying him up into the saddle. He settled feet into stirrups, caught the reins Lullaby flung to him, then let out a wild cowboy yell:

'Yip-yip-yip—yippee-e-e-eee! Hold the fort, Tex. We're comin'!' A moment later he yelled to the rest of the crew, 'Shoot every time you see a head!' From below cries of consternation rose on the air.

The ponies reached the top of the hill, swept down the long slope, kicking back clouds of dust. Guns commenced to bark from among the nearer rocks. A man broke from cover, ran to a nearby horse and vaulted into the saddle. A forty-five barked savagely, and the man toppled to the earth!

Then Tex Malcolm's voice lifted triumphantly across the plain, 'Yip-yip! 3-Bar-O! Give 'em hell-l-l, 3-Bar-O!' His rifle started to bark again, as he came running down from his rock breast-work.

A mounted rider, face white with surprise and anger, swerved around a corner of a high upthrust of granite. His gun was swinging toward Tucson as he appeared. Tucson's six-shooter roared, missed. Lullaby, coming up close, thumbed one swift shot, even as Tucson unleashed a second leaden slug. Horse and rider went down in a mad, scrambled heap. Tucson and Lullaby pounded on, guns ready, heads low.

A man leaped up at Stony, seizing the bridle of his pony. Stony fired once into the wide-open mouth, saw the face drop back. Someplace to Tucson's left a horse screamed and went down kicking. Powdersmoke floated in the air.

Rube Phelps directed his pony close to Tucson. 'Here comes Jake Elliot and some more!' he yelled.

Tucson followed Rube's pointing arm, saw that the other Box-8 men had left the stock and were coming at a gallop. Tucson looked swiftly around, saw with gladness that the 3-Bar-O forces were still mounted.

'Let's go get 'em!' he yelled.

Guns commenced to bark anew, as the two factions closed. Jake Elliot was leading his men, guiding his pony with his knees, a blazing gun in either hand. The riders were spreading out now. Tucson suddenly realized his forty-fives were empty. Shoving them in holsters, he reached to the Winchester rifle in his saddle boot, jerked it to his shoulder and pulled trigger.

Jake Elliot's horse stumbled to its knees. throwing its rider out of the saddle. Elliot came up fighting as Tucson closed in. Tucson reached down, drew a six-shooter. He felt a hot streak of flame on his face as he passed Elliot. His gun-barrel, swinging through the air, toppled Elliot to the earth.

Suddenly the sounds of firing lessened. Somebody yelled, 'Don't shoot! Don't shoot! I give up!' The cry was repeated by another Box-8 man. The savage roaring of guns tapered off to a desultory cracking of weapons, then stopped altogether.

'Round 'em up!' Tucson yelled. 'Throw down your guns, Box-8! It's your last chance!' The Box-8 was quick to take advantage of the order. Ten minutes later the prisoners had been rounded up and ordered off their horses. There were six captives, three of whom had been slightly wounded.

Tucson's crew hadn't escaped unscathed. Rube Phelps had lost some skin off his right ribs and left arm, and was being bandaged with bandannas by Hartigan who had a crimson smear at one side of his face. Stony had had a horse shot from under him and was changing his saddle to the mount of one of the dead Box-8 hands. A ragged furrow showed on Lullaby's left thigh where a strip of trouser leg had been shot away. Tucson's sombrero contained half a dozen holes: his right ear showed a tiny point of blood at the edge of the lobe. Tex Malcolm came riding to join the group. Apparently he bore a charmed life: while his clothing had been ripped at a dozen points, none of the bullets had touched him. Guadalupe was also unharmed.

Tucson said, 'This all the prisoners?'

Malcolm said grimly, 'What's left ain't prisoners—and never will be.' He jerked one thumb over his shoulder, 'Three Mexes are herdin' them cows yonderly. You want 'em? They didn't take any part in the fight.'

Tucson said, 'Go tell 'em to drift pronto, 'less they want to get into a heap of trouble.'

'Want the cows drove back to Box-8 range?'

Tucson shook his head. 'I got a hunch that some of 'em are our animals, anyway, that Ogden stole and blotted the brands on.'

Malcolm wheeled his pony, then asked, 'Bat all right when he got to the ranch?'

'Okay,' Tucson nodded. 'Sort of weak from loss of blood.'

'I wa'n't sure, until you arrived, if he'd made it or not,' Malcolm said. 'From where we was holed up, these Box-8 skunks couldn't see Santone Creek. Bat got his horse, slipped down to the creek, and then swung wide. We'd tossed to see who'd go. I was afraid he might have been spotted, makin' his getaway.'

'Reckon he wasn't,' Lullaby drawled. 'These

skunks was plumb surprised to see us.'

Malcolm wheeled the pony again and started toward the distant herd which was rapidly closing the distance to the regular 3-Bar-O cows a mile away, near a distant bend of the Santone.

The 3-Bar-O riders sat their horses, looking down on the six prisoners they had taken. Jake Elliot started to speak.

Stony said, 'For the tenth time I tell you, shut-up. If I bend a gun-barrel over your conk, it won't be a love tap like Tucson give you a spell back.'

Elliot glared at Tucson, unconsciously felt tenderly of the spot where Tucson's gun-barrel had struck.

'Let him talk, Stony,' Tucson said. 'What you got to say for yourselves?'

All of the prisoners started talking at once. Tucson held up one hand for silence, 'I'll talk to this hombre first,' indicating Elliot.

'My name's Elliot,' the foreman of the Box-8 said angrily. He and Tucson had never seen each other before.

'That right, Rube?' Tucson said.

Rube nodded. 'Yeah, he's Ogden's foreman. These others—' pointing out the ones named, '—are Louis Reece, owner of the Rocking-R, Knight, Merker, Chapman and Decker. All Box-8 hands except Reece.'

Tucson nodded. 'What you got to say, Elliot?'

'Just this,' Elliot exclaimed angrily, 'You 3-Bar-O hombres better drift out of this country. When Steve Ogden hears—'

'Yes, by God!' Reece burst out, 'You hombres have let yourselves in for a heap of trouble.' Reece was a weasel-faced man with muddy eyes and a furtive manner. 'I'm goin' to prefer charges—'

'I reckon it's the Box-8 and Rocking-R that are in for trouble,' Tucson said sternly. 'You've trespassed on 3-Bar-O property—'

'Aw, this is open range,' Elliot blustered. 'We got a right—'

'You know damn well that ain't true, Elliot,' Tucson snapped. 'In addition, you fellers started this, firin' on my men—'

'They killed two of our cows—' Elliot commenced.

'Some of those cows are mine, too,' Reece put in. 'I demand to be taken to Los Potros, right now, and—'

'You're all goin' to town, all right,' Tucson smiled thinly. 'You might as well know you're under arrest.'

'Arrest?' Elliot's jaw dropped. 'Arrest!'

Tucson nodded. 'The law's workin' on our side for a change.' He produced his deputy's badge, displayed it a moment before the eyes of the astonished captives, before replacing it in his pocket. Reece wilted suddenly at sight of the emblem of the law.

'I'm plumb sorry, Mr Smith—Deputy

Smith,' he started in whining tones. 'I didn't know I was doin' anythin' wrong. It's all Ogden's fault. He told me I was free to use this grass and water—'

'Aw, shut yore lousy mouth,' Elliot snarled. 'All of you keep your mouths shut, too. Steve Ogden will straighten this out.'

'Anybody feelin' like tellin' what he knows of Ogden's activities?' Tucson asked. 'It might go a bit easier with you, when you come to trial if you tell anythin' now that you know. Ogden's finished, and you might as well realize that, first as last!'

'I'll tell anythin' I know—' Reece commenced eagerly.

'Shut up!' Elliot snarled. 'This big red-head is just runnin' a bluff. He ain't no deputy. We'll see what Brose Glascow has to say. All right, Smith, take us in. See how far you get. I'll be glad to get to Los Potros. Coupla my men can use a doctor to fix their scratches. C'mon, let's get started.' He grinned nastily, 'We'll see how far you get with a bluff like this. So far as Reece is concerned, do you think Big Steve would trust him? Hell, all he knows is that this is open range as Steve told him. He's a rat anyway. C'mon, Smith, just try to take us in—'

'That's enough,' Tucson said curtly. 'I'll have to show you I ain't bluffin' ... Fellers, round up some hawsses. Bring ropes to tie 'em into saddles.'

Elliot's face dropped. He realized now that

Tucson had been speaking the truth. Reece started whining again, but nobody paid any attention to him. One by one, the captives were assisted to mount and their wrists bound to the horn of the saddle. While this was going on, Tex Malcolm came riding back.

Tucson said, 'The Mexes decide to drift, Tex?'

Tex said, 'They was damn glad to. I don't think they had anything to do with any crookedness that may be laid at Ogden's door. Ogden just hired Mexes to work cattle. He was pro'bly tryin' to pull a show-down when he sent these skunks and those cows over here—'

'He'll get a show-down, all right,' Tucson said grimly. He added, 'Stony and Lullaby can help me get these prisoners into town. The rest of you come back to the ranch. We'll have to send somebody out with shovels to clean up this mess.'

Ten minutes later the 3-Bar-O riders were heading for the ranch, a subdued group of prisoners riding sulkily at their head.

Tucson appeared deep in thought as they proceeded at an easy lope. Finally Lullaby reined his pony close to ask, 'What you thinkin' about, Tucson?'

Tucson raised his head, smiled grimly, 'If it's a show-down Ogden wants, he's due to get it right pronto. We ain't far from the end, Lullaby. From now on, it's me or Ogden. This range ain't big enough for both of us.'

CHAPTER NINETEEN

'JERK YOUR IRON!'

It was shortly past noon when the 3-Bar-O and its prisoners arrived back at the ranch to be greeted with yells of welcome from those who had remained behind. Caroline came running from the backdoor, crying, 'Jeff, oh, Jeff, you're back safe!'

The Guadalupe Kid had blushed crimson, then reined his horse toward the house. In a few moments he and the girl had disappeared inside.

Stony and Lullaby exchanged glances. Lullaby said, 'If the Kid don't tell that girl what's on his mind right soon, I reckon it's goin' to be up to you or me to break the news, Stony.'

The other men grinned. Hartigan mentioned something about getting back to his own place, now that everything appeared to be all right at the 3-Bar-O Ranch, but Tucson invited him to stay for dinner. The prisoners were dismounted, horses fed and watered. Sourdough prepared a hasty dinner at which the prisoners ate sullenly under guard. At the conclusion of the meal, Tucson gave certain orders. The prisoners were tied into saddles again. A detachment of punchers, headed by

Ananias, was told off to return to the scene of the recent fight and look after the cattle. Two of the hands carried shovels.

By two o'clock, Tucson, Lullaby and Stony were again in saddles, pushing the six prisoners before them on the way to Los Potros. The ride through the cut in the Little Escabrosas was made in almost complete silence, except for the whining of Reece whose nerve had broken and who was trying to beg off. Tucson questioned him somewhat, but discovered only that Reece had very little knowledge of Steve Ogden's nefarious activities.

The prisoners were doing their best to hold back now, but the three mesquiteers kept them pushing along and by four that afternoon the little cavalcade entered Los Potros. A pedestrian passing along the street noticed the Box-8 men tied in saddles, and let out a sudden yell. Other men came running to trail along behind the horses.

Passing the Happy Days Saloon, Tucson noticed Happy Hopkins standing in the doorway, open-mouthed. Tucson waved to him, called, 'Better get ready to set 'em up, Happy. We'll be droppin' in on you right soon.'

The horses passed on, drew to a stop at the office of Deputy Glascow. Tucson dismounted and stepped inside the office. The place was empty. Opening the rear door of the office, he walked on through to the jail quarters. No sign of Deputy Glascow there, either.

Tucson returned to the hitchrack, said to Stony and Lullaby, 'You keep an eye on these prisoners. Glascow ain't around. We got to get the keys to the cells.'

'You know where to look for Glascow?' Lullaby asked.

Tucson shook his head, turned to Jake Elliot, 'Elliot, you any idea where Glascow would be?'

Elliot growled, 'I wouldn't tell you if I knew.'

Reece said eagerly, 'Deputy Glascow was out to the Box-8 last night. He and Steve Ogden were to come in to Los Potros this morning.'

'Shut your face, you yellow whelp!' Elliot snarled.

Reece shrank back with a look of fear. Tucson nodded, 'Reckon Glascow ain't come back yet. I'm goin' to drift down to the gunsmith's and—'

'What for?' Stony wanted to know.

Lullaby put in, 'You ain't buyin' another brace of .32-20s, are you?'

Tucson smiled and shook his head. 'That gun feller is a locksmith, too. He'll have keys to open the cells, or he can file some dang quick.'

Stony and Lullaby nodded. Tucson set off at a quick gait. Once he looked back. His two pardners were rolling cigarettes. The prisoners sat their horses in sullen silence, apparently trying to ignore the crowd that had collected around them. Tucson hurried on.

241

A few yards farther on he glanced across the street and saw Deputy Brose Glascow just emerging from the Red Bull Saloon. Tucson stopped and hailed the deputy. Glascow glanced up, frowned, then somewhat reluctantly cut a diagonal course across the street to approach Tucson.

'Back eh?' Tucson snapped.

'Is it anythin' to you?—' Glascow grunted.

'Plenty,' Tucson said.

Glascow didn't say anything for a moment, then he stated carelessly, 'Steve and me rode in from the Box-8 this mornin'. Got here about ten o'clock.'

'I been looking for you, Glascow—'

'That goes two ways,' Glascow snapped. 'A feller just brought me word that you had Reece and some of Steve's Box-8 crew tied in their saddles. Naturally, I didn't believe it, but—'

'You better believe it, Glascow,' Tucson said grimly. 'There's goin' to be a lot more for you to believe too—'

'What kind of a bluff you tryin' to run?' Glascow's eyes narrowed. 'You wouldn't have no right hawg-tyin' any of Steve's crew—'

Tucson laughed scornfully, pointed down the street to the crowd collected before the deputy's office. 'Look for yourself, Glascow.'

The deputy turned, gazed toward the crowd, then jerked back to Tucson. 'What's the idea? You ain't got no right—'

'They trespassed on 3-Bar-O holdin's,'

Tucson said. He paused a moment and let his next words sink in, 'Those six ain't all that trespassed. The rest weren't worth bringin' in.'

Glascow's face turned a shade whiter. He didn't say anything.

Tucson continued, 'I suppose you don't know a thing about Jake Elliot and the rest, pushin' those cows over on our property and throwin' lead at our punchers.'

'What kind of a game you tryin' to run on us—on Ogden?' Glascow demanded. 'Certainly, I don't know anythin'—'

'Don't lie, Glascow. But here's somethin' you really don't know. My pards and I got out there in time to make it right tough for Ogden's hands. Glascow, you might as well give in. Your game's up.'

'I don't know what you're talkin' about.' The deputy tried to keep his voice steady.

'You will, shortly.' Tucson changed the subject abruptly to ask, 'Glascow, where's that deed to the Tresbarro property and that county deed record book?'

The shot went home. A look of fright passed across Glascow's face. He stammered, 'What—what do you mean?'

'Don't try to wiggle out of it, Glascow.' Tucson laughed easily, risked another bluff. 'Gosh, that Elliot hombre sure says somethin' when he talks.'

Blood rushed to Glascow's face. 'By God, did Jake—' He halted suddenly and said

243

lamely, 'I ain't got the least idea what you're talkin' about, Smith. Howsomever, I ain't got time to stand here, wastin' time with you. I got business with Steve Ogden.'

He whirled around and started back across the street. Tucson caught his shoulder, pulled him back. 'What you got to say to Ogden can wait, Glascow. You better get one thing clear: that bunch of Ogden coyotes in front of the jail are under arrest.'

Glascow stiffened. 'Under arrest! You're crazy. I'm the only man that can make arrests in Los Potros. You better untie those hombres, or I will—'

He halted suddenly, eyes bulging. Tucson had produced a deputy-sheriff's badge and was pinning it on his vest. Tucson's eyes were cold but he smiled cheerfully at Glascow.

'Just a little present Sheriff Morgan made to me yesterday, Glascow. How does it look?'

'Yo're—yo're crazy,' Glascow gasped. 'Morgan didn't—Morgan wouldn't—' He broke off and ran one finger around his shirt collar as though the band were cutting off his air supply. 'What sort of a game is this? Morgan wouldn't appoint another deputy here, without tellin' me. I ain't resigned—'

'Morgan's authority is higher'n yours, Glascow, and he passed some of that authority on to me. Enough of it so I can give you orders, anyway. We've talked enough—'

'I don't believe it,' Glascow gasped.

'You can check up with Morgan as soon as you like,' Tucson repeated, 'We've talked enough. I want the keys to the jail.'

'What you want the keys to the jail for?' Glascow was stalling for time, trying to gather his senses to meet this new threat.

'Don't talk foolish, Glascow. Give me those keys.'

Glascow hesitated, his eyes trying to meet the steely glance of Tucson's grey ones. Tucson waited, thumbs resting lightly in belts. Ten seconds drifted past.

Tucson said quietly, 'After I get those coyotes locked up, behind bars, you'n me are goin' to have a talk, Glascow. I'm still curious as to how you got that record book and what you did with it. 'Course, I know you gave it to Steve Ogden, but what did Ogden do with it? He wouldn't dare destroy it. He figures to use it for his own purposes—'

'It's a lie—it's a lie!' Glascow exclaimed hoarsely. His eyes, like those of some cornered rat's, shifted from side to side, seeking some avenue of escape. Involuntarily, his hand dropped to the gun-butt hanging at his right hip. Then he hesitated, face white with fear.

Three or four men had stopped on the sidewalk and were gazing at Tucson and the crooked deputy.

Tucson hadn't missed the motion toward the gun. He said carelessly, 'Suit yourself, Glascow. Either give me those keys or jerk

245

your iron and go to work. What you aim to do? Think fast!'

Slowly, Glascow relinquished hold on his gun-butt. He realized he couldn't beat Tucson in a fair fight. He gulped, swallowing hard. This was a matter for headwork. Forcing a ghastly grin that showed tobacco-stained fangs in his white face, he said slowly, 'I reck—reckon I better resign, Smith. You—you can have the keys. Take my handcuffs, too.'

Reaching his right hand to hip pocket, Glascow produced the handcuffs. Tucson took them with his left hand. Glascow's left hand reached to the other hip-pocket, bringing into sight a bunch of heavy keys. Tucson was watching warily, left hand holding the cuffs.

'Here's the keys,' Glascow muttered, backing away a pace. With his left hand he tossed them to Tucson. figuring to keep Tucson's right hand occupied. Glascow's right hand darted for holster.

Deftly, Tucson's right hand picked the bunch of keys from the air. His left hand released hold of the handcuffs, stabbed toward left holster, before the cuffs had fallen to the earth.

Even as the gun-muzzle cleared leather it commenced to belch smoke and white flame. Two slugs picked up tiny clouds of dirt as Tucson's gun swept up to bear on Glascow's body.

Glascow's six-shooter emitted one wild shot

as he staggered back. His wide-spread legs were swept from under him as though by some huge invisible hand and he went sprawling a half dozen paces away.

Tucson backed two steps, holding his gun in readiness. Glascow was down now, bracing himself on one hand, the look of a hate-maddened animal drawing back his lips in a savage snarl. He raised his right hand, gripping his gun for a last attempt. There came a burst of hot flame. Tucson swayed to one side, his own report blending with that of Glascow's.

Glascow's body jerked. The gun fell from his weakening grasp. For a moment he braced himself on both hands, staring wildly at Tucson. Then his bulky form crumpled and he sank to the roadway.

Methodically, Tucson plugged out the empty shells in his gun cylinder, replaced the chambers with fresh loads. For an instant silence engulfed the long street. Tucson glanced across at the Red Bull Saloon. Two Box-8 punchers, named Auringer and Chap Bell, stood on the porch. Both had their hands on gun-butts.

Tucson eyed them steadily a moment, then, 'Want any of this?' he called across the street.

Chap Bell didn't reply. Auringer shook his head. 'It ain't any of our business,' he replied. The two stepped quickly to the plank sidewalk and hurried away down the street. In a moment their forms were lost among the crowd of men that came running to surround Tucson and the prone Glascow.

There came a quick thudding of hoofs. Men scattered wildly to one side as Lullaby came loping up.

Lullaby's face was white. 'You hurt any, pard?' he said quietly.

And just as quietly, Tucson replied, 'Not any.'

Lullaby said, 'Stony and I were watching from down the street. I didn't think Glascow was that fast.'

'He wasn't fast enough,' Tucson said shortly. 'Here—' handing up the keys, '—you go back and put those prisoners in cells. I'll see you later.' He added, 'I want to see if Glascow will talk any.'

Lullaby took the keys, nodded, and turned his pony to rejoin Stony and the prisoners.

Tucson swung back to Glascow, turned the wounded deputy on his back. Glascow's eyes were open, his face was bloodless. Somebody brought a glass of water. Tucson held it to Glascow's lips. Somebody else said something about getting Doctor Benson. Tucson nodded and gave his attention to the deputy.

Glascow said feebly, 'Reckon I got mine.'

'You made a mistake, Glascow. You should have handed me those keys instead of tossin' 'em to me. You hurried your draw.'

'Am I goin' to die?'

Tucson said, 'We all get it sometime, Glascow.'

A look of anger contorted Glascow's white features. 'Damn Ogden! It's all his fault. He got me into this.'

A large crowd had collected around Tucson and the deputy.

'Ogden's to blame, all right,' Glascow muttered wrathfully. 'By God, he needn't think ... he can go scot-free. He promised me money for—for—for what I done—then laughed at me—when I asked for—it. I'll get even. I'll tell what I know—'

Glascow stopped for breath. Tucson held the glass to his lips again, said, 'I don't reckon you know much.'

Glascow's voice came stronger. 'I know enough to hang Steve Ogden higher'n a kite. It was us raided the ranch the night Don Manuel was killed. Steve led that raid. It was Steve put me up to stealin' Tresbarro's deed. I don't know anythin', eh?' He glared angrily at Tucson. 'I'll even accounts with Steve for not payin' for them jobs.'

'How about that record book?' Tucson asked.

'I stole that from that buildin' they're usin' for a courthouse. No one figured it was strange I was in the courthouse. I went there often to see Sheriff Morgan. There wasn't no vault there. The books weren't locked up. I hid behind some filin' cases, until everybody had left at closin' time an' the doors were locked.

Then I took the book, and got out by a window—'

'Where are the book and the Tresbarro deed now?'

'In Ogden's safe—at the Red Bull—an' I'll tell you somethin' else. Ogden rustled Tresbarro cattle, blotted 'em with a Box-8 brand. You can hold a round-up, get 'em back. He stole over three thousand head—in small bunches—past few years. By Cripes, I may be finished, but I'll finish Ogden before I go!'

CHAPTER TWENTY

TUCSON GOES DOWN

Steve Ogden sat waiting at the table in his office in the Red Bull. The door leading into the bar was closed. Except the barkeep, Gus Trout, there wasn't anybody out there. Ogden reflected he hadn't been getting as many customers as usual of late. At the first sound of shooting between Glascow and Smith, every man at the bar had dashed outside.

'Dammit!' Ogden chewed angrily at the long black cigar clenched between his teeth. 'I wonder what became of Auringer and Chap Bell. Damn skunks! If they've deserted me—' Various thoughts flashed through his mind: 'I hope Smith finished Glascow outright. He'd turn yellow and talk if he had a chance. Wonder what was all that talk about Elliot and the other boys bein' brought in. Reckon I'll have to go find out for myself.'

He started to rise. then dropped back into his chair again. 'I'll wait a few minutes, anyway.' Ogden had told himself that same thing several times. Here, in his office, he felt safe. Outside—well, that was a different matter.

'Hang the luck! Why don't somebody come in? Mebbe Elliot and the boys crossed guns with the 3-Bar-O. I hope so. Now that Smith's shot a legally deputized officer of the county, it'll put him in a bad light. I'll import a crew of good gun-slingers. If I can't shoot Smith off this range, I'll tie the whole business up in litigation. I got to have that Tresbarro Range. I need the water. Hell, whether I need it or not, I'm goin' to have it.' His clenched fist smacked down hard on the table. He raised his voice, 'Gus!'

The bartender came to the door, opened it.

'Bring a bottle of the best.'

Gus Trout departed, came back in a few moments bringing a squat brown bottle and a glass. He pulled the cork, set the bottle and glass on the table.

Ogden said nervously, 'What's doin' out there?'

Trout shrugged his shoulders. 'I can't see anythin'. Too many people gathered around. I

251

heard somebody say somethin' about Smith wearin' a badge.'

Ogden stiffened, then relaxed. 'Some fool shootin' off his mouth. If it was a federal badge, we'd know it by this time. If it's a county—hell! it can't be. Morgan wouldn't make any changes without informin' Glascow ... Is Glascow dead?'

'I don't know, boss.'

'What in hell do you know? Where's Bell and Auringer?'

'They were out front. I heard Smith yell somethin' at 'em—couldn't make out what. Auringer said somethin' about it not bein' his business. Then the two of 'em hiked down the street. They didn't look like they wanted to talk to Smith.'

'Get out of here!' Ogden said wrathfully.

Trout disappeared. The door slammed. Ogden poured a brimming glass of liquor, downed it and poured a second glass. His cigar had gone out. He lighted it again, noticed that the hand that held the flaming match was trembling.

Ogden swore in a low voice. 'I'm gettin' nerves,' he snarled. 'I got to get hold of myself. This won't do. I been in tight spots before. I'll get out of this one, too. There's more than one way of skinning a cow. Smith ain't so fast with his guns. Saunders—damn him!—is faster. Smith just outsmarted him. I'm as tricky as Smith, any day in the week. I'll face him myself—and outtrick him too. Smith is the keystone of that 3-Bar-O outfit. Once he's out of the way, the whole organization will crash—'

A sudden knock at the door sent a look of fear over Ogden's dead-white face. His teeth, clamping down on the cigar, chopped it off short. His heart commenced to drum like mad. He slipped one gun out of his holster, took a second from the harness under his left armpit. His voice shook a trifle, 'Who's there?'

Through the door panel came the response: 'Me—Auringer. And Chap Bell.'

A sigh of relief whistled through Ogden's lips. He snapped, 'C'mon,' and placed the guns on the table before him.

He was brushing sparks and ashes off his vest when Auringer and Bell entered and shut the door behind them, their faces twisted with emotion. The pair stood hesitantly before their chief.

'Is it necessary to break the door down when you knock—?' Ogden commenced, glaring at the two.

Neither of the men replied. Auringer grabbed the bottle, poured himself a glass of liquor. Chap Bell seized the bottle, tilted it to his lips. Ogden stopped talking, eyed the two angrily, then, 'Lay off drinkin'. You two lost your tongues?'

Auringer set down his empty glass. 'We'll be lucky if we don't lose our heads. Me and

Chap's driftin'—'

'T'hell you are. What do you mean?'

'Glascow's spillin' everythin'!'

Ogden swore at the two.

'Take it that way if you want,' Auringer said coloring. 'I'm talkin' straight. Glascow's told the whole thing. We're aimin' to ride. You better do the same.'

Ogden gathered his scattered remnants of nerve, laughed scornfully. 'Well, if you two don't take the prize for yellow streaks—'

'We're playin' wise.'

'Wise hell. If you run you admit your guilt. Stick here and bluff it out. I'm back of you. I put Glascow in office. Do you think I haven't pull in this county? Money talks. Hell, Smith is runnin' a bluff. Don't let him scare you out.'

'He's wearin' a deputy badge—' Auringer commenced.

Ogden forced another laugh. It was true then. He said calmly, 'That ain't news to me.'

Somewhat reassured by their chief's manner, the two quieted down. Ogden said, 'Now tell me what's happened.'

'In the first place,' Auringer related, 'that stunt of pushin' those cows over on 3-Bar-O holdin's didn't work out so well.'

'What do you mean?' Ogden snapped.

'You started the range war you been achin' for,' Auringer said, 'but the 3-Bar-O cleaned us. Jake, Reece, Knight—'

'What about them? I didn't ask for a census.

254

Cut it short.'

'That's the way you'll get it,' Auringer said hotly. 'They're down in the jail now. This Smith has got one fightin' crew—'

'It's like I said,' Chap Bell cut in, 'instead of me'n Auringer comin' to town with you, we should have gone with the other boys. They needed every man—'

'I do the plannin' for this outfit,' Ogden cut in. 'It's my idea to keep you two with me. If I hadn't—well, maybe you'd be lookin' out between bars too ... What about Glascow? Gus Trout tells me one of you said somethin' to Tucson Smith after the shootin'.'

'It was me,' from Auringer. 'Me'n Chap was standin' out in front, sort of itchin' to throw some lead at Smith—'

'Why didn't you?' Ogden snapped.

'He looked up and spotted us, asked if we wanted to take a hand. I didn't, and said as much. Man, I didn't like the look in his eyes, right then. God! They'd send chills runnin' down a feller's back—'

'You've gone yellow,' Ogden accused contemptuously.

'Call it that if you want,' Chap Bell said coldly, taking up the story. 'Me'n Auringer headed down the street, then doubled back and mixed with the crowd that was standin' around Glascow. As soon as we heard Glascow givin' away the whole show, we busted away and come here to tell you.'

'Where's this Lullaby Joslin and Stony Brooke?' Ogden asked.

'Down to the jail, puttin' the boys away for the night.'

Ogden considered a moment, then, 'All right, it's up to you two. Go to the front door of the Red Bull. Smith will be breaking away from that crowd in a minute. Then let him have it—'

'You meanin',' Auringer laughed scornfully, 'it's up to me'n Chap to kill Smith?'

'Exactly.'

'You're all wrong,' Chap Bell refused. 'Nope, Steve, you must be thinkin' of two other hombres. We're leavin' Los Potros plumb pronto. We should be gone now. You ought to give us some credit for takin' time to come in and tell you—'

'And collect what money you got comin', eh?' Ogden sneered.

Auringer nodded. 'That had somethin' to do with it, Steve,' he admitted. 'C'mon, shell out, and we'll be on our way. If you're wise you'll drift too. That Smith is sure making fast dust along a warpath—'

'Wait a minute,' Ogden cut in icily. This was his last chance. He had to persuade this pair to stay. 'Where you goin'? You can't travel far without money. Now, listen, you two have your horses where they'll be handy—'

'The broncs are at the hitchrack out front,' Bell cut in.

'Good. If we can stop Smith, we've blocked the whole 3-Bar-O. You two go out, get on your horses. When Smith steps away from the crowd, let him have it. Both of you. Then ride. After I get things coming my own way again, you can come back and everything will be hunky-dory.'

'T'hell with that, Steve,' Auringer refused. 'You can do your own killin'. We ain't aimin' to do your executin' for you.'

Ogden said slowly, 'I got nearly three thousand dollars in that safe back of me. That amount of money says you'll do what I tell you to do. You're both fast, you're straight shots. One shot apiece ought to be enough. Three thousand dollars. Right good money for two Colt ca'tridges.'

The money was tempting. It sounded easy, Auringer and Bell exchanged understanding glances. Bell nodded. 'We'll do it, Steve. Shell out the money.'

'I'll pay you afterward—'

'We'll be ridin'—fast,' Auringer sneered, 'afterward.'

'I'll mail you the money wherever you go. All you have to do—'

Bell turned toward the door. 'C'mon, Auringer, we can't waste any more time—'

'Wait a minute, wait a minute,' Ogden said hastily. 'I'll pay you now.'

'Kick in,' Auringer said.

Ogden rose from his chair, knelt before the

iron safe, twirled the dial. The handle clicked the door open. Ogden reached in for a canvas sack of money. Rising, he again seated himself at the table and commenced counting bills, gold and silver.

Bell and Auringer waited impatiently. Once Bell said, glancing into the open safe, 'Steve, if you was wise you'd burn that deed record book. I suppose the Tresbarro deed is in it—'

'I'll be needing them some day,' Ogden replied absent-mindedly, and went on counting.

A few minutes later the two men were stuffing the money into pockets and listening impatiently to last minute advice from Ogden. Auringer opened the office door, then closed it with some haste.

'What's the matter?' Ogden asked, 'seen a ghost?'

Auringer said, 'Worse than that. Smith!'

'Comin' here?' hoarsely from Bell.

Auringer nodded.

Ogden laughed confidently. 'Better than ever, boys. You can do it right here. Safer than on the street. You're sure getting the breaks—'

He stopped suddenly, hearing Tucson in conversation with Gus Trout. Auringer and Bell had tip-toed around to the back of the room, stood facing the closed door.

'Get ready to blast,' Ogden snarled in a vicious whisper.

Auringer and Bell nodded, hands reaching to holsters.

*   *   *

Tucson had at last finished listening to Brose Glascow's confession. Even his usually steady features showed evidence of being surprised at the things Glascow had said: there seemed to be no end to the long series of crimes devised by Steve Ogden's iniquitous mind. Tucson heaved a long sigh, his eyes narrowed, as Doctor Benson pushed his way through the crowd.

Benson said, as Tucson rose to his feet, 'Is Glascow hit bad, Tucson?'

'He'll recover to serve a jail sentence, at least,' Tucson said. 'Couple of broken legs and a smashed shoulder. Didn't want to kill him. Figured we'd need his testimony later—'

A snarling exclamation parted Glascow's white lips. 'You—you said,' he accused, 'that I was dyin'.'

Tucson shook his head. 'You're wrong, Glascow. You just jumped to conclusions—'

Glascow broke into a torrent of vile oaths. Tucson turned away, pushed clear of the crowd, and glanced toward the street. Lullaby and Stony were riding toward him. He waited until they came up.

'Got 'em locked tight?' Tucson asked.

'Those cell bars are plenty stout,' Stony nodded. 'Want the keys?'

'Hang on to them for a spell,' Tucson said.

Lullaby asked, 'What about Glascow? Did

259

he have anythin' to say?'

Tucson smiled thinly, 'Plenty plus. He thought he was dyin'. Wanted to even scores with Steve Ogden before his light went out.' Concluding, Tucson gave brief details of the confession.

When he had finished, 'My gosh!' from Stony, 'Glascow spilled it all, didn't he?'

'What's next?' Lullaby asked.

'I'm puttin' Ogden under arrest,' Tucson said grimly. 'He's over to the Red Bull.'

'We better go with you,' Stony suggested.

'Yeah,' Lullaby agreed, 'I was talkin' with a feller down the street. He tells me he saw Ogden and Glascow when they rode in from the Box-8 this mornin'. Those two tough punchers, Bell and Auringer, was with 'em. Bell and Auringer are pro'bly in the Red Bull with Ogden now.'

Tucson shook his head. 'I saw both those coyotes right after I'd downed Glascow. They were just leaving the Red Bull.' He gestured west along the street. 'They went down that way. I want you two to round 'em up. They might be in the Happy Days, tryin' to find out what happened to their pals. Or they may be gettin' away with some of the papers pertainin' to the Tresbarro property. Put 'em under arrest in my name—'

'We ain't got authority to make arrests,' Stony said, 'but we'll bring 'em back to you—'

Tucson said grimly, 'You're wearin' your authority in holsters. I'll square any shootin'

260

that might be done. Go get 'em.'

Lullaby and Stony nodded, wheeled their ponies and went at a lope down the street. Tucson glanced at the swinging doors of the Red Bull, then turned and looked at the crowd surrounding Glascow. Glascow was still cursing. No one noticed Tucson as he started across the street.

His guns were in holsters as he pushed through the swinging doors and stepped into Ogden's saloon. Gus Trout was behind the bar, the only man in sight. Trout was engaged in shoving a pair of shells into a double-barreled shotgun. He looked up in sudden fright as Tucson stepped quietly into the barroom, the shells slipped from his shaking fingers and clattered to the floor.

Tucson's smile was almost as hard as his eyes. He looked steadily at Trout a moment, then said quietly, nodding toward the closed door of Ogden's office, 'Your boss in there?'

Trout's head bobbed up and down. 'I—I guess so.'

'You know damn well he is, Trout. I heard that door slam just before I came in.'

'Y-Y-Yes, sir.' Trout's teeth were chattering.

Tucson said, 'We're startin' to round up undesirables in Los Potros, Gus. We ain't got anythin' definite against you, except your associations. Mebbe if you stay here, we'll get somethin' definite. Take my advice and drift—'

'But—but—'

'Drift,' Tucson said sternly.

Trout didn't hesitate longer to argue the question. By the time he arrived at the swinging doors he was in full flight and not wasting a step.

Tucson watched warily until the man had disappeared. Silence fell over the big empty barroom. Tucson listened. Once he thought he heard voices behind the closed door of the office. He came a few strides nearer, drawing his guns.

'Ogden' he called. 'Come out!'

There was no reply.

Tucson raised his voice, 'Ogden!' sharply.

Reluctantly, Ogden's voice came through the panel. 'What do you want? Who is it?'

'It's Smith. And I want you.'

'What for?'

'You're under arrest.'

Cold, mocking laughter greeted the announcement, then, 'What for?' again.

'Murder, rustling—the list is too long to repeat. I got it all from Glascow. You comin' quiet, or have I got to come after you?'

'I reckon you'll have to come after me,' came the snarled reply through the door panel.

Tucson laughed softly, 'That,' he stated, 'is one plumb welcome job.'

Moving across the floor in quick strides, he hurled his lean muscular length against the door, at the same time turning the knob. The door was locked as he had expected. Spinning on one foot, he whirled sidewise.

And just in time: from the small office came a volley of thundering detonations as hot lead slugs ripped savagely through the door panels at the height of a man's body.

Tucson was three yards to one side of the door now, waiting. He didn't make a sound. From the street came a sudden yelling at the sound of the shooting. Voices approached the swinging doors. A man's head peered over the tops of the doors.

Tucson gestured for silence with one gun. The man's head quickly disappeared. There came the thudding of retreating footsteps. Silence again, except for a buzz of voices from the street.

Thirty seconds drifted past, swelled to a full minute. Tucson hadn't moved an inch. From inside the office came whispers, then louder tones, 'By God! I believe we got him.' That was Bell speaking.

'Told you it would be easy,' Ogden laughed triumphantly. 'Take a look.'

Standing to one side, Tucson saw the door open cautiously for a few inches, then a gun-barrel appeared. The door opened wider to disclose Chap Bell's scowling features. Bell didn't notice Tucson at first. He was glancing toward the street. The office door was suddenly drawn back a full yard. Auringer's face came into the picture, standing at Bell's shoulder.

Auringer let out a frightened yell. Bell's eyes shifted with his gun. The gun roared. Tucson's left hand spat fire, then his right, and his left again.

Bell's form dove full length into the room. Auringer tried to slam the door shut, but Bell's feet were stuck between the door and the jamb. Bell was struggling to rise, fighting to raise his gun.

Auringer cursed, flung the door wide, stepped into full view, both hands blazing. Tucson threw himself sidewise, emptying one gun as he moved. Tucson's movement carried him opposite the door.

Auringer staggered into full view, whirled around and crashed down. From the vicinity of the floor, near Bell, came the roar of a forty-five. Hot steel burned through and through Tucson's body—at least, it felt like steel. As he fell, Tucson's left wrist flicked in Bell's direction, stopped in a burst of flame and powdersmoke.

Bell screamed and jerked his feet clear of the door. Ogden's face appeared a moment, grinning fiendishly down at Tucson. His gun raised. Tucson rolled over and over, heard bullets thudding into the floor near his body, came up, catlike, to his feet, orange fire running from one hand.

He saw wood splinter from the doorframe as Ogden hurriedly slammed the door. Tucson staggered to his feet. Something hot and wet and sticky was trickling freely down his body, inside his shirt. He glanced across the floor, noting the motionless bodies of Bell and Auringer.

'Two down,' he muttered, his lean form swaying a little. He examined his guns, commenced to fumble for fresh cartridges. 'Wonder how much longer I'm good for,' was the thought that coursed his swimming brain as he reloaded. The mists cleared after a moment, and he made his way on uncertain legs toward the door. Fighting to hold his voice steady he called, 'I'm comin' in after you, Ogden.'

Gathering all of his strength, Tucson threw his shoulder against the door. It gave a little, shook on its hinges. Somewhere, it seemed far away, a gun sounded. Tucson felt a bullet rip into his body.

He laughed grimly, stood back, charged the door again. There came a sharp splintering sound as the door was ripped free. Instead of swinging open, it fell inward, wrenched from latch and hinges. Tucson sprawled full length on the door, as two swift slugs whined above his head, the table inside the office preventing the door from crashing to the floor.

Back of the table stood Ogden, lips drawn back in a snarl of hate and triumph as he gazed down on the momentarily helpless Tucson. Ogden's gun swung in a short arc above Tucson's head, roared, as Tucson twisted to one side. Tucson knew he was hit again.

Fighting for his swiftly-failing strength, Tucson scrambled off the door, his thumbs moving in a blur above Colt hammers. The detonations in the small office were terrific. It was all a mad crimson haze of barking guns and pain and powdersmoke. His eyes were blinded with sweat. An acrid gas from burnt powder stung eyes and throat and nostrils.

Tucson felt his legs buckling. His hammers were falling on empty shells now, but he didn't know it. As in a dream he saw Ogden sprawled before him on the floor.

It seemed ages before Tucson realized Ogden was dead. He brushed one hand across his eyes to clear his fading vision, slowly replaced guns in holsters and took one step before he crashed down across Ogden's lifeless body.

From a far distance he heard footsteps thudding into the barroom, then Lullaby's agonized, 'Tucson, oh, Tucson, old pard.' And Stony's, 'He got the three of 'em ....'

But Tucson was beyond hearing now...

CHAPTER TWENTY-ONE

SILENT FORTY-FIVES

Autumn sunshine traced intricate golden patterns through the leaves of the cottonwoods standing before the gallery of the 3-Bar-O ranch house and touched with bright light Tucson Smith's laughing features. A lot of bronze had gone out of Tucson's face in the past two months, but it was gradually being replaced with a flush of returning health.

Tucson sat in an easy chair, wrapped in blankets, on the long gallery. Caroline Sibley stood at his side saying a laughing good-bye to Doctor Benson who was mounting his horse, black bag in hand, a few yards away.

'I wouldn't lie to a friend,' the doctor smiled. 'What I said is truth, Miss Sibley. It's your nursing that has done the trick. We doctors know only so much. We do just that much. After that, well, it depends what sort of convalescent treatment a patient gets, food, care, etc. From now on, it's up to you. There's nothing more for me to do here.'

'I'm owing Caroline a heap, Doc,' Tucson nodded. 'And you too.'

'Never mind my part,' Benson said. 'All I had to do was fish slugs out of your carcass. Don't do that again, Tucson. A man shot up the way you were, hasn't any right to live. You've had a narrow squeak.'

Tucson smiled, 'That ain't worryin' me. In another week I figure to feel fit enough to hairpin a bronc and help on the beef round-up the boys are startin' tomorrow.'

Benson swung his horse around. 'I think your nurse has too much sense to let you do anything that foolish. Take it easy. Good-bye.'

'*Adios*,' Tucson called. He watched until the doctor was some distance away, then looked up at Caroline, 'I reckon he forgets you won't be here to stop me ridin' when I get ready.'

Caroline said, 'I'm aiming to stay, cowboy— for a time, anyway.'

'I don't see the reason,' Tucson protested, watching the girl narrowly. 'Your property is off your hands. You can go visit those relatives you've been wanting to see. The boys can take care of me from now on.'

Caroline seated herself on the gallery railing, opposite Tucson. 'Oh, I'm not so anxious to make that trip.' She wasn't looking at Tucson now.

There was a moment's silence, then Tucson asked, 'What's the matter, Guadalupe lost his tongue?'

Tears came into the girl's eyes. She rose quickly, nodded, and went into the house. Tucson laughed softly. Five minutes passed. The Guadalupe Kid rounded the house, stepped to the gallery and took the seat on the railing that Caroline had vacated shortly before. The Kid looked miserable. Tucson said, 'What's on your mind, Jeff?'

Guadalupe said, not meeting Tucson's eyes, 'I been figurin' you could get somebody else to start round-up tomorrow. I got a hunch to do some ridin'. You can get somebody in my place easy.'

'I ain't so sure of that,' Tucson said gravely. 'What's the matter, restless?'

The Kid nodded. 'It's so long since I heard a gun go off that the quiet is gettin' on my nerves. First thing you know somebody will be callin' this the range of silent forty-fives—'

'Under some circumstances, it could be plumb peaceful here, Jeff. Listen, son, you don't have to lie to me. I've seen how things stood between you and Caroline. Why don't you tell the girl what's on your mind—'

'With my past record?' the Kid demanded. 'Nope, I'm goin' to ride.'

Tucson laughed gently. 'I told Caroline about this terrible record of yours a long spell back, Jeff, told her how you've squared everything up. The point you've missed is that you're all square with Caroline.'

Guadalupe's eyes lighted with joy and gratitude. 'Why—why—' he stammered, 'mebbe I could ask her—' Suddenly his face fell, 'Nope, that's out. Caroline's worth some money now. I can't tie her to puncher's wages.'

'Puncher's wages your eye!' Tucson

exclaimed. 'Foreman's wages, with a share in profits.'

The Kid's jaw dropped. 'Huh?'

'Sure,' Tucson smiled. 'I talked it all over with Stony and Lullaby last night. Somebody's got to rod the 3-Bar-O. We figure you're the man. You've got a good crew. Cripes, Kid, do you expect Stony or Lullaby will settle here the rest of their life? Us three is built to ramble. Only for bein' lucky, we'd be just saddletramps.'

'Gosh, Tucson, you hombres are—are—'

'Forget the thanks, Kid. Look, I figure Sourdough's corns will be frettin' him today. Would you do me a favor and go find Caroline? Ask her will she brew that damn beef broth Benson insists on me drinkin'. She's in the house, someplace.'

'Sure will,' Guadalupe said eagerly. His eyes were shining as he slipped from the railing and hurried into the house. There was a confused scuffle just inside the door and some mumbled words, then Lullaby emerged from the house.

'What in time's doin'?' Lullaby drawled. 'I come through the kitchen and I find Caroline dabbin' at her eyes and refusin' to talk. Then Guadalupe danged nigh killed me in the rush he staged to get past. Where's he headin'?'

Tucson explained the situation. Lullaby grinned, 'Well, I hope that's settled.' His face sobered, 'Tucson, what you aim to do about Sundown Saunders?'

'What about him?'

'I'm afraid he ain't goin' to fit into our outfit. You brought him here when he could be moved. Caroline's done her best to take care of him. All the boys been pleasant as they knew how. Now that Saunders is able to get around, he's talkin' about driftin'. He don't make friends, he's suspicious of everybody, seems to think there's somethin' back of you bringin' him here and bein' decent to him.'

Tucson smiled gravely. 'I reckon he's right.'

'You can't tame a wild cat. This snatchin' a brand from the burnin' is all right for parson's *habla* but it don't work out. You ain't no farther with Saunders now than you was when you met him.'

Tucson denied that. 'He ain't tried to shoot me. Lullaby I want a chance to prove to Saunders that there's a heap of decent hombres in the world. If he'll only stick long enough, I think mebbe we can get him to look at things our way.'

Lullaby shook his head. 'I'm danged if I know how you're goin' to do it—'

At that moment Stony burst from the house, 'Hey, Lullaby, you want to see somethin' swell?'

Lullaby looked suspicious, 'You aimin' to tell me to blow up a rubber balloon?'

'Aw, cripes,' Stony said disgustedly, 'this is serious. It'd make you happy just to look at them two—'

271

'What two?' from Tucson.

Stony explained, 'I come in through the kitchen and there was Caroline and Guadalupe, and they looked so dang happy, smilin' an' all. Gosh, it made me feel good.'

At that moment, Sundown Saunders rounded the corner of the house, walking fast. He checked his steps suddenly, upon seeing Stony and Lullaby. Saunders' wounds had healed but he was still white.

Tucson said quietly, 'Hi-yuh, Sundown. Come up and sit.' Then to Stony and Lullaby, 'You hombres slope down to the bunkhouse, will you, and see if Ananias is there. Tell him he better get some windies ready to spin at a comin' marriage shindig, 'cause Guadalupe has found his tongue, and that while he's foreman here, he ain't aimin' to be boss much longer. The other boys will be glad to hear it too.'

Lullaby and Stony took the hint, nodded to Saunders and disappeared around the side of the house. Saunders stepped to the gallery, sat down on the railing.

Tucson said quietly, 'I understand you're gettin' ready to pull out, Sundown.'

'I was,' Sundown said stiffly. His eyes were as bleak as ever.

'Don't blame you,' Tucson said carelessly. 'A feller's got to ramble now and then. I know you figured I must have some queer business in bringin' you here. You probably thought I'd try to arrest you or somethin' when you got ready to leave—'

'Yeah, I did.'

Tucson nodded. 'We all make mistakes,' he said gently. 'I don't mind tellin' you I did have a reason for wantin' you to stay. Ain't said anythin' before, 'cause I ain't been able to get around yet. Fact of the matter is, I was sort of hopin' you might show me just how you make those fast draws of yours—'

'Tucson!' Saunders could restrain himself no longer. 'I been talkin' to Ananias. He bawled me out for bein' a grouch. Well, I reckon I am. If Ananias hadn't been old enough to be my father, I'd told him to jerk his hardware—'

'A feller gets riled sometimes,' Tucson agreed genially, mentally realizing that a few months before, Ananias' age wouldn't have made any difference. Well, some progress had been made, anyway.

Saunders had stopped. Now he rushed on, 'Ananias spilled the beans, told me how you used .32-20s that day we—we crossed guns—so you wouldn't hurt me, no more than was possible, I'm askin' why? My mind don't take in that sort of a situation.'

'Well,' Tucson said quietly, 'I don't know yet, just why I did that, Sundown. I ain't a killer. I like to see every man have an equal chance. Somethin' about you got to me. Mebbe it was your gameness, mebbe your habit of never breakin' your word. Mebbe it

273

was a certain pride in my own race. Somehow, I got an idea that I simply had to show you that we're not all snake-blooded—'

A sort of dry sob racked Sundown's throat. 'You're makin' me see somethin' I never believed, Tucson,' he said unsteadily, 'but Guadalupe's right. You're a white man—so damn white that I won't feel comfortable stayin' here any longer—'

Tucson laughed softly, 'Don't talk that way, Sundown. Give us a chance. You'll find Stony and Lullaby—all of us—are the same. You know, you been buckin' the world so long, single-handed, that you got an idea that the only straight-shootin' that's done comes out of a gun-barrel. I ain't askin' for nothin' you don't want to do, but I wish you'd leave your blankets unrolled long enough to get acquainted.'

Sundown said a trifle wistfully, 'I'd sort of like to try it, but—'

Tucson played his last card, 'And you know,' he added carelessly, 'the time might come when I'd need your guns. Trouble never stays away very long.'

Saunders' hand came out suddenly to grip Tucson's. 'If that's the case,' he said bashfully, 'reckon I better stick around for a spell. When you get to movin', I'd appreciate a few lessons in straight shootin', strivin' for accuracy at a distance.'

274

'That,' Tucson smiled, 'is just a matter of practice, Sundown, just practice. I think you're catchin' the knack of it.'

(Allan) William Colt MacDonald was born in Detroit, Michigan in 1891. His formal education concluded after his first three months of high school when he went to work as a lathe operator for Dodge Brothers' Motor Company. His first commercial writing consisted of advertising copy and articles for trade publications. While working in the advertising industry, MacDonald began contributing stories of varying lengths to pulp magazines and his first novel, a Western story, was published by Clayton House in *Ace-High Magazine* in 1925. MacDonald later commented that when this first novel appeared in book form as *Restless Guns* in 1929, 'I quit my job cold.' From the time of that decision on, MacDonald's career became a long string of successes in pulp magazines, hardcover books, films, and eventually original and reprint paperback editions. The Three Mesquiteers, MacDonald's most famous characters, were introduced in 1933 in *Law of the Forty-fives*. His other most famous character creation was Gregory Quist, a railroad detective. Some of MacDonald's finest work occurs outside his series, especially the well researched *Stir Up The Dust* which was published first in a British edition in 1950 and *The Mad Marshal* in 1958. MacDonald's only son, Wallace, recalled how much fun his father had writing Western fiction. It is an apt observation since countless readers have enjoyed his stories now for nearly three quarters of a century.

We hope you have enjoyed this Large Print book. Other Chivers Press or G.K. Hall & Co. Large Print books are available at your library or directly from the publishers.

For more information about current and forthcoming titles, please call or write, without obligation, to:

Chivers Press Limited
Windsor Bridge Road
Bath BA2 3AX
England
Tel. (01225) 335336

OR

G.K. Hall & Co.
P.O. Box 159
Thorndike, Maine 04986
USA
Tel. (800) 223–2336

All our Large Print titles are designed for easy reading, and all our books are made to last.